SHADOWS
OF THE NIGHT

SHADOWS
OF THE NIGHT

PHOEBE RAE

To order additional copies of this book, contact:
Xlibris
1-888-795-4274
www.Xlibris.com
Orders@Xlibris.com
731726

DEDICATION

A HUGE thank you to my publisher, Meaghan. I could never thank you enough!

I can't say another word without a hug for my "children"; Matt, Kyl, and Jer-Bear. Never, ever forget that family is EVERYTHING.

To Hope Skibstead-Maca, Ashley Crider, Peggy Hines Morison, Dylan, and Tiffany Schmidt and all people in the Supernatural Can Help forum on Facebook. When I had my finger on the delete button, you wouldn't allow it. I owe this to you!

James Louis Campbell, you get your own paragraph. You are my blooded son. Regardless of what you have been told about me, I love you with all my heart, and every breath in my body. I hope one day you could forgive me, and contact me.

For J.R. Ward, aka Jessica Bird, the greatest writer of all time. You inspired me to do this without even knowing it. Thank you for that, and the most wonderful series of all time, the Black Dagger Brotherhood!

I cannot let this go without thanking one other person, the one that gave me life, Shirley Minor. Mom, we may have had our ups and downs over the years, but we have always come back together. Maybe blood truly is thicker than water. I love you, and thank you for the support throughout the years. This is also for you. I proved the bastard wrong, didn't I?

Most of all, this book goes out to all victims and survivors of domestic violence, female, AND male. There is no excuse for such cowardice, and it is NEVER your fault. There is a way out, always. It is never easy, but you can escape, I promise. I am a survivor myself, and I am now stronger for what happened, and you will be too. Don't let them take your life; you are so much better than that!

CONTENTS

CHAPTER 1

Chicago, Illinois

June 16, 1989

Hope McLeod jolted out of a dead sleep as she normally did, afraid she had overslept again. She couldn't help but moan as the humidity that Chicago is known for bowled over her body like a steam roller. The sweat dripped down her face, making the cuts around her eye and lip from last night's beating sting like a bitch. She reached over and turned the air conditioner on, then slid from the bed, careful not to wake Nickolas Davenport, her boyfriend since high school, and bastard extraordinaire. That would make last night's bout of pissed off seem like nothing at all.

She padded her way into the bathroom in the beat-to-shit-roach-infested-apartment, and turned the cold water on in the shower. The air was just too miserable for the left-handed spigot.

She washed the sweat from her face and body, soaped up her waist-length ginger hair, and then stepped out drying herself off. She ran a brush through her hair, and rolled it up into a bun just to get it off her neck.

God, her mother was going to have an absolute fit when she saw the bruises and cuts on her face, along with her black eye. Normally, her eyes were almost an ice blue, well, one still was, but the other was a nice shade of crimson from when Nick's fist collided with it, making the blue in the iris pop out even harder, although the lid itself was almost swollen shut.

The rest of her face was ordinary, just your stereotypical plain woman in looks, nothing spectacular as Nick and the mirror take great pleasure in telling her every day. She has strange lips, the bottom fuller than the top, but with perfectly straight, white teeth, courtesy of the braces she had to wear for three years during high school. Her nose was a straight shot down the center of her face, with a small bump in the center thanks to Nick having broken it last year during an argument.

She has your typical body, handful of a bosom, narrow hips, and long, muscular legs for only being five foot five. Since she doesn't have a car, she has to walk everywhere or use the bus. She would rather walk, it's better for your body anyway. His majesty the asshole, would really be angry if she started to gain weight. Maybe she was just your plain, average twenty-one year old with self-esteem pounded into the ground.

She padded back to the bedroom, and covered herself with a white, calf-length sundress, then went in and started breakfast. It's a Sunday morning, and Nick likes a huge breakfast, usually consisting of biscuits and sausage gravy, at least one carton of eggs, pancakes, sausage links and patties, a waffle, pancakes, and toast all made from scratch, well, all but the toast.

She sighed as she looked around at the barely functional kitchen. It is so tiny, she could turn her body around, and be at the other side; let alone have any counter space to work in.

Lord, how did I get here? In high school, I had been the student body president, captain of the debate team, and all-American softball player. I was a straight-A student, graduated at the top of my class with an IQ nearly off the charts. Now, I cannot get out of this nightmare of a relationship. If I even tried, my family would die, of that I am certain. Why should I doubt it after all that sick bastard has put me through? At the end of the day, I am reduced to nothing more than a maid, a whore, and punching bag.

She gave herself a mental shake, and started cooking. There was no use crying over things she couldn't change.

After taking out her frustration on the biscuit dough, she stuck the biscuits in the oven, and started on the eggs and sausage. Once they were cooked to his royal assholiness' specifications, usually over hard, she stuck them on a plate, covered them with a paper towel to keep them warm and cut up the bread loaf she baked last night to get an early start on today's breakfast. She stuck two slices in the toaster, pushed the lever down, and started on the sausage gravy.

As she was taking the biscuits out of the oven, Nick crept into the kitchen, which there was barely room for one, let alone two. He kissed her neck, then gave it a hard bite, his way of saying the food smelled good, and he was hungry.

"It should be ready in just a moment or two, as soon as the gravy thickens."

"What about the pancakes and waffles?" he asked in his rough, deep, sleep laded voice.

She looked around, unable to believe she had forgotten that. "All right, as soon as the gravy thickens, I'll make the batter for that, and get them done. It won't take long."

He let out a tortured sigh. "All right, I'll let you cheat this one time. You can use the premixed crap. I'm *hungry!*"

Yah, I'll just bet you are after the coke bender you went on last night, you sorry sack of shit! She would never dare to say such a sentence out loud, even if it is true.

"You do remember that I have to go to my mother's today. She needs help after her stroke last month." Hope reminded him.

"Yah, yah, whatever, just make sure you get these dishes done before you leave."

"I can do them when I get back, it's not like I always leave dishes more than a few hours, Nick."

His eyes turned dark, his lips fell into a straight slant, as if someone cut them out with a knife. He charged at her like a bull seeing red and backhanded her, sending her to the tile floor. "I told you to do them before! Dennis is coming over, and I will not have my kitchen destroyed!"

She nearly rolled her eyes at the thought of his cocaine dealer thinking anything negative about how the kitchen was going to look.

Dennis personifies the word *greasy*. He rarely showers, so his hair is long and straggly. His body odor usually takes a week to get out of the apartment after only one ten-minute visit. His shirts were too small over his gigantic belly, as if he thought the barrel size was sexy and continuously wanted to show it off. His jeans rode low on his hips, showing off the fact that he constantly went without any kind of underwear. Whenever she was home, he did nothing but leer at her, as if he was picturing her without clothes and was determined to get a slice, which Nick had forced on her more than a few times. She had gagged the entire time, wanting to just stab herself into oblivion.

As for this being Nick's kitchen—oh, please! Her name was the only one on the lease, his was never added, and you see how all the attempts to throw him out have fared.

"Get your lazy ass up off my floor and finish my breakfast!" he bellowed.

She slowly stood, her head and jaw throbbing. She finished cooking, and ate slowly, a very small plate of one biscuit with gravy, and a glass of orange juice as sharp pain shot through her jaw making it hard to open, let alone chew. She just hoped that she didn't have to go back to the hospital with another cracked jaw.

After eating, even though she wasn't hungry after Nick's little tirade, she finished dressing, then put makeup over what she was sure was going to be another huge bruise.

"Oh, Hope, two things: One, you had better be back before sunset, and two, when Elaine comes to get you, you *will* have her drop you off at the train station. I don't want you hanging around with her unless absolutely necessary." he said from the doorway.

Even though she had no intentions of listening to him, she nodded her head. She would get there faster, and safer if Elaine took her all the way. Granted, the South Side was a long way from Naperville, but she had the money for gas if she used the money that Nick gave her for the train. The South Side of Chicago was not safe for a woman alone, day or night.

"Answer me, damn it! I'm not talking to hear my head rattle!"

"Yes, Nick."

Just then, a knock came at the door. Nick stared at her for a moment with an air of pure evil just cascading from his pores, and went to answer it. "Hope, the bitch is here!" he called out loudly.

"Excuse me?" Elaine asked, offended.

"No, I don't think I will." Nick said, then pushed past Elaine and walked out the door.

"Oh my god; he is such an asshole!" Elaine said loudly. "What do you see in that monster, Hope?"

"Elaine, please don't talk about him like that. I don't need the fallout from it. You're not the one that has to live with it."

"You don't either! You can get away! It's not like your mother won't take you in!"

"Elaine, Mom doesn't have the room, with Gracie and Kenny there. Gracie's pregnant, and it's a one bedroom townhouse as it is."

"Well, there are shelters, Honey. You can't handle much more of this. I mean, seriously, look at what he did to your eye! He's going to blind you someday!"

"Elaine, I appreciate the concern, but it's not as easy as you think to leave. There are circumstances that you don't know about, and it would destroy me in more ways than I can tell you to leave," Hope said softly.

Elaine Woodrow had been her best friend since birth. They had their diapers changed together, slept in the same crib, started school at the same time, and had many of their firsts together. They had been together through thick and thin, and now Nick was trying to drive a wedge between them. He apparently wanted Hope all to himself, even to the point of almost forbidding her to see her mother and sister.

"Hope, I worry about you. If you don't get away, he's going to kill you."

"Elaine, just drop it already! I can't leave, and that's all there is to it!"

"Can't…or won't?"

"Look, if I have to listen to this all the way to Naperville, then I'm going to take the train. I don't need it right now, Elaine. I have enough to worry about with mom's stroke, and my sister's pregnancy. She's only fifteen for crying out loud!"

Elaine ran her fingers through her long mousy hair, and let out a long sigh. "All right, I'll drop it, but I'm not going to stop looking for ways to help you."

"Elaine, if I leave, then he's going to kill my family. You don't know him like I do. You don't know what he's done to me! He's psychotic, and enjoys hurting others, he gets off on it. I can't leave," Hope said quietly, ashamed of herself for letting it get to this point.

"You truly think he's going to kill your family?" Elaine's eyes were peeled back, stunned that it had come to that.

Hope could only nod, tears tightening her throat, threatening to spill over onto her cheeks, making it almost impossible to speak.

"Then you need to call the police, and have a Restraining Order put on him."

"You're kidding, right? A Restraining Order is nothing more than a piece of paper, not Kevlar."

She finished putting on her makeup and put the makeup brush back into the case. She closed it up and put it back in the cabinet next to the tub where it belonged. "Let's go, please. I don't want to talk about this anymore."

"Damn, you can tell you're Scottish, you're as stubborn as a mule."

"It's kept me alive this long, so you should be grateful!"

Elaine barked out a laugh, and took Hope's arm, leading her out to the hallway. She locked the door, and they went to Elaine's brand new Mustang. Hope was utterly surprised it was still standing with all its parts in this neighborhood! She slid in to the passenger's side, and Elaine made it roar to life. Hope had always wanted something like this, just to feel the power under her. It's sleek, fast, and beautiful. Elaine turned on the radio, and the anthem "Living Years" by Mike and the Mechanics cranked out of the speakers. She couldn't help but sing to it. Hope absolutely loved this song.

Elaine dropped the top in the 'Stang, and they took off like a shot for Hope's mother's house.

"Have you ever thought about trying to go pro with your singing?" Elaine asked carefully.

Hope let out a snort. "Yah sure; I am going to be allowed to sing as soon as hell freezes over! Besides, I suck at singing. There isn't a band around that would take me."

"Hope, that's utter bullshit. There are a lot of people that think you have a real talent, and believe you could make millions."

Hope shook her head. "There is no way in heaven or hell I would ever get up in front of anyone and sing. Not only no, but *hell no*!"

"Yah, stage fright is a bitch, huh?" Elaine gave her a sideways glance. A few minutes later, Elaine pulled up to First Avenue and Ogden, where she had to wait for traffic to clear the intersection so she could hang a left onto Ogden. The light changed to yellow, and seeing a break, Elaine started to pull out of the intersection. It was then that Hope saw the pick-up truck barreling down First Avenue. All she had time for was to look for that ever non-present brake on the passenger side and call out her best friend's name in warning before the sound of screeching tires permeated the air, then total, blessed darkness.

"Hope, come on Hope, come back to us!" A gentle, masculine voice kept calling her name from behind.

"Hope, come on, Honey, I'm not going to let you go! Come back to us, Sweetheart." The kind male voice once again broke through the void. Sirens wailed all around her, but she was too weak to open her eyes. Did Nick finally kill her?

"Hope, come on honey, open your eyes. Come on; let me see those beautiful eyes."

She did as the voice asked, only because she wanted to see if the face matched the attractiveness of the voice. "That's a girl, come back to Davy."

Davy? Who the hell was Davy? "Elaine....where's Elaine?" she asked again; her voice weak even to her own ears, but she needed to know if her best friend was ok.

"Is Elaine your friend that was driving? We....we got her out. You're in much worse shape than she is." he said, running his fingers through her hair, relaxing her.

So this was what a kind touch was like. She'd utterly forgotten how good it felt.

Davy kept talking to her, asking questions, making sure she didn't fall back to sleep. His voice stayed kind, low, and tranquil. "Honey, do you know who the president of the United States is?"

"Ronald Regan."

"Can you tell me your full name?" he asked

"Hope Leslie McLeod."

"How old are you, Honey?"

"I'm twenty-one."

"Well, Sweetheart, let's make sure you have your twenty-second birthday, okay? Can you try to stay awake?"

"I'll try. Why does my face hurt like this?"

"Honey, you were hit by a truck." The back of his forefinger caressed her cheek.

"I....I was hit by a truck?" she just couldn't remember!

"Yes, sweetie; but you're going to be fine. We'll get you out of here, get you to Loyola University Medical Center, and get you fixed up."

"Why can't you get me out of here now?" she asked, panic rising in her chest, making it harder to breathe.

"You're trapped at the moment, between the frame of the car, the dashboard, and the door. We are waiting on the JAWS of Life to get you out, but it's going to take about twenty minutes. Do you have any family you want me to call?"

"M…my mother, oh god, she's just had a stroke. She won't take this very well." Hope gave him her mother's number; he relayed it to someone else, and the person left.

"I want to make you a promise, sweetie. I'm not going to leave your side until I absolutely have to. I'm going to be here with you throughout this entire thing, I swear it."

"I….I just can't understand…." she started, and couldn't finish, as the tears started flowing down her cheeks like Niagara Falls. Her breath came out in short bursts, as she tried to hold in the terror that was coursing through her.

"What don't you understand?" he asked; confusion thick in his voice. She wished she could see his face, but he was sitting behind her in the back seat.

"I don't understand why you're being so kind to me…this is my fault….it's my fault…." Her voice caught in her throat, choking on the sob trying to force its way out.

"Oh no, honey, no! It wasn't your fault, not in the slightest!" he said, soothing her hair.

"Yes, it is…if I would just have listened to him and took the train, none of us would be here right now!" she said, sobbing. Nick was going to be worse than a pissed-off grizzly when he finds out about this! She would be lucky to live through it!

"Listened to whom, Hope?"

"Nickolas Davenport, my boyfriend…oh god, he's going to kill me!" she wailed, unable to keep it in anymore.

"No he won't honey, not if he loves you." His voice was gentle, reassuring, but this time it didn't work.

"No, you don't understand. He's…he truly is going to kill me! I didn't do what he said to do, and he's going to kill me!" she repeated, more terrified than she could begin to fathom.

"Honey, does he…does he hurt you?" Davy asked, dubious.

She could only nod, the words stuck in her throat.

"Well, he won't hurt you as long as I am here Sweetheart; I swear on my life." he vowed, his voice stiff, as if he were angry but trying not to show it.

Hope heard another siren. "Here come your JAWS, honey." She heard the smile in his voice.

"This is going to hurt, isn't it?" she asked, still scared.

"Yes, to be perfectly honest. I will be here with you the whole way, and you can squeeze my hand as hard as you want. It will be over quickly, then you will be out of here, and Loyola will take good care of you."

She heard him whisper something under his breath, but she didn't have time to ask him what he had said, since another voice called from outside the car. "Davy, it's here! We need to cover her, and get it rolling. Traffic is backed up for miles!"

"Ok, Mikey. We're ready here!" Davy loudly called out.

A blanket was put over Hope to keep glass from spraying her face. It vaguely occurred to her how the gapers on the sidewalk would think she was dead, but she honestly didn't care.

"Now Hope, remember, you can squeeze my hand, and scream all you want, even if you go hoarse. You've earned it honey."

As she nodded, she heard a loud motor fire up, sounding ambiguously like a chainsaw with nearly the same amount of decibels. Davy wrapped both arms around her from behind. She tried to use one of her hands, but her left forearm and elbow screamed in protest as she attempted to grab both of his hands, scared to death. He tightened his arms, giving her a kind of a hug, and then loosened them as the JAWS started cutting apart this beautiful Mustang to get her out. She only breathed hard as the steel that was wrapped around her ankle began digging in further, then finally released. She refused to scream since she had lived through much worse than this.

"Honey, let us move your leg now, don't you try to move it, okay?" Davy instructed.

"Okay. Thank you so much for being here, in case I don't get to tell you that later," she said, her breath still coming in short, fast bursts.

"It has been my pleasure, Sweetheart." He gave her another quick hug, then she felt someone grab her under the arms, slowly dragging her out of the car. She was loaded onto a backboard, then onto a rolling gurney; the gapers clapping and cheering wildly from the sidewalk. They loaded her into the ambulance, and immediately, something felt very wrong. Her heart started skipping beats, taking her breath. Her chest tightened painfully, the excruciating agony travelled down her arm, back up into her jaw, and down her back. The back of the ambulance started growing dark, as if the sun descended over the horizon, but it was nine in the morning.

The last thing she heard was: "We're losing her! Grab the defibrillator!" She felt herself being pulled into a different kind of blackness, one that she knew she might not be able to come out of this time. For once, she wasn't afraid, she just let it take her.

CHAPTER 2

Hope again awoke to a strange beeping sound, sort of like a dying battery of a fire alarm although it was every second. She opened her eyes, and realized she was in the hospital!

Her head slowly turned since she was still weak as hell, and the level of pain was off the charts, but the beeping wasn't from a fire alarm, it was from a heart monitor! The most gorgeous man ever known to humanity sat in a chair next to her bed, reading a magazine. She must have made a noise of some kind, as his head snapped up.

She couldn't help but to stare at him. His long, raven hair was tied back in a ponytail; his nose was a straight shot down the center of his face, but not too long. His lips were full, thick, and made for kissing, but the best part of him was his striking eyes--almost a glowing sapphire. She had a hard time dragging her eyes away from his, since she had never seen a color like that on another human being. To say he was tall would be the understatement of the century. He had to be close to six-feet four-inches tall! His arms were the size of her thighs, ones that looked like they could tear her apart without effort. His chest seemed to go on forever, his abs flat, and his legs long and muscle-laden. True. Perfection. Incarnate.

"Hi, Hope, I'm Davy." His voice matched his body--baritone, devastating, and intrinsically male. A delicious shiver ran down the length of her spine, pooling between her legs.

"Hi, Davy..." she stammered. She simply could not take her eyes off of him.

"How are you feeling?" he asked, his eyes wide with worry.

"Well, I was hit by a truck today. I have no memory of the ambulance ride, or getting to the hospital. How do you think I feel?" She tried to keep the sarcasm out of her voice, but it was impossible. That was the one part of her that reared its ugly head at will, and there wasn't a damned thing she could do to stop it.

He gave a snort. "Touché, it was a stupid question." He looked down at the floor as redness crept up his neck, and into his cheeks.

"Listen, I am off duty today; I am an EMT working for the local fire department. I would like to stay around and give you some company, if that is okay with you." he said softly, as if he was afraid of her reaction.

"Isn't that fraternization, and conflict of interest?"

He shrugged. "Well, yes, but I really don't care. There is something… special about you. They'll slap me on the wrist, and call it a day. Since I was off duty there isn't much they can do to me, it's my own time."

"All right, I would like it if you were to keep me company, for however long you want." she smiled and felt her cheeks heat with embarrassment.

He gave a wide smile, one where you could almost see molars, as if she had just made him the happiest man in the world. He pulled up the doctor's stool, and sat beside the bed. "They are going to admit you for observation."

"Oh, thank god!" She couldn't help it; she gets a vacation! What happened to get her here sucked like nothing else, but damn it, it was worth it to get away from *him* for a short time!

He raised an eyebrow, and how bizarre was it that she found that one small movement the sexiest thing she'd ever seen?

"Most people don't think it's a good thing that they're being put in the hospital."

A sardonic snort escaped his lips. "Trust me, it's a good thing. It gives me a break from the epitome of stupid."

His eyes narrowed to slits. God, he had the most expressive eyes she'd ever seen. "Hope, I realize we just met, and you have no reason to trust me, but I would really like you to tell me what gave you the bruises on your face and stomach."

Her heart pounded in her chest. What would happen if he or anyone else knew what was truly going on? She let out a long, drawn-out sigh, not wanting to talk about it. However, to her own horror, the words started spilling out before she could stop them, like an overflowing dam about to devastate an entire village.

"I am dating someone who personifies the word *cruel*. The apartment we live in is in my name, yet he has taken over every aspect of it, and my life. One wrong word, one wrong motion, and he will beat me within an inch of my life. He won't allow me to work; he pushed all of my friends but one out of my life, and doesn't like me having anything to do with my family. If he is really angry, he will have his friends...." She couldn't finish. Her body started shaking uncontrollably, and her lungs constricted, leaving her gasping for air.

He didn't say anything; he just took her hand that didn't have the IV in it.

Once Hope calmed herself, she began again. "He has tried to kill me several times, and has vowed that if I ever leave him, he would kill my family, slowly and painfully. My baby sister is pregnant, and my mother recently had a stroke. My mother, my sister, and future brother-in-law all live in a one bedroom townhouse in Naperville so there is no more room for me. I have no place else to go."

He nodded. "Let me talk to my roommate. Let's see what we can figure out."

She lay in her bed, stunned. "Wait, you want to help me? Why would you do that? You are putting your life in danger just by talking to me!"

"Trust me, I can handle myself. I'm concerned about *you*. Don't worry; you won't be going back there."

She could only give a small smile and shake her head. "I have things I need to pick up there, clothing, etcetera."

"No, you won't. I will get you all new clothes."

"Oh, no! That is where I draw the line! You are not going to spend any money on me whatsoever. Not one penny. Is that in any way unclear?" she demanded vehemently.

He chuckled, unfazed by her vehemence. "My dear, you need clothes and other important items."

"You aren't my boyfriend, or my husband. It isn't your job to spend money on me!"

"Hope, what if I was to say that I would like to get to know you and see if we may be compatible?"

She couldn't move, couldn't speak. Someone this damned gorgeous liked her? What could she say to that? "I...I don't know what to say....I would be honored."

It was then that her mother and sister burst into the room. Her mom took one look at her and almost burst into tears. "Oh god, Hope!" she breathed and covered her mouth.

"Do I look that bad?" she couldn't help but ask, fear making her heart race again.

"Hi, I'm Cassandra, Hope's mother, she said politely, obviously ignoring Hope's question, and offered Davy her hand distractedly, keeping her eyes on Hope.

"I'm Davy Marshall, the EMT that helped get her out of the car."

Her sister shyly ambled up to Davey. "I'm Grace." She also shook his hand.

"Are you ok, Sweetie?" Mom asked, looking at Hope.

Hope almost rolled her eyes. *Why do people ask that when you're lying in the trauma unit of a hospital? If you are here, then no, you're not ok.* "Yah, I'm just peachy. Thought I'd come in here for a vacation. It's much better than the tropics."

Mom barked out a laugh.

"Sis, Kenny went to get Nick." Grace leaned down and gave Hope a kiss on the forehead. *Thank god that it's the only place on my body that doesn't hurt!* Hope's heart beat overtime at the thought that Nick was on his way! She tried to swallow it, but still shuddered, unable to hold it back.

"Ma'am, may I talk to you in the hall for a moment?" Davy asked, looking at her Mother.

"Yes, of course. Grace, stay with your sister."

She nodded, and took Hope's hand. "You scared about ten years off of our lives there, sis!"

God, what is it with these people? "Yah, I talked to the driver just moments before he hit me. I begged for the maximum amount of pain, just leave me alive. I'm a masochist like that."

Grace laughed. "That is the best sound I ever heard. Where do you come up with that shit?"

"I have no clue; it's in the script I guess." Fifteen-year-olds; gotta love 'em.

Mom and Davy came back into the room. "Gracie, let's go grab a bite to eat. My blood sugar is dropping, and I know you haven't eaten since six this morning."

Her sister nodded. "I love you, Hope."

"I love you too sis." Hope said as they walked out.

"They are getting ready to transport you upstairs now, hon. You don't have to move from there; the orderlies are going to move you, sheet and all."

"Sweet, because I don't think I could stand on my ankle right now." Hope said, wincing from a sharp throb. She tried to move it just to see what would happen, and sucked in a sharp breath when pain shot up her leg.

"Yah, they're going to take you to Orthopedics on the way to your room. Your right ankle and left arm are broken in several places, and the ligaments are torn out of your right knee. They are going to put you in medieval torture devices known as casts. You're going to be in a wheelchair for a bit…there's no way in hell you can use crutches."

Oh, crap, I didn't think about that! "Do you know about how long I will be in it?"

"About 6 weeks. But you will graduate to crutches and then a cane. You will need several months of physical therapy."

"So, what did you and my mother talk about?" she asked him, being nosy.

"I wanted to know if you had insurance. Since you don't, I gave your Mom the money for this little descent into the hell we know as the hospital."

An orderly came into the room dressed in a pair of white scrubs before Hope could protest. "Are you ready, Hope? We're going to take you to get you fixed up and then on to your room. But this taxi service is free." He then looked at her arms. "Oh *hell* no, this is unacceptable!" he exclaimed and walked out.

Davy's eyebrows knitted together in confusion. He looked closer, and then rolled his eyes. "Honey, they need to take the glass out of your arm and leg before they can put the casts on."

"Oh god, this hospital is run by geniuses," Hope laughed.

"Honestly, sweetie, this is one of the best hospitals in the Chicago area."

The orderly came back with a plastic bowl and tweezers, and began to pick the glass out piece by piece. Once he was finished with her arms, he moved to her legs. After what seemed forever, he announced he was finished. "That's all I can get, the rest will have to work itself out; the glass is embedded too deep. I'm so sorry that they didn't do this earlier," he said sincerely.

"Yah, well, I never claimed that people are brilliant," Hope laughed.

The orderly unlocked the gurney, and wheeled her out of the trauma unit with Davy beside her all the way. Once they reached Orthopedics, the staff had Davy wait outside while they put the casts on her.

Finally, after what seemed an eternity, Hope reached the door to her room. Her mother and sister were sitting in chairs inside her room when she arrived. Once every few moments, Grace would give a wince, but lately she had been having a lot of Braxton Hicks contractions. It was two months too early for her to go into labor anyway, so Hope wasn't worried. Davy commandeered the third chair, and pulled it up to the bed next to her.

Mere seconds after she got reasonably comfortable in the bed, Davy grabbed her hand. At that exact moment, Kenny and Nick walked into the room. Nick's eyes darkened as he looked at Davy, then at Hope. He came slowly toward her, his face contorted with rage. He didn't say anything, just scowled at her for a few tense seconds. She tried to brace herself, knowing full well what was coming; it was just a question of when. His mouth opened and closed a couple of times, and she could tell he was trying to figure out what to say. "I told you to do the dishes, Bitch!" he finally got out, his voice full of venom. Before anyone could stop him, he hauled back, and his fist connected with the same spot on Hope's temple that the grill of the truck had hit. She saw stars, and obscurity once again fell over her like an old friend.

CHAPTER 3

Davy heard Cassandra cry out in horror and rage, as Hope's head rocked to the side from the blow that son of a bitch delivered, and he erupted like Mt. St. Helen's. "Go get the doctor, Cassandra!" he told her mother. He threw the dumb shit against a wall, holding him there by just his fingers to the throat. It took everything he had to keep from squeezing until he crushed the bastard's windpipe. "You're going to jail, piece of shit, or maybe I'll just put you in the morgue!"

The bastard just laughed, pissing Davy off even more! "You don't know who you're dealing with. Let me go, or you won't walk out of here alive!"

"Does it look like I give a shit, you fucking coward? Does it make you feel like a big bad man to hit a woman? Why don't you hit someone who can liquefy your ass?" It was more of a demand than a question. "Go ahead, asshole, give me a reason, I dare you!" Davy just spat into his face.

At that exact moment, the doctor and security ran into the room, followed by Cassandra. They peeled him off of the bastard. Davy told them what this sorry excuse for a man did, and security carted him off. Davy looked at Hope, who had still not regained consciousness.

The doctor screamed out the door for a nurse, ordering a barrage of tests. Once they were said and done, the doctor had only one alternative. "She is in a coma. We can only sit here and wait for her to wake up. She is breathing, so we don't have to put her on a respirator, but we are going to have to intravenously feed her. We, as in the hospital staff, are going to press charges on Nickolas for attempted murder. If she dies, we will get him for full-blown murder."

"Dies? You mean my daughter could die?" Cassandra asked, her voice thick with terror.

"There is a slim chance of it, Mrs. McLeod. It is mostly going to depend on her stubbornness, and sheer will."

Davy's eyes welled up with tears as Cassandra broke down, her legs completely giving out from under her. Hope's sister and brother-in-law rushed to her, both of them trying to hold Cassandra up. A horrendous, soul-wracking, inhuman wail came from somewhere deep within her. Davy dashed a chair over to sit under Hope's mother before she collapsed to the floor. Tears fell from the older woman like a storm. "Not another baby! Gracie, it's your brother all over again!"

Wait, Hope has a brother?

"Mom, Hope won't die like Corey did. She has a chance. She's stubborn and bullheaded. She's not about to let this take her out. Corey was too little and sickly to stand a chance. I know my sister. She's strong, Mom."

Cassandra nodded, but continued to sob.

Feeling like an intruder, he went over to Hope's bed and grabbed her hand. Damn it all to hell, he should have sprouted wings to keep that bastard from hitting her! An overwhelming urge washed over him. He wanted with everything in him to go downstairs to Security and pummel the son of a bitch until he wasn't breathing any more. Irate with himself that he didn't help her, he just wanted to swing around and hit something but he quickly got himself under control. It wouldn't help Hope or her family in any way.

"Davy, what are you doing over there? You saved my sister; therefore, you are a part of this family. My mother needs you; she needs us all."

He blinked, stunned. They've just met him, and were including him in their inner circle. Astonished, he did as was asked and tried his best to comfort them, but didn't know exactly what to do. He had almost no experience in such things. His parents died in a car accident when he was nine, which is what made him want to be a firefighter. He grew up in a slew of foster homes, none of them wanting him for longer than six months at a time, so he never really had a family, until Andy. He met his best friend and roommate in primary school when a bunch of bullies tried to corner Davy and beat the crap out of him just because he didn't have parents. Andy came up from behind them and attacked them, beating all three of them to the ground. Since then, they became joined at the hip. No matter where Davy went from there on, Andy was with him. Andy's parents even took him in. They treated him like another son, and all but adopted him. They had died soon after Davy and Andy reached adulthood.

When Davy was seventeen and Andy was nineteen, they both got jobs, and moved into an apartment. They joined the fire department together, where Davy became an EMT and Andy went on to bigger and better deals--first, the police academy, then the Chicago Police Department, and then to the FBI. Now that they were in their upper twenties, nothing had changed. They were still joined at the hip, and no one would ever find one without the other. They were brothers in every sense of the word, except by blood.

He shook himself back into the present. All Davy could do was wrap his arms around Hope's mother. Granted, he'd only just met Hope, but he also felt a deep panic that she wouldn't make it.

"Ma'am, why don't you get some rest and come back in a few hours? I will stay with her, and I swear to call you if there are any changes," he suggested, worried about Hope's mother.

"I am not leaving her side, Davy, and I would love it if you call me *mom*."

Close to tears with rectitude swelling in his heart, he agreed, and said: "Then let me have them bring in a cot for you. We can all take turns sitting with her."

"He's right, Mom. You need rest. You are still recovering from your stroke, and it isn't going to help Hope if you are in a bed next to her." Grace said, rubbing her lower back.

"Grace, are you ok?" Davy asked. She wasn't looking well either. Every few seconds, a hard wince pinched her face, and she was continuously rubbing her back, shifting in her chair as if she was uncomfortable.

"Yes, I'm fine. It's just some low back pain. I'm not the important one here; it's my mother and sister." As soon as she got the words out, water gushed out from under her skirt, soaking it through.

He jumped up and bolted just outside the room to the nurse's station. "We have a pregnant woman in labor; her water just broke."

The nurse's station came alive. One nurse picked up the phone to call Labor and Delivery, another called a janitor to clean up the amniotic fluid, while the other came running behind him. Davy broke into a full sprint when a scream pierced the air, the nurse close at his heels. Grace lay on the floor, using Lamaze breathing, and Kenny was holding her hand.

"Ma'am, the baby is too early!" Kenny called out, terror in his eyes.

The nurse rushed back to the door. "Call Neo-Natal Intensive care *now* and get us a Neonatologist!" she yelled out.

"A gurney is on the way." Another nurse came into the room to assist.

Davy went back to Hope's side, taking her hand. He faced away from the birth going on over in the corner, giving Grace privacy. "Hope, you need to come back, sweetie. Your sister is having her baby. Don't you want to see your niece or nephew?" There was no response, no eyelid flicker, no tightening of her hand. It was like she was asleep, a very deep sleep. He saw a slight rise and fall of her chest, so he knew she was breathing, and the EKG she was hooked up to showed that her heart was beating at a steady pace, so she was still alive. But she showed no signs of life whatsoever.

He had never felt so helpless, and he just wanted to scream the walls down! She obviously went through hell, and it's as if the fates want her to go through more! He looked into her peaceful face. "Please, honey, come back. I will give everything I have to see that you are protected for the rest of your life. He will never hurt you or your family again, I swear on my own life!"

A split second later, the gurney came into the room, pushed by an orderly. They loaded Grace onto it, and began wheeling her out. As they hit the door, she looked over at the baby's father. "If you ever touch me again, I will rip it off and shove it in a place that is exit only!"

Davy let out a chuckle and shook his head. She was a lot like her sister.

"I don't know where to go. Both my kids need me!" Hope's mom said, tears streaming down her face, her eyes filled with confusion. That poor woman was so stressed out she couldn't think clearly.

"Cassandra, go with Grace. Hope isn't….here right now, and Grace needs you more. I will stay with her."

After Cassandra rushed out to catch up with her other daughter, his eyes again turned to Hope. When he saw her unconscious in that car for the first time, he about came unglued. He felt like he was seeing someone he had loved from birth dying in front of him. He got what was left of her friend out of the car, and climbed in. He looked around, and saw that she was trapped. That damned driver had been drunk off his ass, and reeked of marijuana. When the cops got there, they arrested him, and towed the truck. The stupid son of a bitch hit them doing close to fifty! He pushed the car close to seventy-five feet, where it jumped the curb! She had to have an angel sitting on her shoulder.

• •

Andy Newcomb sat at the bar in *The Midnight Special,* a local posh club, checking his watch every three minutes. Where the hell was he? This wasn't like Davy to stand him up like this!

"Hi Andy, what can I get ya?" The cute bartender asked. Now that woman as someone Andy would like to know intimately! She had short auburn hair, long, muscular legs, a flat stomach, cute little button nose, and a smile to warm the coldest day, or heart, whichever. You know what they say about red-heads, red in the head, fire in the…"I'll just take the usual, Emily." He winked at her.

She winked back, giving him the once-over. Maybe tonight… .."Whiskey Sour coming right up." She walked away, her hips swinging enticingly. Oh yah, he'd really like a piece of that!

He remembered why he was there, and looked at his watch one more time. He decided to call the station; they may have gotten a call or something. He dropped a quarter into the pay phone, and dialed the number. Lieutenant Jerrod Jackson answered.

"Hey, it's Andy. Have you seen Davy around anywhere?"

"No, Andy, there was a massive accident earlier today and he was on scene, but he never came back from the trauma unit. If you see him, have him call the station, okay?"

"Wait, was he involved? Is he okay?"

"Oh god, no, he was on scene when the accident happened, and he helped to extricate two trapped female victims out of the vehicle. He went with one of them to the trauma unit, and hasn't come back yet."

"He's at Loyola then?"

"Yes." Jerrod said, and said his goodbye.

"Davy, what the hell are you doing? You are going to get yourself fired or suspended!" he mumbled, taking his car keys out of his pocket and hanging up the phone. He finished his drink, left Em a good tip, and headed toward Loyola.

Davy could get himself into some hair-brained scrapes, and had been lucky so far, but this was going to be the mother of them all. Andy could see it now. He was going to get together with this girl, get his ass fired, she would break up with him, shatter his heart into a million pieces, and then he was going to be penniless, jobless, and ruined. There was no way in hell he would allow that to happen to his best friend! Fuck. That.

Wait, what was he doing? Loyola is a huge hospital. Their trauma unit alone sees hundreds of patients a week. What was he supposed to do, go in and ask Gail, the head of the department, to see a woman that was brought in early this morning? He has no name, information, or description, only that Davy was with her.

Yah, that was it, he would ask Gail for Davy, not to see the chick. Gail knew Davy and Andy. She knew they weren't going to cause trouble.

He walked into the unit, and found her at the nurse's station. "Hi Gail." He went up to her, and ran his hands through his thick dark hair.

"Oh, hi, Andy, is everything ok?"

"No, but if you can tell me where my damned roommate is, it will be."

"He came in with a bad car accident earlier. We treated her and put her upstairs. He went with her, and I haven't seen him since."

"How bad are we talking here, Gail?"

"She was hit by a pick-up doing fifty. She came in Code Yellow."

Ok, that explained things a little bit, but he still should have been gone by now. "Are you able to tell me where you put her? The department is looking for Davy, and I have no way to get in touch with him."

"All right, but if I lose my job because you told someone, I will nail your ass to a wall!" she promised.

"You know me better than that!"

She went to the computer to look up the room number, wrote it on a sticky note, and thrust it at Andy.

"Thank you."

She waved off the thank you and went back to doing her paperwork, dismissing him.

He looked at the room number. She wasn't in intensive care, which was a good sign. He wouldn't be able to get into that unit.

He went up to the room, and saw Davy sitting beside the bed, holding the hand of a stunningly beautiful woman about their age. Her long red hair fanned around her face on the pillow, seemingly asleep. Her face had deep cuts and gashes, along with a huge bruise around her right eye, making her look like someone beat the ever-loving hell out of her instead of being in a car accident.

"Davy." Andy whispered, not wanting to wake the accident victim.

Davy came out into the hall and shut the door.

Andy started in immediately. "What the hell do you think you're doing? This will get you fired!"

"You don't understand, Andy. I witnessed a crime, and I will be damned if I just up and leave her. Someone has to protect her."

"That's what Security is for! This is a conflict of interest, and you'll be lucky if they only suspend you!"

"Do you think I give a damn? Her *life* is more important than the department! I can get another job. Hell, I have the band I can fall back on!"

"You would choose a woman you don't even know over the department?" Andy asked derisively.

Davy turned around, and put a hand against the wall, leaning against it. "Dude, seriously. You don't understand."

"You're right, I don't understand. So enlighten me."

He gave it all to Andy. He told him about the accident, the guy that came in here and sent her into a coma, Grace and the baby, everything. "If I don't do something to protect her, when he gets out of jail, he will kill her and her family. I have no problems believing that after what I saw. I am not leaving her side, Andy. I will take a leave of absence if I have to, but I'm not leaving."

Andy felt like punching the shit out of something. So someone did beat the hell out of her. But that certainly didn't excuse blowing off the job that he wanted since he was a kid for a woman he'd just met. "Don't even tell me that you're falling in love with her! I'll knock the shit out of you!"

"Don't be ridiculous! Yes, I am attracted to her, but I don't know her well enough to fall in love with her. I just met her five hours ago! I want to make sure that she and her family are safe. But right now, she is in a coma. When she comes out of it, I am going to bring her home. There is no room at her mother's, and I will not have her go back to numb nuts. There are no shelters around here for her. It's either she comes with us, or she goes onto the street. I won't have that."

Andy looked at him wide eyed. "You have got to be kidding me! You've just told me that her life is in danger, and you're bringing her to our place? Are you nuts?"

He shrugged. "Maybe, but it's going to happen. I am also going to get George and his guys to watch her mother's place. There is a new baby to think of, and I will not let this sick fuck hurt them!"

Suddenly, a suspicion hit Andy. This guy sounds familiar, real familiar. "What is this puke's name?"

"Nickolas Davenport."

Andy's eyes got wide. Holy shit, the woman in there is Hope McLeod! The police and FBI have been investigating Nickolas for a year now on suspicion of mob activity and drug trafficking. They knew that Hope had nothing to do with any of his activities, and they've been trying to think of a way to get her out of there before they made a move on Davenport. It could, and would, turn ugly if they busted into the apartment with Hope there, a hostage situation at best, cleaning her body parts off the walls with a spatula at worst.

"What is it, Andy?" Davy asked.

"You're right; we have to get her out of there. I will call the department and have our place declared a safe house."

"The FBI has a stake in this, don't they?"

He nodded. "Yes, we have a huge stake in this. Don't worry, your job is safe. I will tell the department that I invited her in after I found out who she is, and it's a matter for the FBI to worry about.

"Andy, I don't give a damn about that. All I want to know is how much danger she is in."

"More than you know. Davenport is up there with Lucky Luciano."

Now Davy's eyes grew round as saucers. "We have to get Hope's family out of their house. What about Witness Protection?"

"Possibly, we will have to wait and see. I have to call headquarters first. I am a field operative, not a supervisor; it's their call to contact the Federal Marshals."

"When Hope's mother returns from her other daughter having a baby, we will let her know what is going on. For now, I want to put the family in a motel," Davy seemed to be shaking with worry over them. Andy knew better than anyone the size of Davy's heart, it could encompass the entire northern hemisphere and still have room.

"Let me talk to my supervisor and see if we can arrange something. I will do it when we get back to the house."

"I am not leaving this hospital until Hope wakes up," Davy said; his voice saturated with finality. Andy knew what that tone meant, there was no budging him from this decision. A more stubborn man had never been born, except for maybe himself. Well, there was no *maybe* about it; he was actually more stubborn than Davy was, and damn proud of it!

"All right, Davy. At least do yourself a favor, and take care of yourself. Do things like eat and shower." He gave a long, drawn out sigh. He knew he was making a big mistake by what he was about to say, but it had to be done. "I can come and sit with her while you shower and eat."

"All right, it wouldn't help Hope if I am sitting there while my blood sugar drops."

"Have you eaten anything at all?"

"Yes, I was at McDonald's when the accident happened," he chuckled. "I just left my fries and coke sitting there, and bolted out the door. I had eaten my Big Mac."

Davy went back in the room, followed by Andy. All they could do was sit and watch Hope, hoping she would come out of it, hoping against hope that it didn't kill her.

Andy couldn't help but stare at her. She was positively gorgeous! He was convinced that his heart stopped in his chest the moment he looked at her, he was unable to breathe straight, and he wanted to tear back around and rip Davenport's head off for what he did to her. No one has the right to do that to another human being, woman or not! He just sat in the extra chair next to Davy. However, since Davy was highly attracted to her, this one he needed to keep to himself. She may be positively stunning, but....

"Andy, you ok? You're breathing awfully hard," Davy asked.

"Yah, I'm fine. It's just hard to see what he did to her. I just want to kill him with my bare hands." It was only a partial lie.

"Now you understand why I couldn't leave."

Andy nodded. "Yah I get it. Listen, go and get something to eat and I'll sit here with her. I will call the station when you get back and let them know what's going on."

Davy just nodded and kissed her forehead, then walked out.

Andy just stared at her a moment. Softly, he whispered; "What did he do to you?"

He had never heard any of the recordings, so he had no clue. He just knew some of the people that were assigned to the case. Hell, it was big news over at the Bureau. Davenport was known as someone who was volatile, cruel, and inhumane. They just couldn't pin anything on him right now except beating on Hope, and there was nothing that the FBI could do about that. It was a matter for the police.

If what the bureau knew about Davenport was true, this woman had been to hell and back. Davy was right, she had to be helped. There was no way she could make it through this alone.

A few minutes later, Davy walked back into the room with a woman, an older version of Hope.

"Andy, this is Hope's mother, Cassandra. Cassandra, this is FBI agent Andrew Newcomb." He made the introductions.

"FBI? What would the Federal Bureau of Investigations be doing here?"

"There is a lot to this that you don't know, Ma'am." Davy started. "But it's mainly because Andy is my roommate, and he and I have decided to take Hope in, when she wakes up."

"Wait, what don't I know?" she asked, fear again darkening her eyes.

Andy just broke into his spiel. "Ma'am, Nickolas Davenport is a very dangerous man. The FBI has been investigating him for a year now, with backup from the Chicago PD. We fully believe that he will try to kill you and your family. We are going to get your family out of your house and put you up in a motel with full security. We are also going to make sure that Hope is kept safe."

"Bullshit. Nick is a blowhard, more talk than action."

"No ma'am, he isn't. It is suspected that he is a mafia hit man, with ties to a drug cartel. It is reputed that he killed people with the numbers well into the double digits. With Davy having him arrested, he is going to be angry when he gets out, and he will be out for blood."

"You're serious, aren't you? My god, Hope met him in high school! They were in the same classes together! I have known him for several years! How could he be a hit man?"

"Ma'am, there isn't time to go into that. We have to make sure that you and your family are safe. Either Davy or I are going to be here at all times."

"Do…do you think that Hope is involved in his activities?" Cassandra asked, fear dripping from her voice.

"No, we firmly believe she has no clue about what he is involved in. Nick's arrest puts a kink into our plans, but we are glad it happened. That young lady deserves to be protected, and she needs to get the hell out of that house. We haven't arrested him because he doesn't let her leave unless it is absolutely necessary; and we will not have her become a casualty. We have had that apartment bugged since the beginning of our investigation, so we know precisely what he puts her through, though our hands are tied on doing anything about it. I will say this, should the moment have arrived that she would have been dying; we would have torn that apartment to hell and back to get her out and put him where he belongs."

"All right, I will have Kenny pack up some clothes for all of us."

He answered her, quickly and sharply. "No! *No one* is to go back to your home! We will get clothes for all of you, and anything else you may need, including the baby. Once you get to your motel, you aren't to leave unless it is to come here, and even then, you will come with an armed escort. We will deliver you food, and any important items. You need to understand that this is urgent, your lives are on the line!"

The older woman nodded, her face turning the color of paste. "I understand, and take this seriously. I will make sure my daughter and son in law takes it seriously also." Her hands shook as she brought them to her mouth. "I feel so horrible that I didn't believe Hope when she tried to tell me what was going on!"

"You had no idea, Ma'am. How could you have? He has her positively terrified to even breathe wrong, let alone tell you the full scope of what he is doing to her. Now please, allow me to escort you to dinner. It would be my honor, and my treat. Not on the government, but my tab."

She gave a wan smile. "Thank you, but I can pay for my own meal."

"I insist. Save your money, you're going to need it." He helped her up, and offered her his arm as they left for the cafeteria.

"All right, thank you so much. But after that, I have to get back to Grace."

"It's understandable," Andy smiled.

After they walked out, Davy stared at Hope, just lying in her bed, not moving. A nurse came in, and made sure that atrophy wasn't going to set in by moving her body and massaging her limbs. She would turn Hope over to make sure bed sores didn't set in. It broke his heart to see Hope unresponsive, and near tears when people would beg her to wake, and there was nothing.

God, she was so beautiful. There wasn't a person in Hollywood that could compare to her, they would all fall short. Her mother told him stories of Hope growing up that would make him laugh and cry. She was stubborn, strong-willed, and lately she had been withdrawn, jumping at any sudden sound. She had the symptoms of what the army called *shell shock*, or what the psychiatric venue has started calling *post-traumatic stress disorder*. If and when she woke up, he was going to make sure she goes to therapy, hoping that it would help.

A few hours later, Kenny came racing into the room. "It's a girl, and we're naming her Davianna. We wanted to thank you in some small way for what you did for Hope, Davy."

"Thank you, but you don't have to do that. It is my honor to help her in any way I can." Davy said, and shook his hand. It really feels good to be honored like that, even if it is a bit embarrassing.

Two weeks later, Davy looked up at Andy when he came into the room with hopeful eyes. "Is there any word yet on Davenport?"

Andy shook his head. There hadn't been anything heard about the son of a bitch, who disappeared just this morning. He had returned to the apartment after making bail, and the FBI listened in on the bugs. He ransacked the damn place and by the time the FBI had gotten there to arrest him, he was gone. He had been found yesterday in a hotel about six blocks away from the apartment under an assumed name, but yet again, slippery bastard that he was, had disappeared.

He traced Hope's jawline with the tip of his finger. His heart skipped a beat when her head moved into it!

"Hope?" he asked, his heart thumping double time. Was she coming out of it? There was no response from her. Was it wishful thinking?

"Hey there, Bud, how is she?" Andy came from behind him and asked.

"I don't know...I thought..." He shook his head. "She's the same."

"There was a homicide last night. A woman with long copper-colored hair was found over by I-55. She was raped and shot execution style."

"Did Davenport do it?"

"We don't know for sure, but he is a suspect, just not the only one. The news about Hope has gone main-stream. The press is having a field day over this."

"How did they find out?" Davy's eyes grew wide, scared to death for her now.

Andy smiled. "A little birdie told them. We figure that if the public knows about Davenport, then the safer the family is. People love rewards."

Davy's heart stopped pounding. "What about the nut jobs who call with false sightings?"

"Those are easily weeded out. Do you honestly think we tell the press *everything*?"

Davy couldn't help but laugh. "Well, no, the government never does."

CHAPTER 4

Hope felt herself being pulled out of the nihility. Voices surrounded her, both male. One sounded vaguely familiar, like she should know who it was, but just couldn't place it. They were merely mumbling, with only coherent words slipping through once in a while.

Light started slipping through her lids. *No, I want to stay in this dark, safe vacuum. It is warm, comfortable. No problems, no worries, nothing but peace.*

"Davy...." There was more mumbling, and she heard her name.

"Hope? Sweetheart....." More mumbling came from all around her.

"Andy, go get the doctor!" the male voice shouted.

She turned her head and opened her eyes. "Will you please quit shouting; I am trying to sleep here." Her voice sounded raucous, and weak.

Someone that she didn't recognize came tearing into the room with a doctor, who performed a barrage of tests, and she heard her mother's name over an intercom.

"Where am I?" God, it hurt to talk, she felt like she deep throated a blowtorch.

"Honey, do you not remember anything?" Davy asked.

She just shook her head. The room was precipitously alive with doctors and nurses, and her mother ran in.

"Is she awake?" she asked Davy, and looked over at Hope. "Oh, thank god!" She dissolved into tears.

"Why is everyone freaking out? I have just been asleep for a few minutes."

"Hope, you have been in a coma for two weeks!" Davy answered intensely.

"What? Two weeks? How? When?" She rapid fired questions at them.

"Amnesia is common after a coma," the doctor said calmly. He went into the long explanation.

"Nick did this to me?" The heart monitor started beeping as Hope's heart rate went up, terror filling her. "Oh god, he's going to kill us all!" She started disconnecting wires, and the doctor stopped her when she tried to yank out her IV. "I've got to get out of here! No one is safe with me here!"

"No, Hope, you have to stay here," the doctor said, trying to calm her.

"I can't! You don't know him! He will come back and tear this place apart if I don't leave!"

"Hope, you're safe. Your family is safe, they're in hiding. The government is putting them in witness protection. You will come home with Andy and me when your doctors release you." Davy stroked my hair, his voice low, soothing.

A nurse came in, and injected Hope's IV with something. "This is Radovan; it will help calm you down."

"I don't need drugs; I need to make sure my family is safe!" She moaned when the drug kicked in. She reached out her hand for her mother. "Mom…."

"I'm okay, honey. I promise. I love you!" She heard her mom say as the room went dark again.

Hope awoke after the sun set. Davy was curled up in a chair in the corner, his eyes open. She took a deep, cleansing breath.

His head shot over. "Good morning, sleeping beauty!" He stood up and went over to the bed. "How are you feeling?" He gently took her hand.

"Tired." Her tongue felt thick, like she'd been on a drinking bender. "What happened? What time is it? Where's my mom?"

He took her hand. "It's okay, hon. It's about three in the morning, and your mom is asleep in her hotel room. I have some good news. Your sister had her baby."

"She did? What did she have?" A horrible, bone-crushing guilt washed over Hope that she hadn't been there for the birth.

"She had a beautiful, red-haired girl that she named Davianna." His voice is calm, soothing.

Hope turned her head away from him and looked out the window. Gracie went into labor because she was worried about Hope. She could have died, and it would have been entirely Hope's fault. Granted, Grace got pregnant willingly, but the fact that the baby was born six weeks early proved that Hope was an idiot. God, she should have listened to Nick. No wonder he was angry all the time.

"Hey, what's going on in that mind of yours?" He tilted her chin back around to look at him.

She gave a wan smile. "Nothing, I'm fine." She knew how to hide emotions well.

"Sorry, I'm not buying it," he said. "Let's try again. What are you thinking?"

Okay, maybe she wasn't as good as she thought. "It's my fault that the baby was born early. If I had just listened to Nick...."

He cut her off. "No, that isn't true. We are going to derail that train of thought right now. You had no way of knowing what would happen. Grace could have been at home, safe in her bed when Davianna was born. Plus, we would never have met." He smiled and kissed the back of Hope's hand.

Hope couldn't help but laugh at his boyish charm, or to stare into those dazzling eyes. She could get lost in their deep depths. Her heart leaped in her chest as he leaned down, his face slowly, tentatively coming closer, silently asking for permission. Her eyes moved to his lips, knowing she was about to taste their fullness. She closed her eyes, and....

"Davy, what the hell do you think you're doing?" A vaguely familiar voice called from the door, sharp and demanding.

He sighed and sat back up. "What does it look like I was doing, Andy? I was about to check Hope's tonsils for inflammation." he remarked dryly.

Damn the guy! She was about to get her first kiss from someone who truly feels something for her, and he interrupts it, quite rudely! Who is this guy, anyway?

"Looks like I got here just in time." Andy stared at Hope, accusation stabbed at her like daggers.

"That's a matter of opinion. What the hell do you want, Andy?" Davy did some demanding of his own.

The guy never took his eyes off of her. "Are you going to introduce us, or am I going to have to do it?"

"No, I won't if you're going to continue to be rude," Davy said low, pointedly.

"We will talk later, at home." His eyes returned to Hope. "I'm Agent Andrew Newcomb, Davy's best friend and roommate. You must be Hope McLeod." He extended his hand, which she took timidly, she felt his hatred for her stab her with profound cuts all over her body.

"I am." Her voice sounded small, cowardly, even to her ears.

He dropped her hand like it was a fireball. "I am here because your boyfriend escaped today. Do you know where he could be?"

"Nick escaped? Oh god!" Hope felt her body tremble, and the tears welled up in her eyes. "He's no longer my boyfriend, and I don't know, he could be at his mother's."

"We have already checked there. He wasn't there. Anyplace else he could be?" Andy stood over her, the air around him outright menacing.

"What the hell, Andy? What is this, an interrogation?"

"This is an ongoing investigation, where Hope will be a key witness. I have to question her. Don't get in the way, Davy." Andy still never took his eyes off of her. Hope thought she saw a flash of an unknown emotion, but it was gone before she could name it. His eyes turned gunmetal grey, again all business.

She felt the tears start streaming down her cheeks, her body shook, thinking about her family! If Nick escaped, they're in danger! She had to get out of here! They could go to Florida, or maybe New Zealand would be far enough away. On second thought, Pluto wouldn't be far enough away.

Hope's breath came out in pants, as though she couldn't breathe. She felt like her throat was closing up, and her heart beat triple time in her chest. The walls of the room seemed to close in on her!

"Hope, do you know of any other place he could be?" Andy repeated the question, his tone demanding an immediate answer.

She shook her head, no sound coming from her throat but short spurts of air as she tried in vain to catch a deep breath and to answer him, but no words would form. Her chest and arm felt like they wanted to explode.

"Andy, stop already; damn it! Look at her!" Davy thundered as she lay in her bed, gasping for air, the tears streaming down her cheeks like Niagara Falls.

"She's having an anxiety attack," Andy said as if it was something he saw every day. "I have to wonder why, Hope. Are you hiding him?"

"Oh yes, Andy, I forgot to tell you, she made a dozen phone calls to people trying to find a place for him to go to, all while she was in a coma." Davy glared daggers at his best friend. "Jesus, you're an asshole! What the hell is wrong with you?"

"I am doing my damned job, which is where you should be *right now*!"

Hope cried out, and curled into a ball at the sound of their anger. In her experience, that emotion was never a good one. It always got her hurt.

Davy jumped onto the bed, and wrapped his arms around her. "Ssssh, its ok," he murmured and smoothed her hair.

She heard Andy sigh. "I…I'm sorry, Hope. We have to find out where he is; there are too many lives at stake here, including your own. But I realize I am being too harsh. Please forgive me." he said in a much kinder, gentler tone.

Once she was able to breathe normally, Andy looked at her. "Please, tell me anything you can about him. Maybe you know something we don't."

"I know he is insane." She stopped, and sighed. "Look, I don't know what you want to know."

"Maybe if you start at the beginning of your relationship with him, it could give us some insight into the way he thinks." Andy suggested.

Hope sighed and nodded. "I met him while we were both in High School. He was a senior, I was a freshman. Back then, he was quite good-looking, and popular. He was a defensive lineman for the football team, and I was all but invisible to a lot of the school's populace, including the teachers. A mutual friend introduced us, and he sat beside me at the lunch table. He made me feel special, beautiful, and most of all, visible. After a month, we were full-fledged dating. My mother liked him, at first. He was kind, respectful to all of us. Then at the end of my freshman year, his house burned down, and Mom went to get him in the middle of the night, and let me sleep. I woke up to him sitting on my bed. She invited him to live with us, but he was to sleep on the couch, and look for work while I was in school. As far as I knew, everything was going fine. He had gotten a job in a cold storage warehouse, but the constant cold hurt his knee. So, he got another job where it wasn't cold. He worked that for about a year.

"One day, he and my mother got into a huge fight, and she kicked him out. To me, it just came out of nowhere. I was angry, and threatened to go with him. I didn't know it at the time, but Mom caught him selling cocaine. She didn't tell me *that* until recently. He told her that he would kill my sister and me slowly and painfully if she ever told me. I was going into my junior year of high school at this point. My relationship with my mother had deteriorated to the point where we could hardly stand to look at each other. We were constantly fighting over Nick, and I could do nothing right. So, I got a job, both working and going to school full-time. I moved out, got an attorney, and was emancipated.

"Slowly, Nick became abusive. It started with a slap across the face. He cried for hours, telling me how sorry he was, and that he would never do it again. We were having dire money problems, and then all of a sudden, we were fine. All of our bills were paid, and he was talking about buying us a house, then he talked about getting married. But, he said that I wasn't pulling my own weight, I just wasn't making enough money to suit him, so he made me quit my job, and he started pimping me out. If I didn't make three thousand dollars a night, he would beat me, and….force me to sleep with his ruthless friends."

Neither Davy nor Andy said a word. They merely stared at her with stunned expressions. Davy took Hope's hand again, and Andy put a hand on her shoulder, both seeming to lend her strength to finish. She had never told a soul any of this before, and it scared the shit out of her to do it now, but Agent Newcomb was right. It needed to be told.

She took a deep breath and continued. "I graduated in '84, and had started talking to my mother again. I wanted to patch things up; she is my mother after all. I tried telling her what he was doing, although I left out a lot of stuff, and she didn't believe me. I never felt so alone in my life. He threw an absolute fit that I was talking to her, but he would allow me to go see her. By this time, he had complete control over me. I don't know how he got it, or when, but it had happened.

"Mom had moved into a one-bedroom townhouse, and started having health issues. So Grace and her fiancé moved in with her, and stayed in the loft at the top of the stairs. Grace had been living with our father since Mom had kicked out Nick, not wanting to deal with the drama that it had created. But every time I would go to visit Mom, Nick would throw a conniption. I wouldn't even be there an hour when he would call, demanding I come home, and would pick a small thing that I had to come home for, like he couldn't find a pan, or that his mother wants us over for dinner, when he had never told me about it before. If I didn't leave immediately, he would call every ten minutes, pissing my mother off until I left. Then, when I got home, I would be beaten for some imagined violation or another.

"He started becoming increasingly paranoid, that me, and everyone else was out to kill him, even members of my family. Even though he knew I was at my mother's, he would accuse me of going out with other men, cheating on him, then that they were going to kill him. He put tin foil on all the windows, convinced that people were watching him. Then, seven months ago, Grace learned that she was pregnant, and four months after that, Mom had a stroke. I was on my way to help them cook and clean when I got into the accident."

Andy looked at Davy, who had tears rolling down his cheeks. "We have to put this guy away."

"I agree." Davy wiped his tears, and looked at her. "We are going to keep you safe, sweetheart, even if it costs me my life."

"So you believe me?" she asked, shaken to her very core.

"Yes Hope, we do. There are things you don't know. He is a member of a large crime syndicate here in the area. He is a hit man, Hope, and we think he may be moonlighting as a serial killer. Lately, thin, burgundy-haired women have been coming up dead in horrible, brutal ways. Does that description sound familiar, Hope?" Andy took a deep breath, and continued in a softer, gentler tone. "We now have what we need to put him away for a very long time, but we can't make a move with you in the house. We knew he would use you as a shield."

Hope shuddered at the thought. She, of all people, knew how deranged Nick was, which made this situation even more deadly. She knew that she would freeze up when he grabbed her, with the guns pointed at them.

A month after Hope's accident, the doctors performed a barrage of testing on her to determine if she had suffered any brain damage.

Somehow, she made it out with no brain damage, and no cognitive dysfunction. The doctors called her a medical miracle, and determined her well enough to go home. Davy was as proud as a peacock of her--this just goes went to show how strong she truly was.

Something was happening to him, and he had no clue what it was. When he looked at her, something welled up in him, something powerful. What he felt for his ex-girlfriend, Holly, was nothing compared to what he felt for this woman that was getting dressed in the room, and he almost married Holly.

Oh, he knew that he wasn't falling in love with Hope, not yet. He didn't know her well enough for that. She was, however, the most stunning woman he had ever had the good fortune to meet, not to mention the sweetest. There truly wasn't a mean bone in her body. She took his hand earlier, ecstatic that she was being released, and his heart jumped into his throat. He lost count of all the times he wanted to kiss her, even tried, and every time they had been interrupted either by Andy, her mom, or her sister.

Andy had pulled some strings and gotten Hope's family relocated to another state just this morning under new identities. The FBI was working on getting Hope another identity, but for some reason, it was taking some time, and in the meantime, it was frustrating Davy to no end. You would think with her being the victim that she would have been the first with getting a new identity, not the last. But Davy and Andy would keep her safe, come hell or high water.

Andy had the house set up with a temporary wheelchair ramp since she would only be in one for a few weeks. Then, she was going to have to use a cane for a bit until she could keep her balance.

As much as he loved Andy, Davy was about to beat the hell out of him. He was constantly harsh with Hope, throwing her into a tailspin. She had gone through enough without having to deal with his aggression too. Once Andy got home from the office, Davy was going to have a long talk with him. It wasn't going to be tolerated any more.

Speaking of Andy, he needed to call him and let him know that Hope was being discharged. He went to the nurse's station, and used the phone, calling Andy's direct line at the Bureau.

"Andrew Newcomb." His voice sounds exasperated, as if Davy is interrupting something important.

"Andy, it's me. Hope is being discharged as we speak. She is getting dressed."

"What, so soon? Davy, *do not* leave until I get there! I am dead serious about this!"

"All right, Andy." Davy said, thoroughly confused.

"I will be there in about twenty minutes. I am leaving right now," he said, and then Davy was listening to dead silence.

"Well, I guess that settles that," he said to no one in particular, and hung up the receiver. He thanked the nurse, and returned to Hope's door. A moment later, her nurse emerged, and handed him her discharge instructions.

"Can we wait in the waiting room for my roommate? He is going to escort us out."

"You are welcome to wait in this room for now. We are in no hurry to fill it again." Her doctor came up from behind the nurse, and looked toward the room. "We are going to miss that young lady. She was a model patient, and the sweetest woman I have ever met. We are however glad she is leaving." The doctor smiled.

"She is quite special, isn't she?" Davy also smiled.

"That she is. Well, take good care of her, and we hope that we never see her again," he added humorously. Davy refrained from rolling his eyes. Doctor humor....something he can live without.

"I'm sure she feels the same, doctor."

Davy shook the doctor's hand, and went into Hope's room. He stopped, looking at her in the wheelchair. When the light from the window hit her hair, it seemed almost like her hair caught fire. The light framed her face from behind her, giving her a halo effect. His body tightened as he couldn't stop staring at her. By god, she was the most exquisite woman he had ever known.

The nurses had all gotten together, and gotten her clothing to wear out of the hospital. A long, flowing, plum-colored peasant skirt flowed to her ankles, with a black and plum tunic, both fitting her like a glove. They bought her under-garments, and makeup which they themselves applied for her. They were determined that she would leave this hospital with beauty, grace, and dignity.

His heart hurt for her, for the long road she was going to have recovering from what Nick had done to her, physically, mentally, and emotionally.

CHAPTER 5

Andy came tearing into Hope's room, out of breath. She inwardly groaned, truly not wanting to deal with his egotistical attitude; with his *all must go my way or no way* approach that he wore like a cloak. She had gotten to where she couldn't stand him. He had done nothing but start arguments, and generally treat her like dirt. She was really getting sick of it, though she wouldn't dare say anything about it. He and Davy are were taking her in, protecting her, so it would be stupid of her to complain.

"Wow, you look great for just coming out of the hospital." He gave her the once over, and as soon as his eyes returned to Hope's face, they turned stony, the color of gun metal. He jerked his chin up, and looked down his nose at her. "Are you ready?" he asked; his voice just as hard as his eyes.

"Yah, she's ready, Andy." Davy's voice turned dark as pitch.

She was not one to complain, but something had to be said before they left. It could affect the outcome. "Guys, may I say something before we leave?"

They both looked at her, waiting. "If I am coming between you, then I am not going with you. You two have known each other a hell of a lot longer than you have known me, and I am not about to break up that friendship."

"You aren't, Hope. There are some things that Andy and I have to discuss is all. Don't you worry about anything; there is nothing on earth that could end this friendship."

Another look that she couldn't decipher crossed Andy's eyes, and was gone before she knew what it was. Andy truly was a hard one to read, he kept his feelings close to his chest. She knew that she was going to have to find a way to get along with him, for Davy's sake. There had to be a way that she could find to make peace with him.

An orderly came in, and wheeled her out of the hospital room for the last time. Davy walked on one side of her; with Andy on the other. Andy kept his hand on the butt of his sidearm, his eyes tracking everything and everyone around them, while Davy just held her good hand.

Davy went to get his car, while Andy stayed glued to Hope like the secret service guarding the president. She half expected him to talk into his watch.

Davy pulled up in a gorgeous piece of machinery, a midnight blue Camaro! He got out and looked at Andy. "I am taking her shopping; she has no clothes or anything, so she needs some. We're going to Sears."

"All right, I will follow you there. I am not leaving your side." Andy picked Hope up and put her into the passenger's seat, then took her wheelchair with him, since it wouldn't fit in the muscle car.

Andy slammed the car door once Hope was comfortable, making her wince with the sound. "He *really* doesn't like me," she muttered.

"What makes you say that?" Davy looked at her, stunned.

"Just the way he acts when he's around me. I don't understand. I have never treated either one of you badly."

"Don't worry sweetheart, I will have a talk with him and find out what is going on. He's not usually like this, I promise."

"Gee, aren't I the lucky one then?" she asked flatly, and looked out the window.

A car with a BMW emblem emblazoned on the hood pulled up behind Davy, and gave a short honk. He gave a wave, and pulled out.

They went to Oak Brook Terrace, where the guys brought Hope the rented wheelchair, and stayed ever-vigilant. Davy bought her several skirts; which were easier to put on over her cast, along with short-sleeved shirts, and some jeans. He bought several bras and panties, to Hope's complete mortification. She had to admit that even though she hated every penny Davy spent on her, all three of them had a good time. Even the ever-uninterested Andy had cracked a smile occasionally. Davy was like a kid in a candy store, he couldn't make up his mind what he wanted to buy for her. He would bring out items that he thought she would like, but she actually couldn't fathom wearing.

Hope had such an eclectic taste in clothing that she was hard to buy for. There was a time, just after graduation that she had thought about going Victorian Goth, but that was only if she would leave Nick. He hated anything different from what he liked, and would have beaten the ever-loving hell out of her if she had come home with anything resembling what she truly liked. To her, the long skirts and the corsets were more beautiful, classier. Nick would have said she looked trashy, even slutty.

After seeing the way the nurses made her up, she was starting to like the natural look. For the first time in her life, she felt beautiful, like a model.

Davy wheeled her into the mall proper, and entered other stores. He spent more money in *The Deb*, where he got her some nicer clothes, then to a jewelry store, where he bought two watches, one for every-day use, and another for dressy evenings. He also bought some earrings, necklaces, and bracelets.

"Davy, where are you getting the money for all of this? You can't possibly afford this on an EMT's salary." She couldn't help but ask.

"I have an inheritance from my parents. Don't worry; this is everyday money for me, Hope. I can afford it."

Andy looked at them. "Hey, are you two getting hungry? I'm starving over here."

Davy looked at her when she didn't say anything. She hated the thought of him spending more money on her, but she decided to tell the truth. "Yes, I am a little hungry. I got sick of hospital food real quick."

"Good! Andy, the usual place?"

He gave a snort. "Of course, like we would go anywhere else. By the way, don't even think of pulling that card out, it's my turn to pay."

Davy rolled his eyes, and wheeled her back to the car. It took both vehicles to put all of the bags in, and they even had condensed some. No one had ever bought so much stuff at one time for her. She felt saddened by the amount of money spent on her, yet at the same time, delighted. She thought about the clothes that she had back at the apartment. Everything in there was second-hand with holes and stains, stuff no one wanted. Never before have any of her closets been filled with such nice things as what had been bought for her today. She just had no idea how she would ever pay him back!

Andy again lifted her and carefully put her into the car. He softly shut the door this time, and sat there for a moment, just looking at her as Davy put the wheelchair in Andy's trunk. His eyes this time held a softness that she couldn't believe. It made her stomach do a flip, and her palms broke out into a cold sweat. His eyes turned to granite again as Davy came around the car to get in and he walked over to his car. Before she knew it, they were off again, to the other side of the mall. Davy pulled into the Red Lobster! She had always wanted to eat at one. Her mother hated seafood of any kind, so she refused to take them to one and Hope was never able to afford it once she moved out.

Andy put her back into the wheelchair, and wheeled her in. She sat looking at the live lobsters in the tank as Davy got them a table. It was almost sad to watch the beautiful creatures, knowing they were going to be eaten by someone.

Davy wheeled her away from the tank, and to a table with one less chair than the rest. He smiled and sat beside Hope. She couldn't help but smile at him, his was so infectious. She opened her menu one-handed, and looked at the prices of everything. *Oh dear god! Soup and salad it is!*

"Hope, I want you to order whatever you want." Davy said as if he had read her mind.

"I will just take the soup and salad."

Her eyes wandered to Andy for some reason. His own pools turned dark, suspicious. "I will bet you have never eaten at a Red Lobster before, have you?"

"No, I haven't. How did you know?"

"If you had, you wouldn't order just a soup and salad. Davy, order for the lady," he instructed from behind his menu.

"I can order for myself! I am not a complete invalid!" she hissed, and then clapped her hand over her mouth. *Damn it, damn it, damn it! When am I ever going to learn to keep my big trap shut?*

Both men looked at her in stunned silence. *Oh hell, I have really done it this time!*

Both broke out in laughter. "Well, the lady does have some backbone after all," Andy said between peals.

Mortified, she buried her face into her menu. When the server came for their orders, Hope let Davy order for her, and sat there in silence. *I can't believe I did that!* Looking into her lap, she said, "I'm sorry for my outburst. It was uncalled for, and I hope you can forgive me."

"Are you kidding me, Hope? I haven't been so thoroughly put in my place in a long time! I have to say that my respect for you has upped a notch," Andy said.

Her head snapped up, looking to see if he was joking. His eyes said he was completely sincere, so she nodded. "Thank you."

"Now, with that said, there are a few other places I need to go after this. We have to get Hope a dresser, and unless she wants to sleep in the same bed with me, we have to get her a bed, and some clothes hangers, not to mention a jewelry box."

"Well, aren't you just a good boyfriend? You think of everything," Andy said sardonically.

"Andy, listen to me right now. First, I am not her boyfriend, yet. Second, tone down the hostility. Trust me, you and I are going to talk about this, but now is not the time."

Andy leaned into the table, his eyes spitting fire. "Fine, but let me just say this." He swiveled his head slowly to look at Hope. "If you do to him what I think you're going to do, there will be no place you can hide from me." His eyes snapped with the promise of unspeakable malevolence.

Hope rocked back in her chair, shaken to the core. "I am not planning anything, Andy. I swear that to you." Even she heard the fear in her voice. She knew he was capable of a tremendous amount of violence, and she couldn't help but be petrified that he would direct it at her.

"Don't you dare threaten her, Andy; I'm not going to have it." Davy's tone, although soft, lent truth to his fury.

"You will thank me when she tries to do what Holly did."

"You think she is after my money? What are you, stupid? She didn't even know I had any kind of money until we were in Sears. She has had enough violence in her life for you to say something like that to her; you know it as well as me!" he susurrated quietly so he didn't disturb anyone around them.

She could only sit there, staring at the table. At that point, she made an executive decision. "I want everything returned."

Both men looked at her as if she'd completely lost her mind. "Hope? What did you say?" Davy asked.

"You heard me, Davy. I want everything returned. I am going back to Nick. I won't have this man accuse me of using anyone, least of all you."

"We can't have you go back there, Hope," Andy said.

"Then you tell me, Agent Andrew Newcomb, where do you suggest I go? You carted my family off to parts unknown and gave them new names. I am unable to go and retrieve my belongings; therefore, I have nothing to wear, yet when Davy steps up to the plate and buys what I need, you accuse me of using him for his money. The FBI isn't stepping in to get them for me, and you are dragging your heels on my new identity. So, Agent Andrew Newcomb, tell me what the *hell* you want me to do, because I am out of options," Hope demanded softly, but it seemed to have a whiplash effect on both Andy and Davy.

Davy looked at her with pride in his eyes, and Andy had the good grace to look sheepish.

"I.....I'm sorry Hope. I didn't think of it that way." He toyed with his fork instead of looking at her.

"Maybe you should start thinking before you open your mouth and insert your foot, asshole," Davy shot back, grabbing her hand, showing unity.

"Davy, I need some air," she said, not taking her eyes off of Andy. He wheeled her outside, where a line of people were starting to form for lunch.

He took out a pack of cigarettes, and lit one.

"Let me have one of those, please," she asked of him. He looked at her, shocked.

"What, you don't think I ever smoked?" she asked as he handed her one. She lit it, and exhaled.

He gave a long sigh. "I am sorry about Andy. I had no idea that he would act like this."

"Davy, he is a cop by nature. He is suspicious of everyone, except you." She gave a snort. "I can't believe I am making excuses for the asshole." She took another drag. "Something has to give though, because I am not going to be able to live with his attitude. I am scared to death as it is. I know this isn't going to end well."

"It is going to end just fine. We aren't going to let anything happen to you, I promise."

She looked at the burning cigarette. *How do I tell him that it's not me I am worried about, it's him?*

She had to be perfectly honest with herself; she was highly attracted to Davy. He was the sweetest, kindest, most gentle man she had ever known, not to mention gorgeous. What was nice was that he seemed to like her too. He was exactly what she needed.

She had never known anyone like him. Oh yes, she had a few male friends in high school that were sweethearts, but nothing like Davy. She felt more than privileged to know him. When he threw out the *"unless she wants to sleep with me"* comment, her heart gave a flutter. She couldn't help it; the thought of waking up to him every morning gave her the warm and fuzzies. However, she also knew it was entirely too soon. She truly didn't want Davy to be a rebound relationship.

"Hope, I want you to know that I truly do like you. You are unlike anyone I ever met." He took another drag on his cigarette, and exhaled, seemingly nervous. "I have to be honest; I have purely selfish reasons for asking you to come and live with us. I couldn't bear the thought of having to leave that hospital and never see you again. When I saw you in that mangled car, I felt like I had known you all my life, and it almost killed me to see you unconscious. I have been an EMT now for close to ten years, and I have never had that kind of reaction for any of the victims I have helped, let alone anyone else. Instinctively, I knew you were something special. Then when you coded in the ambulance, I had never been so terrified in my life."

"What do you mean, I coded?" she asked, confusion clouding her eyes.

"I mean, you were clinically dead for three minutes. I had to use the defibrillator on you to bring you back."

"That's why I don't remember the ambulance ride."

He flicked his cigarette into the parking lot. "Well, lunch should be at the table by now. What do you say we go in?"

"Before we do, I have a question. My friend that was with me in the car never came to see me in the hospital. I have known her all my life, and it isn't like her to never speak to me again."

"You mean no one told you?" he asked, his eyes wide. "Told me what, Davy?"

"Hope, she died on the scene. She never made it; her injuries were too severe."

She closed her eyes as the tears welled up. She was the best friend a person could ever have. She saw Hope through so much, held her hand when she cried, jumped up and down together when she had good news; they went to kindergarten together, all through school together. They talked about their first kisses, first time having sex, everything. Now she's dead, and Hope couldn't help but feel it was her fault!

"Hope, we need to eat, then we are going to get your furniture. Then we will go back to the house, and you can have some time to yourself."

She followed his lead with the cigarette, putting a reign on her tears. Davy wheeled her back in to see Andy worriedly picking at his food. He wasn't eating it, merely rearranging it on his plate.

He straightened up in his chair when he noticed them approaching. "Thank goodness. I was getting worried."

"Sorry, I just needed some air," she said with a small smile, her voice still slightly shaky.

"Hope, I'm sorry. I truly am. I have been sitting here, thinking about what you said, and you were absolutely right. I haven't given you a fair chance. If I try to do better from now on, will you forgive me?"

"I absolutely can, Andy. I understand why you misjudged me. I was the girlfriend of a mobster who is trying to get away from said mobster. You are a cop through and through; therefore, you are going to be suspicious of everyone, including, and especially me. But I swear to you, I mean no harm to you, or to Davy. He saved my life, and you are his best friend. I would rather die than to have either one of you hurt, by anything. I like Davy a lot, and I would like to get to know him better. Maybe somewhere down the road, we can even have a romantic relationship."

Hope felt Davy straighten beside her. "I would like that, Hope."

She looked at him and they both smiled.

The three of them ate in a jovial manner; easily laughing as Davy told her about some of the trouble they had gotten themselves into as kids. After they finished eating, Davy put his arm around the back of Hope's chair, and she leaned toward him. Before she knew it, she found herself wrapped in his arms. For the first time in her life, she felt warm, safe, as if nothing could ever touch her, purposefully not thinking about Elaine.

Andy looked at his watch. "Oh shit, if we're going to go to those other stores, we need to get going!" He picked up the check, and whipped his wallet out of the back pocket of his trousers.

"At least let me pay for Hope and me," Davy offered.

"Nope, it's the least I could do for what I put her through."

She couldn't help it; she put her hand on Andy's, and looked into his eyes. When she did, a jolt of electricity shot through her from the tip of her hair to her core, stunning her. She hid it by taking her hand off of his, and said, "Thank you, Andy, for everything."

He obviously felt the jolt also, since he looked at her with astonishment registering in his eyes.

Oh, no! She was so not going to go there. It was Davy she liked, not Andy. It was Davy that she wanted a relationship with, not this arrogant cop.

Andy coughed; clearing his throat, then went to the podium to pay for the meal.

Davy wheeled her out to the car. He lifted her up and ever so gently put her in the seat. As he leaned over to put the seat belt over her, he looked deep into her eyes. They stared at each other, seemingly for an endless amount of time. He leaned in, and when his lips touched Hope's, a feeling went through her, warming her blood. It was one of peace, and sheer joy. In that instant, only three words went through her head. *I am home.*

Her good arm wrapped itself around his neck as he deepened the kiss, tasting her as she tasted him. A moan escaped from somewhere deep inside of her as her stomach did a delicious turn.

"Yo, D-man, her tonsils are fine. Let's go."

Hope broke off the kiss. "Yo, A-Rod, Here's a real nice bird in flight for you." She raised a middle finger in salute. "You're number one in my book!"

Davy broke into hysterical laughter, while Andy looked at her, unsure what to say, or think. After thinking about it for a few heartbeats, a slow, wide grin spread across his face, and he too broke into frenzied laughter.

"She got you there, Andy." Davy shut the door, and went around to the driver's side. "Let's go to the furniture store at the other side of the mall. Maybe if I drop some major green, they will deliver by tonight."

Andy pulled Davy aside, and they talked for a moment. Hope heard Davy say excitedly: "That sounds like a great idea, Andy!"

Andy got into his beamer and headed toward the exit of the mall proper. She turned back around, and shot Davy a questioning look.

"You'll see, I promise." He grinned, and started up the car.

"Wait Davy…he has my wheelchair in his trunk!"

"I know honey, he's going to meet us at the furniture store, and then he's going to take off for a few minutes."

She couldn't help but feel a bit twitchy, especially where these two were concerned.

Andy put her back into the chair, and returned to his car. Andy put the car into gear. "Be right back, you two. Don't cause any trouble while I'm gone." He said.

"Oh yah, Andy, I'm going to jump on all the beds, overturn the sofas, then have hot monkey sex with Davy right in the middle of the showroom. If you hurry back, you can join us."

All three laughed as Davy wheeled Hope inside, and Andy left.

"I have to admit that I like your sarcasm. It's refreshing."

"It's gotten me into many tight scrapes, especially with Nick. He truly hated it. I'm sure it made him feel like the idiot that I had proved him to be."

Fortunately, both the glass doors in the showroom were open, so he just wheeled her through them. He seemed to know exactly where to go, so he took them straight to the bedroom furniture.

"How do you like your mattresses, Hope? Do you like them firm, medium, soft?"

"I like to sink into them like I'm lying on a cloud," she said, smiling up at him.

He smiled back. "That's the way I like them too."

A beautiful bedroom furniture suite made of cherry oak came into Hope's line of vision. She couldn't suppress a moan as he began to wheel her by it.

He immediately stopped, and looked over at the suite. The king-sized bed frame had a bookshelf at the head, enough to fit fifty books or so into it. The footboard was solid with random etchings. The matching dresser, wardrobe, and two nightstands gave it a true homey feel. The more she looked at it, the more she fell in love with it; however, the price tag broke her heart, knowing she would never be able to pay Davy back for it, and she fully intended to pay him back for every penny.

"So, this is what you like then?" Davy asked, smiling.

"It's my taste, yes," she said in all honesty, wanting to cry.

He nodded, and said, "I'll be right back." He moved her over to the side, yet inside the bedroom suite area to keep her out of the way of other customers, and went to find a sales person.

"I'll wait right here!" she called out while he was walking down the aisle, being her general smartass self.

He laughed and shook his head. A few minutes later, he and a tall, gangly salesperson that could moonlight as an actor playing Ichabod Crane came back to the suite.

"Yes, sir, we can sell you this suite, it has been here for quite a while, and we could easily get another. I think you will be able to take it home today like you wanted."

Hope looked at him, shocked. She turned to the sales person. "Could you please give us a moment?"

"Yes, ma'am." He turned and walked away.

Once he was out of ear shot, she looked at Davy. "No, Davy. This is entirely too much. I can never pay you back for something like this."

"Hope, I don't want you to pay me back. I want to give you something that you could use for years. Plus, you deserve it. I highly doubt you've ever had anything like it."

She shook her head, even though he was right. "I can't let you do this."

"You don't have a choice." He leaned down and kissed her, then walked away. She watched as Davy gave the salesman his credit card. She then saw Andy hurrying past the suite, so she called out to him.

He stopped and looked at her. "Is this what you are getting?"

"Apparently, I am. I protested, loudly, and was ignored."

"Well, you have good taste," he smiled.

Her heart skipped a beat for some reason. She couldn't help but notice his white teeth, a stark contrast against his olive skin. She looked away, trying to hide a flush. "Thank you."

A few moments later, Davy came back with five burly guys. "Hey, Andy, so did you get it?"

"Yes. It's in the parking lot." He turned to Hope. "I got a U-Haul so we could bring your stuff home."

It was at that moment, the tears wouldn't be denied and a sob escaped from somewhere deep in her. The kindness that they were showing her was completely foreign to Hope, not to mention overwhelming. To complete her ride on the humiliation train, she couldn't go anywhere, and cried around everyone. Someone took notice, and wheeled her outside, away from prying eyes. A strong hand rubbed her back, as she buried her face in her hand, unable to hold back the sobbing. Strong arms wrapped themselves around her, and she didn't care who it was, she just buried her face in their chest, and let go. It all came out, the pain and terror from the last seven years, all the way down to the death of her best friend; it came out in the form of banshee wails and a perfect storm of tears.

Once she could gather a coherent thought, she pulled away. "I'm sorry; you must think I am a real head case," Hope said as someone handed her a tissue box.

"No, Hope, I don't think that at all. You have been through a lot in a short time, and it's bound to take a toll." She expected it to be Davy, and sat up, surprised, when it was Andy's voice coming from the one comforting her.

"Hope, I promise you, I'm not heartless, even though it may seem that way at times."

"I promise too that I don't have a meltdown constantly." She gave a small smile.

"Even if you do, I can handle it, as can Davy. He just stayed inside to finalize the sale of the furniture, and then he will be out here. Are you ok now?"

She nodded. "I think so."

"Good, here he is now, he's signaling for the truck, so they must be ready." He grabbed the back of the chair and wheeled Hope over to him.

"It's all ready." Davy smiled, and turned concerned eyes over to me. "Are you ok?"

"Yes, I'm fine. I'm sorry about that. I'm not used to kindness, and it just got a little prodigious is all."

"Well, get used to it, because if anyone treats you with anything less, they'll answer to me," Davy promised.

"You better beat me to it, my man, because I won't be as nice as you will," Andy said, his eyes wide with sincerity.

With seven brawny men, the furniture was loaded in a matter of minutes. Hope was loaded back into the Camaro, and they made a return trip to Sears. Two bedding sets were bought along with a large standing jewelry armoire, also made of cherry oak, and several pillows. Davy then had a stroke of insight, and took Hope over to Waldenbooks where he bought more books than she could read in a month, along with a lap desk, some bookmarks, a journal, and some pens. He took a quick trip over to Walgreens where he picked up her prescriptions, and some toiletry items.

"All right, I think we can go to your new home, Hope." Davy smiled down at her. "If there is anything else you need, just let one of us know, and we will pick it up for you."

He wheeled her out to the truck, where he put everything he had just bought into the back of it. I looked inside, and it was jam-packed. "Um, Davy, I think I have everything I am going to need for the next century," she breathed.

He laughed and put her into the car. She heard the back door shut, then a bunch of grunts, and something fell onto the back of the truck. She realized then that they were attaching a tow bar for the car. Someone drove it up onto it, hooked it in, and Davy got into the driver's seat of the truck and started the engine. Without looking at her, he said, "Hope, I just want to see you happy is all. Over the last month that I have known you, I have come to like you, a *lot*. You deserve nothing less than the best, and I intend to see to it that you have it."

Hope felt a blush creep up her neck. "I like you too, Davy. You have been kinder to me than anyone ever has, and I don't just mean today. You were there for my family while I was in the coma, you saved my life, and you have treated me with such dignity and respect." She touched his arm, wanting to show her sincerity. "Please, just give me some time. The pain from Nick is still fresh, and I can't help but be afraid of a lot of things, but I would like it if things progressed between us. I just don't want you to be a rebound."

"Hope, I have a friend of mine who is a counselor, and she owes me a huge favor. Would it be ok if I were to call her and set up an appointment for you? It's not that I think you're crazy; it's that I think you need help putting things straight in your head. What Davenport did to you would mess anyone up, including me. And yes, I would love it if you and I started dating. In fact, I would be honored."

"All right Davy, if you think it would help me, I would be willing to try."

He started driving. They went in relative silence, since no words were needed between them. He took her hand, and held it the entire way.

They pulled into an affluent neighborhood back over by Loyola Hospital, and into the driveway of a large Tudor-style house. So large in fact, it could be considered a mansion. Hope couldn't help but to stare in awe. She had never even dreamed she could stay in such a place! When her parents were married, they were more than poor. After her dad got out of the Army, he and mom bought a farm, and Dad became a truck driver when the farm hadn't produced enough money. The combined income was barely enough to squeak by.

When her mom left her dad, she tried to provide a good home for Grace and her, but it wasn't easy. Mom worked a few jobs at one time: waiting tables, and as a dispatcher for a limousine service. There wasn't much money in either of those, so they lived with Hope's grandparents. Dad never paid any kind of child support, and it made things even harder on her mom. Now, she was with Davy and Andy in this huge home, in which she was certain she could get lost.

Davy wheeled her inside, and she stared at the opulent entryway, her mouth wide with shock. The skylight in the hall gave the home an open feel, with lots of sunlight. The cathedral ceilings towered above her, making her feel about the size of an ant. Directly in front of her, a long staircase climbed up into the second floor, the thick oak banister polished and shining. The floors of the ground level were made of hard wood, also freshly waxed.

He brought Hope into a living room to the right of the staircase, where a black leather sectional wound around a large red brick fireplace. A life-sized picture hung above the massive structure, the man portrayed in it must have been from the Napoleonic years, since he was wearing a military uniform that reminded her of the French Dictator.

An oriental rug spanned the length of the room, without any stains or tears in it whatsoever. The furniture sat on top of it as if it were made specifically for this rug. The walls had been painted a soft mauve, giving it a peaceful, homey feel.

Everything was polished and spotless, including the oak shelving over the fireplace that boasted of a few masculine knick-knacks. Off in a corner sat a television in a black pressed-wood entertainment center, along with some VHS tapes of different movies encased in glass. On top of the television, a VCR sat waiting for someone to use it.

She couldn't help but be in awe of the true beauty of the room.

"Welcome home, Hope," Davy said from behind her.

"It's beautiful!" she breathed.

"I found out it was my parent's home before they died. I was little, and don't remember much of anything about them. But when I found out where they had lived, and when it went up for sale I bought it."

He wheeled her into the living room, and put her on the sectional. "Andy and I are going to bring everything in. I am going to put you into the bedroom next to mine, which I will bring you into once we put everything in it." He turned on the television, and handed her the remote.

"Thank you Davy, but I don't watch much television. I don't even know what shows are on anymore."

He smiled, and put the remote next to her on the arm of the couch anyway.

They went out to the truck, and started hauling everything in. All of her bags went into the living room first so they could bring in the furniture without worrying about tripping all over the place. She couldn't help but watch them. Hope heard a lot of hisses, grunts, and swearing, along with *this son of a bitch is heavy*! Andy grunted in pain.

"I told you we should have used the hand cart!" Davy grunted.

"It's too big for the hand cart! Even sideways it won't go on it, even if it is industrial."

"Fine, let's get the bastard in there." There was more grunting, some scraping of wood against wood, and they both rested a moment in the living room with her.

"I'm sorry guys. I didn't realize that it would be so heavy."

"Don't apologize, Hope. You haven't done anything to apologize for. It's a beautiful bedroom suite, and it suits you," Andy said, panting from exertion, sweat rolling off his forehead. He took his shirt off, and used it to mop his face. She turned away as a flush heated her face, and that was something she wouldn't want Davy to see. Andy has one hell of a body, not an ounce of fat on him. He had a six-pack; his pectorals and arms were massive, as if he worked out continuously.

"You should have heard us trying to bring everything in when he and I moved in. There was much more cussing, and even a shoving match started." Davy laughed, remembering; sweat also rolling from his forehead as he tried to pull in a deep breath. Either he didn't notice her staring at Andy, or he ignored it.

"Yah, I still say that I was right, you should have let me go in first, you asshole. My knuckle still hurts from scraping it against the sliding glass door in the kitchen."

"Why didn't you guys just hire a moving company? I mean, if you guys can afford this place, you can afford a moving company." Hope asked.

"Oh, well gee, why didn't I think of that?" Andy said acerbically, shooting a pointed look at Davy.

"I didn't want to, Hope. I figured we could do it. Granted, it took a couple of days, but we got it all in."

"All right, let's go get the rest of this. I need to get the truck back."

After more struggling, they finally got everything in, and Davy took Hope down a long hallway and into the bedroom on the other side of the stairs to figure out where she wanted to put everything. She thought it looked perfect the way it was, and told him so.

The room itself was gigantic, about the same size of the old apartment. The walls were painted in rich plum, which accentuated the cherry in the wood of the furniture. The curtains over the windows were taupe in color, and the floor, like the rest of the house was hard wood, polished to a beautiful shine.

"I am going to take you through the rest of the house, then come back to put the bed together."

"It's all right Davy, I've got it," Andy offered.

"Thank you, bud," Davy said, and wheeled her out.

"There are ten bedrooms in the house; I guess Mom and Dad were planning a large family." He kind of chuckled. "Dad was a sports agent, and mom taught medicine at the University of Chicago, so there was plenty of money." He stopped at the room next to Hope's, and opened the door. "This is my room," he said, and wheeled her in. It was beautiful, in a masculine sort of way. The entire room was decorated in deep, rich earth tones, without an ounce of clutter anywhere. He too obviously believed in keeping things as clean as she did. Even his bed was perfectly made.

The rest of the house was just as immaculate as the living room. The kitchen itself was gigantic, large enough for a catering business to set up shop. The island in the center of the kitchen boasted a large stove, and plenty of cabinets. Behind the stove, was a counter with the sink, oven, and microwave built into the wall, and more cabinets bolted into the wall. He took Hope over to a doorway, where a large butler's pantry overflowed with cans of food, among other culinary items. At the other side of the room was another door that led down to the basement.

"Should you want some wine, just tell one of us and we will go into the cellar to get it. I have enough wine down there to outfit a liquor store." "I haven't had wine in eons. Maybe with dinner we could have a bottle to celebrate my getting out of the hospital and away from Nick?"

"That sounds excellent," he smiled, and wheeled her over to the smaller breakfast nook in the corner of the room. He sat in the chair in front of her, and took her hand, looking deep into her eyes. "Hope, I want you to consider this your home. You are welcome here as long as you want, which in all honesty, I hope is the rest of your life."

She didn't know what to say, so she just smiled, and leaned in to kiss his cheek, only she missed. He turned his head at just the right moment, and she felt his lips move ever so gently on hers. Tender warmth again spread through her as he deepened the kiss. She wrapped her arm around him, and he picked her up, putting her on his lap.

He looked deep into her eyes. "I could go on kissing you forever."

"Then why stop to tell me?" she asked, only half-joking. She positively loved the way he kissed. It made her think of warm summer days and walking through a meadow barefoot, soft grass between her toes.

His kiss turned a bit more urgent, even though he kept his hands on her back; she felt the bulge begin in his jeans. He broke it off, and moaned her name. "I had better stop this before it goes too far. I want to take this slow and easy, I don't want to scare you, or hurt you."

She had to admit, disappointment flooded her as he put her back in the chair. She didn't know why, but she wanted to know how it felt to not be forced, but she didn't want to say anything to him. She just let him stop it. He turned toward the window, readjusted himself, and turned back.

"There you guys are. The bed is put together, and made," Andy called from the doorway.

"Thank you, Andy." She gave a small smile; she tried to make it bright, but it was one she truly didn't feel.

Hope couldn't help but think about the two men she was now living with. They were as different as night and day. Andy was balls-to-the-wall intense while Davy was more laid back, easygoing. It was amazing that they were as close as they were.

"Hey Davy, I'm going to check the mail," Andy said.

"Okay, bud, I'm going to put Hope to bed."

CHAPTER 6

Davy took Hope into her bedroom, and got out one of her new nightgowns. He took her top off, and couldn't help but stare at her. By god, she was the most beautiful woman that ever walked the face of the earth. She was a tiny thing; he could wrap his fingers around her waist and still have room left over. Both of her breasts could fit into the palm of one of his hands. Her legs were long and muscular, pure perfection in every way a woman could be and more.

His jeans grew just a bit tighter as he felt himself start to harden again. She had this massive effect on him, something he had never felt before. He had never been this randy around a woman, never wanted to touch her constantly, to be near her every moment of the day.

He finished helping her dress for bed. "Do you want one of your books to read while I get dinner? I was thinking of ordering some Chinese delivery."

"Sure. I can't take my medications on an empty stomach anyway."

Andy came into the room, his eyes stormy slits, his face red with fury.

"What's wrong, Andy?" Hope asked.

He looked at Davy. "He's made it personal." He thrust out a piece of paper, and Davy took it. He looked at the magazine lettered piece of paper.

You have my property
If you don't return my property
I will kill you all
Bring it to the park
In downtown Oak Brook
Tomorrow at Noon
Or you will all die.

"He can go straight to hell! In fact, I'd like to send him there myself!" Davy exclaimed, more pissed off than he'd ever been.

Hope sat up as much as she could in the bed, and said, her voice shaky; "I have an idea. If you want to catch him, why not use me as bait?"

"Oh hell no, it's too dangerous!" Davy shot down the idea, his heart pounding in his chest at the thought of her in that kind of danger.

"That is so not happening!" Andy seconded.

"Guys, listen to me. Nick has gotten away from every attempt to capture him. If I show up, then he's sure to be there. Canvas the park first. Put some plain clothed police out there. I will be safe if you do that."

"That is very brave of you, but I'm not going to put you at risk like that," Andy said with a tone of finality.

"So you would rather me have to live in fear every day than to end this once and for all before someone gets hurt or killed?" It was more of a statement than a question, although her hard tone made Davy's blood freeze in his veins.

He thought about what she said. It made sense, but it killed him. All different kinds of scenarios went through his head, each one worse than the last. What if this was a trap to get everyone together to take them out? On second thought, since there was no postal stamp on the letter, it was obviously hand-delivered, so he knew where they lived. He could just take them all out here. There was definitely something fishy about this, but he just couldn't put his finger on it. She was, however, right about one thing. It would bring a fast end to this either way.

"Davy, maybe she's right," Andy choked out in a small, barely audible voice.

"Yah, I know.....but I don't have to like it," he said grimly.

"Let me call my boss," Andy said, and reluctantly left the room.

"Honey, you don't have to do this." Davy continued to try and talk her out of it.

"Yes I do. He's not going to stop until someone is dead, and I sure as hell don't want it to be you. I'm not worried about myself, Davy. I don't give a rat's ass what he does to me, there isn't much more he could do that he hasn't already done except flat out kill me. It's you, Andy, and my family that I care about."

"And we care about you, Hope. We don't want to see anything happen to you. I just found you, damn it!" Davy felt himself start to lose control of his emotions. Terror gripped him as he saw this backfiring.

"You won't lose me, not with the backup that is going to be there. Davy, I have to do this. No one else could. Not only that, but have faith in yourselves; I do."

He sighed and ran his fingers through his hair. He knew he lost this debate. He also knew beyond the shadow of a doubt that it was going to end up as one big cluster-fuck.

"My boss gave the go ahead," Andy said, walking back into the room. He looked at Hope with respect, and a good dose of fear. "He thinks you are one hell of a brave woman to volunteer for this."

"Andy, it isn't like we have a plethora of choices here. I really don't want to live in fear for the rest of my life."

Davy wanted to scream over this whole situation. Instead he gave her a kiss on the forehead, and asked Andy to order delivery.

Davy climbed onto her bed and pulled her into his arms. He just wants to hold her once, if only for a bit. A sense of semi-peace came over him when she molded her body to his, and put her hand on his chest. The warmth of her body, the feel of her heart beating in her chest, seemed to help to bring him out of this moment of terror--the likes of which he had never known. Since every part of her body is flush against his, he noticed one thing, she wasn't shaking. She was completely calm, relaxed even.

"Aren't you scared, Hope?"

"Oh yes, I am scared to death. The thing is, though, what you aren't understanding is that he has put me through all kinds of hell, things that most people could never even come close to imagining. I have already lived the nightmare, and I am more worried about what he will do to you, Andy, and my family. What I told you in the hospital is just the tip of the iceberg, Davy. There is more, so much more."

He chuckled to himself. "You truly are amazing, Hope. You are so willing to walk into the lion's den to save others."

She leaned her head up to look at him. "I'm not amazing, Davy. I am merely doing what I know needs to be done. I am the only one that is going to be able to do it. He won't give a rat's hind end about my mother, or my sister, or even the two of you. It's me he wants."

He couldn't help but to pull her in close for a hug. Regardless of what she thought, she was the most astounding woman he had ever had the pleasure of knowing. Brave, intelligent, and beautiful; she was the ultimate package. He knew then that he could fall in love with her, if he allowed it. He heard a tiny voice come from her, the words jumbled. "I'm sorry Hope, what did you say?"

She again lifted her head. "Kiss me, Davy. Make me feel alive."

An erection punched the inside of his jeans so hard he could pound a wood screw into a two-by-four! His breath rushed out in a hiss; he almost came right then and there. He pulled himself together enough to be able to warn her. "Hope, before I do, you need to know something. I don't know if I can stop with just a kiss. I don't know what it is I feel for you, but I do know this, I want you like no one else on the earth. Are you ready for that?"

She nodded. "Please, Davy." It wasn't the words, or even the pleading. The heat in her eyes seared him completely through, down to his soul!

A growl came from somewhere deep inside him, and he carefully turned his body so he was semi laying on her. He took a firm but gentle hold of either side of her face, and brought his lips to hers. Her taste is so divine that he can't get enough of her kiss. Mindful of her casts, he completely laid over her. Their tongues warred, each trying to own the other. He broke off the kiss as her one good arm ran the length of his back, sending shivers up his spine. He had to taste her neck, her collar, all of her, or he knew he would lose his mind.

She whispered his name, and it all but threw him over the edge. He had to be in her, now! He needed more than just to possess her, he needed to mark her, brand her, and worship her like the goddess she was. He needed it like he needed air to breathe.

He slowly removed her nightclothes so he didn't hurt her, and then removed his. He stared at her body for a moment, and took in how exquisite she was.

"Hope, you are the most beautiful woman ever created." He breathed, and carefully climbed above her. He held back for one more moment, needing to make sure. "Are you positive this is what you want?"

"Yes, Davy. Take me, please." she begged breathlessly.

The hunger in her eyes shattered all control he had left. Her moist tightness clamped around him as he entered her body inch by glorious inch. He stopped as his base touched her silken entrance, almost exploding right there. She wrapped her legs around his, and arched her hips. He sucked in a breath as he felt her hand slowly moving up his spine; her moist sheath around his cock sent him into a helix that he never knew could possibly exist. He started to move in her body, plunging him into the deepest recesses of heaven. Every guttural moan, every arch of her back, every cry of his name intensified the animalistic instinct in him, and made him want to give her the orgasm of her life. He didn't even care if he had one; that meant he could be in her even longer. At that very moment, he knew he was home.

Her movements and breathing became frenzied, as she rotated her hips with his, and he knew she was close. Before he knew what happened, she flipped them over so she was above him, her long, soft, beautiful hair framing them. Slowly, she moved her hips in a circular motion, driving him insane. She gained momentum above him until she rode him hard, and fast, and Hope cried out in shock and fear as her walls became vice grips. She pulsated all around him, and arched her back, thrusting her breasts out, shoving him as deep inside of her as is humanly possible. He grabbed her hips as he screamed her name with pure bliss at the feel of her release all over him. It sent him over the edge, as he exploded deep inside of her with one last brutal thrust.

She cried out his name, and collapsed on top of him. Both of them panted heavily, and he rubbed his hands along her spine ever so gently. To say that this was fantastic doesn't even begin to cover it! This moment was one that would stay with him as the best of his life every second that he breathed.

"Davy, I have never…that was my first." Her face began to turn red, and she turned her head to avoid looking at him.

"Was that your first orgasm, Hope?" he asked, stunned.

She nodded, burying her face in his chest.

He placed his finger under her chin and lifted it so she would look at him in the eye. "It's nothing to be ashamed of, it's his fault. He wasn't attentive to you enough."

"It's not that, Davy. He forced me from the get-go, and he….he was my first," she said, humiliation swimming in her eyes as she rolled off of him, and stretched out.

"He's raped you?" he demanded, wanting to kill the son of a bitch.

She had no response, she merely stared him in the eyes. He knew then that Davenport in fact had raped her. Throw the fact that he was her first lover on top of it, and it made Davy quite homicidal. He started to shake from the pure pissed-off feeling he had. How could anyone do that to her? Hell, how could anyone do that to another person?

Davy forced himself to calm down; he didn't want to scare her. When he realized that she *wanted* him to make love to her, it somewhat helped to calm him. After enduring what she had for that long, that she would want anyone to be that intimate with her--that she could trust anyone like that--let alone him, made him feel ten feet tall.

"Hey, dinner's here," Andy called through the door.

"Thanks, dude, I will be right there," Davy said loud enough for Andy to hear him.

He kissed her forehead. "Are you ready to eat?"

"Yes, I'm famished," she tried to smile, and failed miserably. Her eyes crinkled but they were still dull and filled with deep-seated pain.

He kissed her forehead, and got dressed so he could grab her dinner and bring it to her.

Andy sat at the kitchen table, eating his General Tso's Chicken, trying not to think about what was going on in Hope's bedroom. Since she came into their lives, everything had turned upside down. What was even worse than that, Andy was beginning to have feelings for that gutsy little woman in her room. That was not something he could allow. She obviously wanted Davy, and Andy would be damned if he would do anything to hurt his best friend.

Davy padded into the kitchen, scratching his bare chest.

"How is she, man?" Andy couldn't help but ask.

"She'll be okay. That is one fine woman in there. I have never met anyone like her before. She's got beauty, brains, and bravery."

Andy couldn't argue with that analysis. Once she got past what dipshit did to her, she was going to be one formidable force, nearly indestructible.

"Dude, I was thinking….when she gets back on her feet, literally, let's teach her self-defense. It will empower her, and make her feel a bit more secure."

Andy thought about it for a moment. Maybe it would be a good idea. She would need something on her side in case one of them couldn't be around. And it would make her a bit more self-assured, maybe even raise her self-esteem. "Yah, that's a good idea."

Davy grabbed the tubs of food, and looked at Andy. "Dude, what's wrong? Something's been eating at you all day."

"It's nothing. I'm just trying to figure out how we're going to do this tomorrow without getting any of us killed, especially our star witness." He didn't like referring to her as that, but he had to get some kind of distance between them, or he just knew he would be in deep, way over his head.

"Andy, she has a name; I would appreciate it if you used it."

"Fine, I am trying to keep *Hope* from getting killed, Davy! Deal with it!" Andy grabbed his meal, and went to his room, not wanting to deal with the shit-storm that he could feel coming a mile away. This could get ugly quick, and not just from Davenport.

Andy kicked his door shut with the sole of his sneakers, and put the plate down on his desk. Sinking into the chair, he put his head in his hands. God, what the hell was he supposed to do? As Davy said, she was one fine woman. He wasn't enjoying the thought of spending the rest of his life watching the two of them making lovey-dovey eyes at each other. He was going to have to find a way to purge her somehow. Maybe he just needed to find a woman, get laid, and go on with his miserable life. Besides, being the better half of an FBI field agent wasn't very advantageous. Odds say that they would be alone inside of a year.

A sharp knock came to the door, almost like a SWAT battering ram.

"Yah!" Andy barked, wanting to be alone and knowing that Davy wouldn't let it be.

He opened the door, and stuck his head in. "Can I come in for a minute?"

Andy swept his arm out toward the room, and went back to eating his meal.

Davy opened the oak door, and walked in. "I don't know what your problem is, but it has got to stop. You and I have been friends for too long for us to argue like this, and it's getting old."

Andy felt himself snap. *Who the hell does he think he is?* "Davy, don't chastise me like I'm a child. You and Hope aren't the only ones with a lot of shit on their plate. I only have eight hours to come up with a game plan to keep us all alive! Even stake-outs take time to plan. I don't have any! If I make one wrong move, one wrong decision, one or all of us could die! Do you think I relish knowing that I have your lives in my hands? If that's what you think, you're effing insane!" At the end of the tirade, Andy was panting and shaking.

"Man, I understand all of that, but at the same time that's not what all of this is about. This started the day of Hope's accident. What else is going on?"

Oh hell no, he's so not going there! "Dude, just drop it. It's a need to know basis, and you don't need to know."

Davy's eyes narrowed into fine slits. "It had better be work-related, or so help me, I will give you a beat-down like you read about for being such an asshole."

Andy inwardly groaned. He so didn't need this right now. "Yah, it's work-related, are you happy?"

Davy just stared at him for a second, trying to size him up. He was apparently satisfied, because he nodded. "Fine, whatever, just quit taking it out on Hope and me." He again stared at Andy, realization widening his eyes. "This is about Caleb, isn't it?"

Andy's heart skipped a beat. Caleb hadn't crossed his mind in a few months, and that not only surprised him, but also angered him. "Do. Not. Go. There." He made sure Davy knew to back off quick. The subject of his old partner was a trigger of nuclear proportions.

Davy threw his hands up in a show of surrender. "Sorry man, I didn't know it still bothered you that much."

He deflated. "I'm sorry." He took a deep breath, and slowly let it out. "In a way, I guess it does have something to do with him. I just don't want to lose you too, bro. I'm tired of having to bury people that I love."

"Do you really think he's insane enough to try anything in front of the public? There are cameras everywhere, which will make it easy to convict him. I think he's crazy, not stupid."

Andy nodded. Davy might be right, but at the same time, something was very wrong and he couldn't put his finger on it. Something didn't jive, didn't fit into the puzzle. Yes, Davenport wanted Hope back; he saw her as his and would do what he had to in order to get her back. However, he also knew that all manners of law enforcement was after him. He knew they all have his picture, and fingerprints, and they knew where he lived. Andy had proof positive that Davenport threatened a law enforcement officer in the form of a letter, yet he wanted to meet Andy,

Davy, and Hope inside of a public park? No, there was something very wrong there. The bastard was planning something.

He told Davy his suspicions, and with every word, his eyes grew wide as saucers.

"We can't close the park; the ass-wipe will suspect something. With all those people there, everyone is in danger, not just the three of us. We absolutely cannot go. It isn't worth that kind of risk. It's why the police don't do many high speed car chases anymore; it's putting innocent civilians at risk."

"What about putting an undercover in there instead of Hope?"

"It's the same thing; too many innocent lives are at risk. What if he shows up, we're not there, and he loses it? Civilians can die then too. Andy, we can't let that happen!"

"You're right." He went over to the phone on his nightstand, and called his Supervisor. He told him quickly of their thought process, and he agreed, it was entirely too dangerous. The FBI was going to get in touch with the proper authorities and have the park shut down tomorrow, under the guise of maintenance on the playground equipment. If Davenport showed up, the "maintenance workers" would make an arrest on the spot.

"I also don't think that the three of us should be here tomorrow, just in case. We need to find something to do for the day. Davenport knows where we live; therefore, it's too dangerous to be here," Davy pointed out. He then told Andy what Hope had told him in the bedroom.

"Dude, right now, do not tell me anymore; this has become way too personal for me. I am not going to be able to effectively do my job--I am enraged enough," Andy said, shaking from it. So help him, he knew that if he were to look at Davenport, he would wrap his fingers around his throat and laugh with glee as he died. To take a woman's virginity in such a way, while professing love the entire time was beyond abhorrent.

"Gentlemen, will you two please come in here? I need to talk to you," Hope called from down the hall.

They looked at each other and laughed. "Sure, sweetheart," Davy answered her.

They walked into her room, and she was sitting up on the bed. "I heard every word you two said. Yes, it makes sense, but I don't like it. Nick will see right through it."

"Yes, Hope, he will. We are counting on that, it will have to happen. We want him to get angry, therefore he will make a mistake and we can catch him." Andy said.

The phone rang, and Davy answered it.

Andy sat on the corner of her bed. "Hope, you have to know that not only will Davy and I keep you safe, but so will the FBI. We are not going to allow him to get anywhere near you. You may not have much of a life for a little while, but in the end, you will be free to do what you've always wanted to do."

She nodded her head. "I wish I had known about this a long time ago. I have wanted to leave him for so long, but didn't think I could without my family getting hurt. I know since they are in witness protection that I will never see them again, but at least they are alive. That means more than anything." The pain was naked in her voice. She truly missed them, maybe even blamed herself for what was going on. He knew that it wasn't her fault, not in the least bit, and he needed to find a way to help to ease her suffering.

"We can find ways to communicate to them, one of us in the bureau could always send messages back and forth once in a great while to keep you updated on each other."

Davy returned to her bedroom, all energy that was in him deflated like a popped balloon. He looked at both of them. "I just got put on suspension pending an investigation. Essentially, I just got fired."

CHAPTER 7

The next morning, Hope opened her eyes to the sun shining through the window. She looked around; scared in unfamiliar surroundings, and then everything came flooding back. She was at Davy and Andy's house, safe. Neither one of those two were about to let anything happen to her, or to them. Davy had left the wheelchair next to the bed in case she needed to go to the bathroom in the middle of the night. It was harder than she thought to use her opposite leg and arm to move, but she was going to have to get used to it. She couldn't allow the guys to carry her all the time; she was much more independent than that.

She used her one good leg to push herself into the restroom at the other side of the bedroom, and struggled to get herself situated.

She did her thing, and got herself back into the wheelchair. By the time she sat back down, she was gasping for breath, feeling like she'd run a marathon.

"Hope, what are you doing?" Andy's sleepy voice with a slight edge came from behind her.

She jumped, feeling like a child with her hand caught in the cookie jar. "I was just coming back from the bathroom."

"How did you get into your chair?" he asked, surprised.

"I do have one good leg and one good arm, Andy. I can't let you or Davy keep carrying me around. Besides, the casts should be coming off in a few weeks, and I need to build strength back up in them."

"Well, give yourself a break and let me wheel you into the living room."

Exhausted and out of breath, she let him.

"Do you need anything? Are you thirsty?" he asked, getting ready to go into the kitchen.

"Some hot tea would be great."

A smile tugged at the corners of his mouth. "Don't like coffee?"

"I can't stand the taste of the stuff. I love to smell it brewing, but the taste is awful."

"All right, would you like some breakfast?" He gave her a look that was almost hot, smoldering, like a large wooden structure about to detonate in flames.

Even though she wasn't hungry, she never was when she first got up; she would be by the time he finished cooking. "Um, sure Andy, thank you." He started walking away, and she suddenly wanted to go in there, and try to do something to help.

"Could you wheel me in there with you, please? I want to do something to help. I can't just sit here doing nothing."

He gave a chuckle, and shook his head. "I will wheel you in there, but there isn't much that you can do like that. You can just sit and talk to me, how does that sound?"

She nodded. God, she positively hated not being able to do anything. She was so used to having to do it all; it had been that way her entire life. To let others do everything for her was a blow that she didn't know if she could take.

He wheeled her over to the breakfast table, and placed her so she was facing him. "I was thinking that we could go to a few different places today. Maybe go to a movie, or even into the city. Taste of Chicago is supposed to start today."

"I have never been to Taste. Won't it be packed?"

"It was last year. But since you've never been, it would be fun for all of us. They have bands, and a whole bunch of other stuff. Plus, it's ideal; Davenport won't try anything, even if he figures out that we are there. It risks too much exposure."

"All right, if that is what you two want to do, it's fine with me." She gave him a smile, and actually meant it.

"Now, what do you want for breakfast?"

"I honestly don't care. I am so used to cooking enough breakfast for an army that I am not particular."

"Why would you cook enough breakfast for an army?" he asked, confused.

"When Nick wanted breakfast, he wanted a lot of it. Every weekend, I was to make a dozen eggs, pancakes, waffles, homemade biscuits with sausage gravy, both sausage links and patties, and fried potatoes. If there was anything left, which was rare, then I could eat. Any deviation from the menu and I would catch hell for it like you've never seen. That is why now, when I start cooking again, then I don't eat until you guys are done. It is how it's been done for so long that I don't know any other way."

Andy sat in a chair, and opened his mouth to say something, and shut it when Davy's voice came up from behind them. "Good morning, you two." He leaned down and gave Hope a kiss.

"Davy, listen to this." He wanted her to relay what she had just told him, which she did. To her, it was no big deal, merely a fact of life.

"Well, I want you to eat with us. That is not the right way to do things, ok?"

She could only nod. She didn't know how to act with these two. Everything Nick taught her, or made her do, seemed to be wrong. What if she made the wrong decision based on something Nick made her do before, and royally screwed something up? What would happen then? They didn't seem the type to throw her out, but if they got angry enough, could they.....?

No, she couldn't let herself think like that. They didn't seem the type to hurt her in that way. They were both too protective of her, even if for different reasons. Davy was wholly attracted to her, and wanted to date her, while Andy....well, Andy wanted her to testify against Nick. While yes, they were getting along better, it still felt like he hated her deep down, that he was merely tolerating her and she had no clue what to do about that. She kept telling herself that she cared because he was Davy's friend, and she had to live with him, but was it true?

Of course it is, stupid! A small voice inside of her screamed.

No, it's not, and you know it, another said. *You have to live with him. You like things interlacing, and any kind of stress drives you nuts. Besides, you like him, admit it.*

Yes, she liked him; she just liked Davy more. There was nothing wrong with that.

You mean besides the fact that Andy abhors you! Who the hell needed Nick when someone's own mind abused them just as meticulously?

"Hope, what are you thinking? It's nothing good if your eyes are welling up with tears like that." Davy asked, worry clouding his own eyes.

"I...I am ok, I promise." She buried her thoughts with a show of bravado. She decided to change the subject, hoping that they would just let it go. "So, I'm looking forward to going to Taste of Chicago. Having you both there should make it fun!"

Andy and Davy looked at each other, and Andy gave a shrug of his shoulders, but they did drop it.

"So, let's get some breakfast. Instead of cooking, let's go to IHOP. I have a sudden craving for some blueberry crêpes," Davy said.

Davy wheeled her into the bedroom and helped her change into a long, bohemian skirt and peasant blouse. He fastened one of her new watches on her good wrist, and helped her put earrings in her ears, and one of the necklaces around her neck. She had to admit, when he was done, she looked....nice.

She couldn't help but to meet his eyes, and smiled at him. She had never met a more helpful man in her life.

"Hope, before I take you out of the room, there is something I need to tell you." He came around and sat down on the bed, taking her hand. "Yesterday, when we made love, it was....god, I can't describe it. I have never been exactly celibate....I never had a problem finding a woman. But yesterday was incredible. I have never felt like that in my life. I wanted to let you know that I am officially off the market. I never want anyone else but you."

She sat there for a moment, stunned. "I....I don't know what to say, Davy. It was extraordinary for me too. I think we can officially say we are dating now." Her heart swelled with pride, and unadulterated happiness. He leaned in and kissed her, his taste sweet, gentle, interlaced with mint toothpaste. His tongue snaked between her lips, and her stomach flipped. Her fingers threaded through his long, soft hair, reveling in the instant warmth that flooded through her.

He slowly broke off the kiss, and put his forehead against hers. "Hope, I think I may be falling in love with you."

She didn't know what she felt for Davy, but she knew that it was wonderful, exciting, and calming at the same time. "I think I may be falling in love with you too." She pulled her forehead from his, and kissed him again.

He pulled away. "If we don't get out of here now, we will never leave. I will keep you in bed for the rest of your life."

He wheeled her out into the living room where Andy waited. "It's about damned time!" he said sourly. "I think we should take the Beamer. It would be easier for all three of us to fit into it, and Hope's chair."

"Andy, have you ever thought about having your head checked out? You go through moods faster than a manic depressive," she pointed out.

If looks could kill, Hope would have dropped dead on the spot! Without another word, he turned and stalked out of the house.

She let out a sigh. "God, if I don't start checking my tongue, I am going to get into serious trouble with you two."

"Your inner monologue is broken. I like that." Davy laughed. "Besides, here lately, it's been true with him. But, we do need to get going. I don't want to take the chance of being here if your ex shows up."

"Have you ever thought about getting a home security system?" She asked, looking around for a security box.

"I've looked into it, but here in Maywood, it's not like crime is abundant. But now that you are here, maybe I will get one. I will look into it tomorrow, okay?"

She nodded, thinking that it was his house, he didn't need her permission.

He wheeled her outside to the Beamer, and put her in the passenger's seat. Morose, Andy tossed Davy the keys, put the chair in the trunk, and sat behind Hope in the backseat.

She could feel his eyes boring into the back of her head as if daggers were piercing her skull.

Davy turned right onto First Avenue going toward Interstate 55, and his head whipped back around toward where we came from. He did a U-turn at the next intersection, and pulled into an empty restaurant. He just sat there at the driver's seat, looking at the building for several moments.

"Davy, what are you doing?" Andy asked.

He didn't say anything for several moments. When he did finally speak, it was soft. "We all know I lost my job last night. The conclusion of the investigation is going to be that I acted unethically."

Oh, that one hurt. He lost his job because of her. Hope's stomach churned like she swallowed a vat of bacon grease. She wrapped her arm around her stomach, and pulled her good leg up into herself. Davy deserved so much better than what she had given him so far.

"Yah, so, what are we doing here?" Andy demanded.

He looked at the building for a few more moments, and said in a much stronger voice, "We're going to eat, and then we're going to go to the real estate office."

He peeled out of the parking lot, and went to IHOP down the street, next to the Real Estate office they need.

After they were seated, and had ordered, Davy turned to Hope and Andy. "I am thinking about buying that empty building, and starting a restaurant."

Andy looked at him. "Man, you're crazy if you think you could do this! Granted, no one cooks better than you do, but there is more to running a restaurant than cooking! You don't know the first thing about running a business! You'll go under within five years!"

"Hope, what do you think?" Davy looked at her, his eyes holding the hope of the universe.

She sighed, hating being put in the middle of this, but since he had asked, she had to tell the truth. "I think you could do anything you put your mind to. However, I will say this. My mother opened a restaurant several years after she and my father divorced. The only reason she still doesn't own it is because she had to sell it when she got sick. It is tougher than most people think, but I can help you. I know the inner workings of a restaurant backwards and forwards, I ran Mom's when she couldn't be there. I cooked, did maintenance, ordered the trucks, hired, terminated, and waited tables, all mess and manners of paperwork, all of it. There is a process to all of it, even though it seems arbitrary, it truly isn't. I could show you the management end of it."

"And I suppose I can come in while I'm not at the bureau," Andy offered.

"Yes, that's it, Andy! Let's back him up!" I said, getting excited for Davy.

"I don't know; I just have a real bad feeling about this. Nothing is going to turn out the way we want."

"Andy, you know I trust your instincts; I've known you too long not to. Let's just hope that this one time, you're wrong."

Andy just concentrated on his napkin in front of him, not saying anything.

Hope didn't know what to think. What if Andy was right and something went horribly wrong? Davy would be crushed. But then again, any business venture was a huge risk. If no one took that risk, there would be no stores, no farms, nothing.

"So Davy, by the size of the restaurant, you want a full service. That means servers, cooks, prep cooks, everything. Do you know what kind of food you'd like to serve, and what age bracket you want to aim for customer-wise?" Hope asked, trying to find out exactly how far he'd thought this through.

"I'm thinking Greek. We have plenty of Italian and German restaurants, but there are hardly any true Greek places in this area. I would like it to be a family atmosphere."

"All right, when we get back home, we can all sit down and work out a business plan to give to the city. It is something they are going to require." Hope then thought of something new. "Are you going to want to serve alcohol?"

"I haven't thought about it, but yes, that is a good idea."

"Then what about putting a bar in the back of it, you can serve it there, and also have live music. That would bring in a lot of money, and provide some entertainment. You can put the front of the restaurant for families, yet still serve alcohol."

"I like the way you think." Davy grinned and took her hand.

It was then that the food came. They ate, and excitedly talked about getting this new venture off the ground. Even Andy started getting into it, throwing out ideas.

"Davy, what do you think of naming it *Sparta*, after the best known and toughest of the Greek cities?" Hope suggested.

"Yes, that's perfect!"

Once they were through eating, Davy paid, and they went next door. The agent took them back to the restaurant, and gave them a tour of the place. It had obviously been Italian; the booths and walls were a bright red, with rust-colored carpeting in the dining room. The server area still had the soda fountain, along with a reach-in freezer that needed a desperate cleaning, along with other things that servers need, like trays.

The kitchen still had the original oven and stove, and the walk-in freezer and cooler were still intact. Some of the shelving for the dry goods was rusted and bent, so it would need to be replaced. A part of the ceiling in the prep area had some water damage to it, so that would also need to be replaced, but otherwise it was in decent shape. Davy started taking notes on the changes that needed to take place, and he fell in love with the entire building.

They went back to the real estate office, where Davy made an offer of fifty thousand dollars, cash! Hope's jaw hit the floor. She just couldn't believe he had that much money that he could just drop it as if it were nothing! Andy just sat there like it was something he'd seen every day of his life!

The agent said that he would get with the owners, and let them know what was said.

After they got back into the car, Davy turned in the seat and looked at Hope and Andy. "This is our restaurant, not mine. I want to put it in all three of our names."

"Have you completely gone around the bend?" Andy demanded. "What the hell am I supposed to do with a restaurant? I work for the FBI! The United States Government is my boss! I don't have the time to deal with a restaurant!"

"So be a silent partner!" Davy shot back. He then looked at Hope, begging her with his eyes. "Hope, what do you say? I know you've done this before."

She couldn't speak for a moment. She could only open her mouth like a fish out of water. "I…I don't know, Davy. I am perfectly capable of running a restaurant, and making it profitable. But can I run my boyfriend's restaurant? I honestly don't know. Are you thinking about making things permanent with us? That is something I needed to know, because if god forbid we break up, it is going to get pretty awkward between us at work."

"She has a point there, Davy. You have to look at the bigger picture here. This isn't something to just jump into as you tend to do. This will change your whole life."

He took both of Hope's hands. "If everything goes the way it has been, then yes, Hope. I fully intend to marry you. I am just not going to ask you right now, this is the most un-romantic place humanly possible."

"Whoa, David, this is going a bit fast here! You just met Hope a month ago, and you've spent one night with her! You couldn't possibly know whether you want to spend the rest of your life with her or not! Use your head man, not your hormones!"

"When it's the real thing, you know it, Andrew! I know I love Hope. I have spent every waking moment with her since the day we met. A more perfect woman has never been born." He looked directly into her eyes.

She couldn't say anything. She was absolutely, completely thunderstruck.

Then Andy said something stupid, plunging headfirst into one of Hope's biggest pet peeves. "See, she agrees!"

Hope whipped around to look at him. "Do not speak for me! I have a voice of my own, and I am more than capable of using it!" she snapped, her voice echoing in the car.

He lifted his hands in surrender, "I'm sorry."

Hope realized then what she'd done. Her eyes widened in stark terror as she silently begged the earth to open up and swallow her. Her hand clapped over her mouth, and she burst into hysterical tears. "I'm so sorry!" She just kept repeating the apology. She absolutely could not believe she'd just yelled at someone like that. Nick would have ripped her head from her body. If she could have, she would have climbed under the seat, certain that Andy was about to kill her.

"Davy, let's get her out of here--someplace private," Andy said softly.

She didn't know where he was headed; only that he was driving. When she looked up, they were pulling into a slough. She started choking on her sobs and her stomach churned like it wanted to evacuate the contents of her breakfast. Her one good arm wrapped itself around her stomach, trying to hold the contents in. Her door opened, and Andy was suddenly next to her, sitting on his haunches.

"Honey, it's okay. It's perfectly normal to stand up for yourself, and I am glad that you did."

She could feel Davy's hand gently rubbing her back. It seemed to help to calm her.

Surprised that they weren't angry, she asked them why.

"Honey, you have every right to stand up and be counted when someone or something upsets you. It's a basic human right, you aren't a door mat," Davy said softly from the other side of her.

After a few minutes, her tears finally dried up.

She looked up at Andy once she was able to draw a breath, and think coherently.

He looked into her eyes, and said gently, almost like the caress of a lover, "I want to make a deal with you. I won't be such an asshole if you will start standing up for yourself more often."

She barked out a laugh and nodded. "Am I that scary when I'm angry?"

Davy laughed. "To see your eyes flash like that about made me wet myself."

"Now I know you guys are full of shit; if there was anything scary about me, we wouldn't be here right now!"

"No, it just means that Davenport doesn't have two brain cells to rub hard enough together to fart!" Andy said, laughter dancing in his eyes.

"Besides, it's the quiet ones you have to worry about," Davy said, continuing to rub Hope's back.

Another one of Andy's mysterious emotions flew across his face, and he immediately hid it again. He kissed her forehead, and got back into the car. "Let's get going. I'm looking forward to seeing the bands they have at Taste."

Davy switched on the radio, and a Styx tune was playing. Halfway through the song, she realized she was singing with it, and instantly stopped. She knew she had the world's worst singing voice, and she felt her face heat with embarrassment that she subjected these two wonderful men to it.

She saw Davy look in the rear view mirror at Andy, and saw Andy smile back. "Hope, Davy and I are part of a cover band. We actually have practice this weekend. What do you say you come with us?"

"Um, sure, as long as I don't have to get up and sing. As you just found out, I can set dogs to howling."

"Are you serious? You have one of the best voices I have ever heard! I would put you up there with Pat Benatar!" Andy piped up from the back seat.

"Now I *know* you're lying! *Nobody* is as good as Pat," she laughed.

"Hope, I'm dead serious here. You are," Davy said, his tone lending truth to his words.

"Guys, I was just goofing around, singing with the radio! It was *Renegade* for crying out loud!"

"If that was goofing around, what do you sound like when you're really trying?" Andy asked breathlessly.

"Hope, would you do a favor for us please? I'm going to stick in a tape and I want you to sing it, please. Do it for me?" Davy begged.

She sighed, frustrated. "It depends on what it is."

He shoved in the tape, and *Total Eclipse of the Heart* came through the speakers. She loved that song, so it was easy for her, not to mention that Hope and Bonnie have the same type of voice, gravelly, with a five-octave range.

Once the last note faded, Davy ejected the tape and turned the radio off. There was dead silence in the car for the span of minutes, until Andy broke it.

"Are you thinking what I am thinking, Dave?"

"Yah, we need to get in touch with Tristan and Chris, as soon as possible. In fact..." He got off at the Pulaski Street exit, and turned around, heading back west.

"We're not far Hope; they're just at the Cicero exit."

"Davy, I demand to know what the hell you're doing."

"I am hoping to help you. You need a hobby of some kind, Hope. You don't know how you sounded or looked when you were singing, Baby. Whether you want to admit it or not, you enjoyed it. You were closing your eyes, and truly getting into it. You love to sing, you just don't think you're very good at it, which is dead wrong. You truly are fantastic, Sweetheart. Your years of obvious training cannot go to waste."

"I've never had any training," she said honestly.

"Wait, what was that?" Andy asked.

"I've never had any formalized vocal training!" she said a little louder.

Davy's voice dripped with shock, "Sweetheart, if you have a voice like that and have never had lessons, you can really make it."

He pulled into a nice split-level house surrounded by houses exactly like it. A nice, brand new Mustang, her favorite car, sat in the driveway, looking forlorn.

"Wait right here, I will be right back," Andy said, opening the door. He all but sprinted into the house. Within moments, he came back with two other guys, both of them the stereotypical rocker types. They were tall and skinny, with long hair. The taller one had long, light brown hair, almost mousy-colored, with a pair of drum sticks in his hand. The other had a spiked mullet, the back of his hair falling to his waist under his bass guitar. They looked enough alike that they were probably related, maybe brothers.

"Guys, this is the one I was just telling you about, this is Hope. Wait until you hear her sing!" He looked down at me. "Hope, this is Tristan." He pointed to the bass guitarist. "And this is Chris." He pointed to the drummer.

She smiled and nodded to each of them in turn. "It's nice to meet you both."

"Well, do you want to come in and we'll jam a bit?" Tristan asked, sounding a bit like Matt Spiccoli from *Fast Times at Ridgemont High*. She half expected to hear "duuude" come out of his mouth.

"Hope, do you mind?" Davy asked.

She let out a sigh. She really didn't want to do this. The thought of singing in front of people she didn't know scared the bejeezus out of her, but she would do anything for Davy. She owed him her life, so she nodded. "All right, I will do it for you."

He smiled widely, and got her chair out of the trunk. Chris and Tristan didn't seem surprised when she got in it.

Davy wheeled her in the house. The living room was cluttered with pizza boxes, and cans of soda and beer were all over the place. One side was a musician's wet dream. A full drum set and keyboard, a guitar stand sat next to the drum set, and a microphone in its stand sat in front of it all. To the right of the drum set, stood a large mixer, and a couple of smaller amplifiers sat around where Andy and Chris would stand. Chris went into a back room, and came back with an electric guitar, handing it to Andy. Davy wheeled her in front of the band, and handed her the microphone. He went to stand in front of the keyboard.

Davy started the opening notes to *Total Eclipse of the Heart*, on his keyboard and she chimed in at the right beat.

Once the last note faded, Chris and Tristan both let out a loud "whoop".

"Damn, Dude, where did you find this angel?" Chris asked.

Davy told them a condensed story of how they met. When he looked at Hope, his eyes shone with pride, happiness, and love. It made her smile back, and she began to relax.

"Let's do *Love is a Battlefield*," Andy piped in.

Chris started the short drum solo and everyone else chimed in at the right moment. When the last note died, there were high fives all around, the excitement tangible in the air. For the first time in a long time, she felt relaxed, truly enjoying herself.

"So guys, if Hope okays it, do we have a lead singer?" Davy asked, hope evident in his voice.

"Hell yes!" both Chris and Tristan said at the same time.

"Dude, this girl is a godsend! I have never heard anything like her in my life! We could actually win next year with a voice like hers!" Tristan beamed brighter than a beacon on a lighthouse.

"Wait, win what?" she asked, suddenly nervous.

"Every year, for Taste of Chicago, they have a battle of the bands. The winner gets to sing at Taste, and gets a recording contract. We have tried several times and have never even come close to winning. We recently fired our lead singer for doing acid, and I have been filling in." Tristan said.

"Oh, I don't know if I'm ready for anything like that," she said, starting to shake.

"Right now you're not. But we have a year to practice, and get gigs," Andy said to her. "I personally think this will be good for you. When you sing, it's like you are in a totally different universe. You can almost see your stress lift off of you."

"I don't know....I honestly think you guys are barking up the wrong tree here. I'm not that good."

"Are you kidding me? Lady, you are the best I have heard in a hell of a long time!" Chris said emphatically. "You have a true talent here, and it would be a sin to let it go unused."

Could she really do this? Maybe they were right, and Nick had been wrong the whole time. She had always enjoyed singing. She stopped because Nick hated it. Maybe she could test this, if they knew her favorite song, then that would tell her if this was meant to be or not.

"Do you guys know Journey's *Faithfully*?"

Davy started the opening riff on his keyboard, and she sang the best she ever had, her voice obviously warmed up. Once the song was over, Davy looked at her. "Well, what do you say, Hope?"

She found herself truly wanting to do it. These guys were truly fantastic when they played, and they made her feel like she could do it. "All right, I accept." It was then that the celebrating really started. Before it could get too loud, she thought they should know about the problem with Nick, and had Davy relay some of what was going on, at least the more important parts.

"Oh hell no, there is no way in hell you are going to be hurt on my watch! I'll help protect you, Hope," Tristan promised.

"I will too." Chris also promised.

"So, do you guys want to do an unscheduled practice, or do you want to wait until Saturday?" Davy asked.

"Just a question here, guys; who is the leader of this band?"

Andy raised his hand. "I put it together about three years ago. It started as a project, something for fun. Now everyone wants to do gigs."

"Is there anywhere special you want to play?" she asked.

"There are a lot of places. But now, I think we have a real chance of being a true band, something to be taken seriously with you on board, Hope," Tristan said.

"Will you at least give me a chance to get out of the chair? I will only be in it a few more weeks, tops."

"Oh, of course we can!" Chris chimed in. "Is there anything you want to sing in particular?"

"I was thinking of doing something we could harmonize with, maybe *Seven Bridges Road* by *The Eagles*." She thought that sounded like a good idea, something they could come together on.

"I've always been good with singing The Eagles. I could do it, and we all harmonize," Tristan said.

"Shall we try it?" she suggested. She had to stop for a second. Was she really doing this? This was something she never dreamed she would do in a million years.

"Three, two, one," she counted down, and they started at the same time, and damned if it didn't sound fantastic!

"Now, Hope, we want you to take the lead on something. Let's do something sultry, something that would bring the roof off," Tristan said.

"How about Fleetwood Mac's *Hold Me*?"

"No, something we can back you up with," Davy offered.

She gave an evil grin, and turned her chair one-handed. She gripped the microphone hard, and started the opening refrain of *Shadows of the Night* by Pat Benatar. She thought all four men's eyes were going to pop out of their skulls. Their shock wore off quickly, and they played the music. She gave everything she had to the song, putting as much stage presence into it as she could since she was in a wheelchair.

"Was that sultry enough for you, Tristan?" she asked when the song ended, knowing her eyes were glowing with pure happiness. She had to admit, Andy's guitar solo was the best she'd ever heard.

"Hope, I am speechless. You are fantastic!" Tristan put down his bass, and hugged her. "Davy, she truly is a gem."

He laughed. "I wholly agree; she is the best, behind the microphone, and away from it."

She blushed brightly under all the praise.

"Tristan and Chris, would you believe she has never had a single voice lesson?" Andy piped up; his eyes had again turned icy.

Damn it, what did she do now? Her shoulders deflated, and her smile withered, crushed under the weight of his anger. She didn't know why she cared so much, it seemed she could do nothing right in his eyes, and likely never would; but, she did care, and damn it all, it hurt!

"No way in hell! It's like she was born having voice lessons!" Chris said.

"Dude, I am just stunned!" Tristan said.

She refused to look at Andy, she knew she would be devastated by the look in his eyes, so she turned to Davy, whose eyes shone and shimmered with tears of pride.

Andy stared at Hope as she sang. *Dear god, she was fantastic*! He hadn't seen her look so beautiful in the month or so that they'd known each other. All the layers of stress seemed to peel off of her like a flower opening up to the sun. When she sang the last song, she completely let go and allowed the music to just flow from her like nothing he had ever heard. Her cheeks flushed with happiness, and he knew that if she was capable of it, she would be all over this room, showing a massive amount of stage presence. As it was, she showed real talent in dancing and keeping a beat in her chair, well, as much as she could with half her body wrapped in plaster. Damn it, he wanted nothing more than to take her in his arms, and kiss her until she couldn't think.

No, this was wrong! She was Davy's girl, not his! He didn't have the right to these feelings, *at all.*

He put his guitar down, and murmured about needing some air. He went out onto the back porch, and leaned against the railing of the deck.

Trying not to think about that woman in the practice room, he turned his mind to the day he bought this house, and moved Chris and Tristan in.

Those boys were brothers, and as different as night and day. They had witnessed a crime as horrible as any that he could ever imagine, and had gone on the run. He ran into them, literally, after they had broken into his and Davy's apartment, and were stealing food. There was nothing else gone, just food. They were teenagers, and starving.

Tristan spilled the beans about what they had witnessed. They had both come home from school just a week prior, and walked in on their mother being brutally raped, tortured, and murdered. The four men had tied them up, and made a real attempt at beating them to death. It was a miracle that both of the boys lived through what was done to them. When Davy was buying his parents' old house, Andy went house hunting on his own. He had put the boys into a foster home, but he couldn't stop thinking about them. He involved himself with their case, and desperately wanted to help them. He found this beauty of a house for a good price and bought it. He moved the boys in, and made sure they had everything. They have been so grateful that they keep the place semi clean, and they practice music every day, wanting nothing more than to make it and pay him back, not that he intends to take anything for helping them.

Finally, two years ago, the men that had murdered their mother were caught, and sent to prison for the rest of their lives with no chance of parole.

Tristan opened the back door, and came out, "Yo, Andy, what's wrong, dude?"

He shook his head. "Nothing is wrong, my man. Go ahead and go back inside. I will be back in a few. It was just a bit hot in the house, so I needed some air."

"I call bullshit. I may be fresh out of my teens, but I am not an idiot. You've got it bad for Hope, don't you?"

Andy made a move to try and deny it, but saw the look in Tristan's eyes. Damn the kid, he's always been ultra-perceptive. "Yah, I do."

"Let me guess, she doesn't like you in the same way." It was more of a statement of fact than a question.

"No, she likes Davy. They just officially got together last night."

"Oh man, dude! While yah, I'm happy for Davy, that's got to blow chunks for you!"

"I'll be ok." He let go of the railing. "It wasn't meant to be. Besides, Davy deserves good dose of happy. He just got sacked from the department."

"So let me see if I get this right, you two rescued Hope from a madman, moved her in with you, Davy gets canned, you rescued my brother and I from hell, formed this band for us, saved our asses, and only Davy deserves happiness? Dude, your perceptions are bent."

"No, Tris, they aren't. There is a lot more to this than you know. This madman that we are trying to get Hope away from is a mafia hit man. I can't talk much more about the case, but she is in very real danger. I don't want to make light of what you and your family went through, but Hope's case made what happened to you look like a dime store novel."

Tristan stopped for a moment. "Are you serious? Is it worse than what my mother went through?"

"It's not even in the same zip code. The woman you see here, the carefree woman, just emerged. I met her a month ago, the same day that Davy met her, and she is so full of terror that this is the first time I have seen her relaxed."

Tristan took a deep breath, and slowly let it out. "What she must have gone through to be that afraid."

"My man, if I wasn't an agent, and I met him on the streets, no one would ever find his body," he said in a vehement whisper.

"You are one scary individual when you get like that." Tristan laughed uneasily.

"Go ahead and go back inside. I will be there in a moment. Not a word to anyone, even your brother about what we discussed out here," Andy said, clapping Tris on the back.

"I don't even remember what we talked about, dude."

Andy turned back around, and looked out into the back yard. All the talk about Hope's case, and thinking about the boys brought back another memory, one he has never been able to shake.

He was walking up to a two-story house, and a single gunshot had irrevocably changed his life.

He shook himself of that memory before he got too deeply in it, and walked back in. He just couldn't handle the memory, so he shoved it into a room in his head, slammed and locked that door.

He smiled at everyone, including Hope, and said: "Is this a band practice, or are we just going to stand around and shoot the shit? It does tend to splatter you know!"

It was then that Andy saw the television. It was on to a local news channel, where a beautiful woman was standing in a park, and the banner underneath said *Downtown Oak Brook*. "Wait, guys, turn that up!" He pointed to the television.

Another woman at the news desk said: "To reiterate, a bomb has gone off in a park in downtown Oak Brook; it was near the enclosed public facilities. Three people are dead, and ten injured."

He heard Hope suck in a breath. "Davy...." she said in a small voice as all the color drained from her face.

"I know, honey," he said, and held her close.

"What's going on?" Chris asked.

Andy told him about the situation going on, how she wanted to use herself as bait to catch Davenport, and explained about that park, and the boys too, went white as a sheet.

"You were all supposed to meet this maniac there today?" Tris asked, his voice quaking.

"Yes, I am sure the bomb was meant for us, guys."

"If you need a place to hide, come over here."

"No! I will not put you two in danger like that!" Hope put her foot down. "I hate it that Andy and Davy are in danger because of me, I couldn't handle it if something happened to you two over this!"

"This guy really is whacked!" Chris exclaimed, running his fingers through his long hair.

"Chris, you really have no idea," Hope said; her voice soft but terror-filled.

Davy pulled back into the driveway at home, with Hope asleep in the passenger's seat. God, she was so beautiful, and looked so peaceful. There was such a difference than how she was earlier, not that he could blame her.

"I am going to check the perimeter," Andy said softly, and opened the door. When the dome light came on, Hope stirred, and took a deep breath.

"We're home already?" she asked, stretching.

He beamed, ecstatic that she considered this her home. "Yes, Andy is going to check the area around the house, make sure no one is in it."

Andy closed the door softly to make sure that no one that might be inside could hear him. A few moments later, he came back around and gave the thumbs up.

Davy exited the car, and got Hope's wheelchair. He and Andy stood by while she got into it.

Once inside, he took her into her room, and helped her get ready for bed. As he was getting her clothes out, he stopped for a moment, thinking she might want a bath.

"Honey, I am going to grab a couple of garbage bags to wrap around your casts. Would you like to have a bath?"

"Oh yes, that would be heaven!" Her eyes lit up like they did at practice. He marveled at how easy it was to please her.

Oh, he was in deep shit when it came to her. Since she came into his life, all other women have ceased to exist. All he was capable of thinking about was her; and how to bring her self-esteem up, along with some pleasure.

He took some trash bags out of the box under the sink, and started to head back. Andy came out of the den, his eyes wide. "Davy, you got a call from the real estate agent. The owners of the restaurant accepted your offer. You are now an entrepreneur."

He stood there, dumbfounded. "I'm.....wow, I'm amazed! It never happens that quickly."

"They probably want to just get rid of it. It has been sitting there empty for a few years now.

"That's true. Well, I guess I had better get that business plan made up, and get things rolling." He gave a small smile. "Wow, this is really happening. I guess it was meant to be."

"Davy, what's going on? You don't seem too excited."

"Yah, I am. I really am; I just have a lot on my mind with taking care of Hope and trying to keep her safe, along with everything else. Right now, that is my first priority."

"She's a good woman Davy, a real keeper. But you also have to take care of yourself. How can you take care of her if you don't?"

"Yah, you're right." He started back toward the bedroom and then stopped. "Andy, can I ask you a question?" Davy asked without turning back around.

"You just did," he joked.

"I've had a bad feeling off and on today. If something happens to me, I want you to take care of Hope. You're the only one I trust enough. I am going to go see Sonny tomorrow morning, and have a new will made up. You and Hope are going to get everything."

"Davy, don't you think you're jumping the gun a bit? This is only her second night here. I mean, making out a will is always a good idea, but you're young, healthy, and vibrant. Nothing is going to happen to you."

"Do you know why I want to leave it to her?"

Andy released a long, drawn out sigh. "No, but I'm sure you're going to tell me."

"She doesn't want it. Granted, she doesn't know how much is there, but even if she did, she wouldn't want it. She's not with me for the money, she genuinely likes me, if not loves me." He continued to the bedroom, knowing that she is waiting for him.

"Is everything ok?" she asked, worry swimming in her eyes.

"Oh yes, everything is fine, Sweetheart." He started wrapping the garbage bags around her arm and leg. He told her about the real estate agent's call.

"Oh Davy, that's great!" she beamed, and hugged him with her good arm.

"Listen, I have to go out for a bit tomorrow morning. Andy is going to stay here with you. I just have a few errands I need to take care of."

"I can imagine, the starting of the close of the sale of the restaurant, and applying for the permits, I'll bet you do."

"Then yes, I will be gone all day." He laughed. "That's not all I have to do, Honey." He looked directly into her lovely eyes, the loveliest shade of blue he had ever seen. He could stare into them the rest of his life and never get sick of it.

"I am going to my attorney's office tomorrow, Hope. I am going to change my will. I am leaving everything to you and Andy."

"Whoa, wait one moment." She took a deep breath. "Davy, nothing is going to happen to you for one. Two, I don't want anything from you, only your love. Plus, we haven't been together long enough for you to know whether or not you want to leave half of everything to me."

"Yes, Hope, we have." He stood up, and ran his fingers through his long hair. "Look, I know that I love you. I realized that today during practice. Hope, you are everything a woman can be. I plan to one day make you my wife. Right now, neither one of us is ready for a step like that, but I think that one day soon we will be. Just in case something does happen to me, I want to make sure you are taken care of. I am not saying that it will, but you never know."

"Well, since it seems that I don't have a choice in the matter, what am I getting?" she asked; her voice flat.

He wrote on a piece of paper, and handed it to her.

"How many digits is that, Davy?"

"That would be twelve, plus half the house."

Davy watched the blood drain from her face as she looked at the paper a second time. "That is nearly a billion dollars! No....I cannot accept that," she said in a small voice, beyond stunned.

"I'm not doing it out of any misplaced charity, Honey. I'm doing it because I love you, and I want to make sure you never have to worry again, about anything. Besides, as I said, it's not like I'm going to keel over tomorrow."

"I would still rather you give it all to Andy. You've known him a lot longer, and he is more deserving of it than I."

"Hope, there is no one other than him that is more deserving of it than you. You can do with it what you will after I am gone. If you don't want it, give it to charity. But you *are* getting it. Deal with it."

CHAPTER 8

"All right, Hope; the casts can come off now," her primary doctor said, grabbing the saw to remove the detested plaster.

"Oh, I have some more news for you. Your blood test came back today. Congrats, mom!"

She sat there in silence for a few moments, the implication sinking in. "Wait, what doc?"

He shut off the small saw. "Hope, you're pregnant. I am going to give you the address and phone number of an OB/GYN. I still can't believe it. I've been your doctor since you were ten, and now you're going to be a mother. Where has the time gone?"

She walked out of the office with her cane, numb to the core.

"How did it go?" Andy asked, obviously seeing the fear in her eyes.

"I will tell you in the car, but please, don't say anything. I want to tell Davy."

"Tell him what, Hope? Are you ok? he asked, grabbing her arm in a loose grip, his eyes wide with worry.

"Again, Andy, I will tell you in the car."

Once the car doors were shut, he turned to Hope. "Now, what is going on?" he all but demanded.

"I'm pregnant," she whispered.

He sucked in a breath, and started the car. "I'm not going to tell Davy, that is completely yours." His jaw started working overtime, a sure sign that he was irritated, *again*.

When they got home, she opened the door to find Davy, Tris and Chris in the living room. She hugged all three of them, genuinely happy to see them. She looked up to see a banner above the window saying *Congratulations Hope.*

"What's going on here, fellas?" she asked, confused.

"You are back on your feet, Baby! That is a huge milestone, worthy of celebration!" Davy's face lit up with excitement, and he hugged her. The boys soon followed; Chris and Tristan both picking her up in their arms, bear-hugging her.

Those two were great. They had been over every day since they met her, helping out, keeping Hope entertained if Davy and Andy both had to be out at the same time. Her eyes filled with tears as they all hugged her in turn, congratulating her for finally being on her feet.

"Now that you're out of that chair, and we know you have a hell of a set of pipes, you can show us your stage presence," Tristan joked.

She laughed. "Yes, Tris, as soon as I get my land legs back."

"Hope, I did something for you. We are going to have a real party. While yes, I am no longer with the department, I am still friends with everyone, and everyone who is off duty is going to be there. Everyone from Andy's office will be there too, along with all the off-duty police. There will also be a band. Civil Service people know how to party!" Davy said.

"Davy, this house is big, but it's not that big. Where are we going to put everyone?" she asked, stalling. She looked at Andy, and by the look in his eye, he knew it, too.

"Go get yourself dolled up and I will show you. The party doesn't start for two hours."

She gave a small smile, and went into her bedroom. For the first time since the day of the accident, she was able to take a long shower, and it felt so good she didn't want to get out. As she dried her hair, she looked for something to wear, wondering how she was going to tell Davy the news that Doctor Pritchard gave her today. She had never been so nervous in her life. What if he didn't want kids? What if when he found out, he no longer loved her, and didn't want to be saddled down with a baby and a girlfriend? What would she do then? She knew she had to tell him before they left for the party, and it could just ruin it all. Then again, if he broke up with her, then she would know that he was a selfish jackass, and didn't deserve her. Then again, he has thus far shown that there wasn't a selfish bone in his body, so that likely wouldn't happen.

She went ahead and slipped on an ankle-length black cotton skirt and a plum-colored ruffled blouse. She slipped on a pair of hose and flats. She wasn't exactly ready for the heels as of yet; she just got out of the casts, for crying out loud. She had a bit of atrophy in the arm and leg that were in the casts; they were both paper-white and a touch difficult to use from stiffness. The doctor had given her some exercises to do so the muscles would get back into shape and loosen up. Maybe if she did some sun bathing, she would get color back into the limbs too.

For now, she plugged in her curling iron, and started applying her makeup, which was something she hadn't been able to do since high school. Nick hated her wearing it; then again, he hated anything that made her feel good about herself.

It didn't take long before she started on her hair, curling the length into ringlets. She separated a few wisps in the front, and tied the rest into a ponytail, the soft curls falling down her back. She curled the front wisps into long, tight spiral curls that framed her face. Thinking that was as good as it was going to get, she shut the curling iron off, and unplugged it. Grabbing her cane, she went out to face the music, expecting the guys to laugh their asses off, telling her that she looked like a damned clown.

When she got out to the living room, instead of laughter, she was met with complete silence. No one moved a muscle; not an eye blinked. Even Andy seemed dumbstruck, which had never happened.

"Do I look that bad? Damn it, give me a few minutes, and I will go change."

"No Hope, you are stunning!" Davy breathed.

It seemed to break the spell, and everyone gave a nervous laugh as Davy kissed her. The men were all dressed in suits of different colors ranging from all black, which had been Andy's choice, to black and plum, which was Davy's choice. Chris was dressed to the nines in a pair of black dress pants, red shirt, and black suit jacket, with no tie; while Tristan was dressed in a pair of black pants, white shirt, black leather tie, and black suit jacket. All four wore their hair down, but neatly combed. Hope guessed they figured out that she liked guys with long hair, so they decided to wear it down.

"All four of you look gorgeous tonight. I had better get at least one dance with each of you."

Chris and Tristan turned a nice shade of crimson, while Andy looked stoic as usual. Davy just beamed. He wrapped his arms around her waist. "I love you, Hope."

"I love you too," she smiled, and kissed him.

"Do you mean it?" Davy pulled back, shock registering in his eyes.

"Yes, I do. How could I not? You have given everything to me, your home, your heart, and you got me into this band. But, I have something to tell you. Before we go, I need you all to sit down for a moment."

They went to the couch, and she sat in the chair so she could face them. "The doctor drew blood the other day when I went for my checkup, if you remember, Davy." She's certain he did; she has a horrendous phobia of needles, and Davy had to keep kissing her to keep her mind off of it.

"Yes, I remember."

"Well, I got the results back from the test today," she stopped and took a deep breath, scared to death. Was this when he was going to throw her out? No, he wouldn't. He had given no indication that he would ever do that. She had to trust him.

"Hope, what is it? What did the doctor say?" Davy asked, nervous.

"I'm pregnant. I know exactly how far along I am, since you are the only one I have had sex with since February. I am five weeks along."

Again, such silence filled the room that you could hear a needle hit carpeting. Davy stood up, and went over to her. He gently lifted her from the chair, and planted a kiss on her that took her breath away.

"You have made me the happiest man alive. You don't even know how happy I am!" He lifted her up, and spun her around until she thought she would faint. She laughed, giddy that he still loved her.

He put her down, and kissed her again. "God, I love you so much." He turned to the guys. "I'm going to be a father!"

Tristan and Chris congratulated him in the typical manly way, slapping him on the back and chiding him on his virility. Andy hung back, a black look spreading across his face before hiding it with a look of indifference. You would think that it was the first time he heard it the way he reacted, or maybe he was hoping that Davy would break up with her.

She just didn't understand Andy. You would think that he'd be happy for his best friend; instead, he was being such an ass, yet again. Any news, especially pertaining to Hope, and Andy looked like he wanted to murder someone. *Did he still hate her that much?* There were times that she started to think he was over that hatred; at others she felt like his eyes were shooting daggers straight at her heart. She knew Andy wanted her to remain safe so she could testify against Nick so he was protective of her. Other than that, it seemed he couldn't stand to be around Hope.

Andy congratulated both Hope and Davy, and suggested they head for the party. His eyes still black and narrowed into fine slits, he turned and headed for the BMW.

A few minutes later, they pulled into the local Hyatt Regency where Davy had booked a banquet hall! The caterers were there setting up for the food, and the band was setting up and tuning their instruments.

"Davy, this is way too extravagant a celebration for me getting out of the casts! Are you insane?"

"Yes, Hope, I am. I'm crazy about you, and I wanted you to know how happy you have made me. I love you so much that I wanted to give you a slice of that happiness."

A wave of love and appreciation washed over her. She lifted her hand to caress his gorgeous cheek. "Davy, you do, every day, when you just look into my eyes. I am alive because of you. I intend to show you how much I appreciate it by staying that way. Yes, I do love you, but that is because of you, not because you saved my life."

He smiled, and kissed her. "You really are an incredible woman, Hope McLeod. I am proud to be yours."

She blushed under all his praise.

People in uniform started pouring in. Police, firefighters, and FBI all approached Davy and Hope, and introduced themselves to her. All of them were warm, hugging her, talking to her like they had known her all her life.

Within an hour, the party swelled to a fever pitch. The band played the latest in music, and the food is beyond fantastic. People flocked to the floor, dancing their hearts out.

Hope had been standing over by the bar talking to Tristan when she heard her name over the speakers. "Hope, please come to the stage, Sweetheart," Davy's voice again projected.

She groaned inwardly, but pasted a smile on her face, and did as she had been asked. A chair was placed next to the microphone stand, where Davy had her sit, facing him. *What in the world is he doing?*

She gasped when he got down on one knee, with the microphone in hand. *Oh god, is he doing what I think he's doing?* He reached into his pocket with the other and pulled out a tiny black box. He opened it, and inside sat the most beautiful sapphire and diamond ring she had ever seen. Her hand fluttered to her mouth.

He brought the microphone to his mouth, while looking straight into her eyes. "Hope, I have loved you from the moment I saw you in that mangled car. I know that I broke all kinds of rules and regulations, but I knew somehow that we would have something special. You are my life, and I love you with every beat of my heart, every breath that I take. Will you do me the honor of becoming my wife?"

She could only sit there, stunned, so much so that she forgot to breathe, forgot to answer. When it hit her that he was waiting for a response, she nodded, and said, "Yes!" She held out her hand and he placed the ring on her finger.

The room erupted into cheers and cat calls. She planted her cane, and stood up, moving into his arms where he gave her a kiss that stole her breath, and made her knees weak.

When he broke off the kiss, she took the microphone, and said to the crowd, "You have all been a part of Davy's life for such a long time that you are all invited."

The cheering became deafening. Someone started chanting her name, and within seconds, the whole room was doing it. She buried her face in Davy's chest, embarrassed to her toes. She felt rather than heard him rumble from laughter.

"This has officially turned into an engagement party! Oh, and one more thing, I am going to be a father!" She heard him say into the microphone. A stunned silence filled the room for a moment, then a roar filled every space, every nuance of the room exploded into a cheer so deafening that Hope thought her eardrums would explode. As they exited the stage, people came up and congratulated them, bear-hugging Davy, and gently hugging Hope as if she was made of porcelain.

For some reason, Hope's eyes sought out Andy, and she found him over by the bar. His eyes held so much pain, more than she ever noticed before. For a moment, her heart broke for him. She never really thought about it before, but it made sense. There was something in his past that had him so wrapped up in knots that it was tearing him apart. She had to wonder who he or she was that would hurt him so badly. She would gladly tear the person apart with her bare hands. She said he or she, not because she thought Andy was gay--and it wouldn't matter to her if he was--but it was purely because it didn't always have to be someone of a romantic interest that could hurt another person that badly. She had worked so hard to try and gain his trust, and his friendship; she wondered now if she would *ever* have it.

His eyes met hers, and the pain faded into obscurity, replaced by the usual anger. He slammed his empty glass on the bar, and bolted out of the room.

Davy gave a sigh. "I'll go talk to him."

"No, let me," she said. She gave Davy a kiss, and followed Andy.

She found him outside in the parking lot lighting a cigarette. He was facing away from the building, staring out into the street.

"Andy, what's wrong?"

He whipped around when he heard her voice, going for a gun that wasn't at his side.

"God, Hope! Never sneak up from behind an FBI agent unless you want to die!" he roared.

"I'm sorry, Andy. I didn't mean to sneak up on you. I am worried about you."

"Well, don't. I'm perfectly fine."

"Oh, yes, you're so perfectly fine that a trained cop like you didn't hear my shoes and cane clicking on the asphalt." She let out a sigh. "You know, Andy, we have to live together. You need to trust me sometime. I am not your enemy."

"Hope, don't do this right now. Trust me you don't want to do this."

She ignored his warning. "Who hurt you so badly that you hate me this deeply?"

"You really think I hate you?" he asked softly, disbelief dripping from his voice.

"You certainly make it obvious to me that you do," she said with no accusation in her voice, merely a statement of fact.

"No, I don't hate you. I think you're a sweet woman that has been put through a lifetime of hell."

"Then why is it that every time I turn around you are looking at me with contempt?"

He sighed, and put his hands on the hood of the BMW. "It's not you, Hope. I don't want to talk about it with you, or with anyone else for that matter, but it's not you I hate."

"So you're going to shut me out when I have done nothing more than try to be your friend?" It actually wasn't a question, but more of a demand for answers.

Andy erupted, ripping her heart out and stomping it into the ground. "We're not friends, Hope! We can never be friends! Don't you get it? I am the FBI agent that is trying to keep your gorgeous ass alive! If I get involved with you on any level, it can get us all killed! Now get back inside with your fiancé, and leave me the hell alone!"

Tears filled her eyes, and a sob escaped before she could stop it. "You unmitigated bastard, you can't even pretend to be friends with me for Davy's sake. You are a poor excuse of a man! Worse than that, you are a poor excuse of a best friend!" She spun around, and all but ran back into the hotel, straight to the bathroom.

Andy felt like an ass for what he said to her, but he didn't have much of a choice. *She hit too close to the truth, and he couldn't have her knowing how he felt for her. She was Davy's woman, damn it, and he has no right to these feelings! He would not betray his best friend like this! She was right; he was a full-fledged bastard! But damn it all to hell and back, he had to stay away from her on all personal levels, or he would do something he would regret later! He hated causing her pain, but it was better for them both. He stopped for a moment. Oh dear god, he did! He told her she was gorgeous! Fortunately, she didn't seem to notice!*

He finished his cigarette and went back to the party. He found Davy, and congratulated him.

"Where's Hope?" Andy asked, shaking his hand, wanting to apologize to her.

"I thought she was with you!" Andy dropped Davy's hand as fear clenched his stomach.

"No, she went outside to talk to you."

"We had a disagreement, and she ran back in here. I really need to apologize to her; I was beyond cruel."

They shot each other a look, and without another word, they tore out of the room. As soon as they got to the lobby, a scream shattered the air, shrill, full of terror and pain!

"Hope!" Andy screamed, and tore off toward the sound, his heart pounding in his chest. If she was dead, he would never forgive himself!

He found the women's bathroom and burst inside, not giving a shit if anyone was in there or not.

A smashed window lay open next to the sink, the broken pieces outside. "Andy, it was Nick! He got out through the window!" Hope panted, tears streaming down her face. Andy looked out, and saw the bastard running across the parking lot toward the street, but he was too far away for Andy to catch him. He hauled back and with all his strength, punched the dingy, painted brick wall beside the window. His knuckles throbbed unmercifully, but he ignored it, beyond infuriated.

Andy hadn't heard Davy come in, but he was there holding her close as she cried, her sobs wracking her body.

"Are you hurt, Hope?" Andy asked, going into full FBI mode, but as her friend, his heart was breaking for her.

She shook her head. "He didn't touch me this time. He didn't have time."

"Good." He turned to Davy. "Take her back into the party. Grab Captain Huntsford and tell him what just happened." Andy looked back to Hope. "You do not leave his side, got it?"

She nodded, tears still streaming down her face, although the sobs quieted. "I mean it, Hope. You are glued to him like a second skin. If you have to go to the bathroom, he stands outside the door."

"We get it, Andy," Davy said, and walked out with her.

Once the door closed, Andy leaned against the sink, taking a few deep breaths. It was either that, or his knees would collapse. He had never been so scared in his life, not that he would admit it to either one of them.

He would have to take her aside when he was done with the manager and question her about the specifics.

When his heartbeat returned to normal, he left for the front desk.

He informed the manager of what had happened, and offered to pay for the window. The manager first sincerely inquired after Hope's welfare, and then refused the payment, stating that it was no one's fault, except Davenport's, so the manager would bill the state for reimbursement of the window.

He went back into the party, where everyone was in an uproar. Word traveled fast among Civil Service personnel, and everyone seemed to be surrounding Hope, including the firefighters. There was no way in hell that anyone was going to allow her to be hurt, including and especially him.

He grabbed Hope and Davy, and took them out into the lobby. "Hope, I need to know exactly what happened, and we have to do it now before you forget any details."

She sighed. "I've already told your Captain what happened."

"That's good, but I am the one assigned to your case. I need to know."

"I went into a stall for privacy after you told me off, and he came in, locking the door. He said '*I hear you're engaged, slut! Break it off, or you both die! Your baby is going to die anyway!*' I screamed, and he broke the window to get out. I started out of the room to get one of you, and I had just unlocked the door when you came in. I had forgotten my cane, so I went to get it when you burst through."

"I want to know how he found out," Davy pointed out.

"There has to be a leak within the bureau." Andy sighed, trying to hide the terror gripping every part of his body.

"Wait, you mean someone is feeding him information? Who in the hell would do that? He's wanted for murder!" Davy demanded.

"I don't know, but I am going to damn well find out! Do not trust anybody, except my captain!"

Andy turned to Hope. "I am sorry for what I said earlier. I didn't mean a word of it. I am trying to protect you, and I figured that by staying at a distance from you, it would keep you safer. I was wrong. Please forgive me."

She nodded, but looked away. He knew then that he had a major bridge to repair. She was absolutely right; they needed to get along if for nothing more than Davy and his own mental health.

But he had to be honest with himself. He really was beginning to care for her, in ways that he didn't have the right to. She was beautiful, with a heart as big as Texas. She didn't deserve what she was being put through, hell, no one did. He was more than willing to put his life on the line, along with his heart and soul to keep her safe. Either way, he knew that he was going to be a casualty in this, so he might as well go full throttle. Davy deserved this kind of happiness, and Andy would be damned if he saw it torn apart by him, or anyone else.

"Let's get back into the party. We need to break up this cloud that is forming. This night belongs to the two of you. Don't let Davenport ruin it for you," he said, and went into the banquet hall.

He made a beeline for the stage where the band was sitting around the edges, and grabbed the microphone. "Hey everyone, I thought this was a party. Yah, shit went down, but it happens. Let's celebrate my best friend's engagement to a great girl, and their pregnancy. Come on, band, get off your asses, and start playing! Hope, get up here, I want everyone in here to hear you sing!"

"Andy, no, I'm not…."

"I don't care. You don't need to dwell on this."

She gave him a black look, and headed toward the stage. He ignored it, and looked at the band. "Sweet Home Alabama in C."

He turned to the lead guitar player. "Do you mind?"

The guy shook his head, happy to have a break.

As soon as she reached the mic, Andy started the opening riff. She looked at him with murder in her eyes, but he didn't care. She needed this. After a few moments, she started getting into it, and had the room clapping and dancing. Hope was all over that stage like someone that had been born on it, her presence demanding the audience's attention, if for nothing more than to see what she was going to do next.

During the background singer's solo, she had the room singing with him, making them a part of the show. She became aggressive, a totally different person than she truly was. When she was on that stage, she indubitably cut loose, and it was more than a beautiful sight. She was relaxed, yet so full of energy that she could light the city of Chicago with it. She exuded an overabundance of sex appeal, which was driving him to the brink of insanity. Davy was one lucky man, and Andy prayed that he could find someone just like Hope one day.

Once the song was over, the room erupted. She moved to leave the stage, and Andy turned to give the guitar back, but the lead singer of the band said into his own microphone, "Do you want to hear one more from the pretty lady?"

The applause and cheering was deafening. Chanting started up: "One more song…one more song…" One thing about police and firefighters, they can be such frat boys.

She looked at the guys in the band. She covered the mic, and asked, "Do you know *Black Velvet* by *Alannah Miles*?"

Hope never missed a beat or flubbed a note. Andy couldn't help but watch her; that she could pull a song like this off and sound that good was beyond amazing to him. Alannah herself would be staring at her in awe.

Andy's heart swelled with a pride he had no right to feel, but he couldn't help it. He told himself that it was because she was his best friend's fiancée, and they were in a band together. He had a right to be proud that she had such an astounding voice. He had to admit it for once, they were friends, but he could not let them get too close.

Davy opened the door for everyone, and walked in to find the house in shambles. The furniture was overturned, bric-a-brac lay shattered all over the floor, and couch cushions had been shredded. He motioned for the other two to stay outside while he searched the house. He went into Hope's bedroom, and found her beautiful furniture overturned, her bed torn apart on the floor, and all of her belongings scattered to hell and back. The wall next to the window had been vandalized--*'The baby and the whore must die'*—the red paint dripping from the words like blood.

He went back outside, and had Andy go to the local store and call the police. Davy didn't want to touch anything, including the phone. This bastard had gone too far. He had to be stopped, and soon.

The police arrived and took pictures of the place. Davy shook with rage and fear for Hope. He looked at her and terror had flooded her eyes. Never had he felt as helpless as he did in this moment. How was he supposed to protect her against someone that no one seemed to be able to catch?

Davenport had gotten in through the back door of the house, breaking the window above the lock. Nothing was sacred to this bastard. He obviously meant to scare Davy. Well, he didn't scare off that easily, and neither would Andy.

After the police took statements and left, Davy decided they were going to the Double Tree and booking a room. They grabbed enough clothes for a week and left the house.

He let Andy drive the car as he was still shaking with absolute ferocity. Plus, he wanted to be next to Hope to hold her. She had not uttered one sound, not one syllable since she saw the inside of the house. She really didn't have to, it was written in her eyes how she was feeling.

It was in her movements, the stiff way she walked, and was startled at every sound around her.

Her fluttering fingers found her ring, and twisted it around.

Nervous that she was having second thoughts, he kissed the top of her head. "Honey, what are you thinking?"

She shook her head. When no other sound came from her; his heart leapt in his chest.

"Hope? What's going on?"

"He's going to kill us all, Davy. He knows our every movement, where we live, everything. Nothing can stop him. He will never allow us to marry. That is what he was telling us by destroying the house and threatening me at the party."

"He doesn't have a say in the matter, Hope. That is our decision, not his."

"He will if he kills us," she said in a small voice and turned her head to look out the window.

What could he say to that? She was right.

"Hope, we are going to make certain that doesn't happen," Andy said from the front seat.

"How are you going to do that? No one can catch him. He got away from us at the party and he ransacked your house. The security system company hasn't gotten back to us about installing an alarm, so he can get into the house in the middle of the night while we are sleeping, and we could all wake up with our throats cut."

"First of all, Hope, it's your house also. Second of all...." Davy interjected and let out a long, drawn out sigh. "Andy, she has a point."

"Damn it, I know she does," Andy retorted. "I am going to talk to my Captain tomorrow. Something is very wrong with this. I know we have a leak somewhere in the bureau and we have to flush them out. I am going to do a complete background check on Davenport, his family, and friends. If any of them are in the bureau, we will have our man. I am sick to death of him staying one step ahead of us."

"I think that's why my identity change hasn't gone through," she said softly.

Andy suddenly cranked the car over to the right, pulling into a 7/11, throwing Davy and Hope around in the vehicle.

"Damn it Andy! Was that absolutely necessary?" Davy complained.

"That's it! I know who it is!" he all but shouted back.

He ran to the pay phone right in front of the car and talked excitedly for several minutes. He finally came back to the car, and didn't say a word until he shut the door. "The Captain is going to investigate him. Collins is the one handling your name change. It makes sense. But, we can't accuse him until we have proof."

"Did he handle my family's identity changes?" she asked, her voice trembling.

"No, I handled that personally," Andy said and started the car. He pulled back out into the empty street, heading toward Oak Brook.

Davy could see Hope silently crying in the seat next to him. He wanted to tear Davenport apart with his bare hands, limb by limb, but all he could do was hold her close. "I love you, Hope. That will never change."

"I love you too, Davy," she said never looking up at him.

He just held her closer, his heart shattering.

"I hate having to run," she said in a small voice.

"I know, baby." He kissed the top of her head and left her alone.

They got two rooms at the Doubletree, one for Andy and one for Hope and Davy. Once inside their suite, Hope changed clothes, and lay down. She flipped on the television, and veg'd out. When he lay beside her, she curled into him without saying anything, and put her head on his chest. "I'm so scared, Davy. I just found you. I don't want anything to happen to you."

"I know, honey. I'm not going to let anything happen. You're stuck with me." He tried to smile, but it seemed like too much effort.

She tilted her head up, and looked into his eyes. "I wouldn't have it any other way."

Over the next week, he left Hope in the hotel, knowing that Davenport didn't know where they were. Davy continued to work on the restaurant as he wanted to have the grand opening in three months. There was so much to do: renovating, bringing things up to code, ordering booths, tables, kitchen supplies, and everything else that was needed. He had added her to his bank account, and gotten her a debit and credit card, so she could go shopping anytime she wanted; but, all she would do was eat when she needed to. She refused to spend money, unless it was on him.

Andy finally had a talk with Hope, letting her know that she would need maternity clothes in just a few short weeks. She shrugged it off, saying that she could get them when she needed them. Davy couldn't help but feel that she didn't think she would need them.

After a long week into their exile, she went over to the mall while he was at the restaurant and surprised him with something he never thought of--a computer. She said it would be easier to do his bookkeeping and other business-related tasks for the restaurant. Although it was a clunky, heavy thing, he had to admit, it was a very good, practical idea.

"Honey, did you even look at anything for yourself?"

"No, I don't need anything," she shrugged.

"Come on." He took her hand.

"No, Davy, I really don't want to go anywhere."

"You need a distraction, Baby. We're going out, just the two of us."

She grumbled and stood up, slipping her shoes on. They stopped off at Andy's room, and Davy let him know they were going out for a bit.

Hope and Davy went over to the mall, where they just wandered around, holding hands. She stopped in front of a Waldenbooks, looking at the books in the store window.

"You left all your books at the house, didn't you?"

She nodded, and he took her inside. She went over to her favorite section, romance of course, and began browsing. He watched as she read every blurb, smiled at a few, but put them back.

"Hope, I want you to buy some things."

"No. I don't need or want anything, Davy. I'm fine."

"Alright, I tell you what. If you don't get anything, then I am going to get you something expensive as all hell. It will be my choice of what I get, and I can guarantee, it will be a lot of money."

She shot him a venom-filled look. "Alright, fine, but it won't be in here. I have somewhere else in mind."

"That's my girl! Where are we going?"

"A musical instrument store, but what I'm going to get will have to be stored at the restaurant until we can go back home. But remember, you asked for this!"

His eyes grew wide as saucers as he registered what she said. *What the hell was she going to get?*

The store was right around the corner from the mall entrance, so they walked over. Hope went straight for a Remo Mastertouch Drum Kit. Wow, this girl has taste! She grabbed the sticks sitting on the bass, sat down, and wailed one hell of a beat on it. All he could do was stand there with his mouth wide open as she drew a crowd. Once she was done, the gapers clapped and cheered.

She looked at him and shrugged. "I've been playing since I was eight."

"Why didn't you tell me?" he asked, dumbfounded.

She again lifted her shoulders. "It just never came up." She looked at the salesman sensing a sale, and said, "I'll take it, but I want a few other things too." She went in the back to where they kept the microphones and stands. She picked up a wireless microphone, a headset with a built-in microphone, a battery pack for it, a stand, clip, and batteries for the wireless, all top of the line.

"For someone that never wanted to be in a band, you know what you're doing." Davy couldn't help but laugh.

"I thought about it at one time, but was told I would never be good enough. I want to get one more thing. Yes, it's for you."

She went over to the keyboards and picked out a Yamaha keyboard. He tried to tell her no, but she wouldn't hear of it. As they passed by the guitars, she picked out a Fender Voodoo Stratocaster with red and black flames for Andy.

"You wanted me to spend money, so I'm spending money," she looked at him and laughed.

Hope had gone through that store like a whirlwind and had left no stone unturned.

Davy gave them the address of the restaurant, telling them that he would be there at nine in the morning for the delivery of the drums. They would take everything else now. Since they had spent so much money in the store, the salesman threw in a free case for the Fender. Davy put the Fender into the case to make things easier to carry, and Hope and Davy carried everything else out. It was then he realized she'd forgotten the cane.

"Hope, where's your cane?"

"Oh, I must have left it at the hotel! I forgot all about it!"

As Andy picked up the TV remote and began channel surfing, someone knocked on his door. When he answered it, shirtless, Davy stood on the other side, grinning like a Cheshire cat. "My man, you need to come over to our room a moment. Hope has something for you."

"You can't be serious! Why did you let her spend money on me?"

"Now, you sound like her! Just get your ass over there."

"Let me get a shirt on…."

"There's no time, she's bursting at the seams." Davy smiled hugely, knowing that Andy was going to love this!

Andy sighed, and scratching his chest, he went out without a shirt, and barefoot. Realizing he forgot his keycard, he went back to get it before he locked himself out. He came out a second later and followed Davy. Against the far wall in the sitting room of the suite sat a guitar case. "Hope, I really wish you hadn't spent money on me."

"You won't say that when you see what's inside," Davy said.

Andy sighed, and went over to the case. He picked it up, noticing it was heavy. He put it on the love seat. "I don't think it is Hope bursting at the seams," he said, unlatching it.

When he opened the top of the case, he sucked in a breath, and his head whipped around to look at her. "Hope, you got me a Fender Voodoo Stratocaster?" he breathed, his voice dripping with awe and surprise.

Davy watched as Andy stroked the neck of the guitar like it was a lover. "Pick it up, Andy. It won't do any good sitting in there."

"Hope, do you realize what you have done?" Andy asked, ignoring what Davy said.

"Yes, Andy. I realize that the Voodoo was played by Jimi Hendrix. I wanted you two to have something from me; something that I knew would be special to you."

"If you didn't get anything for yourself, then I won't accept this."

"Dude, you have *no idea*! She got herself something alright. It's being delivered to the restaurant tomorrow."

"What did you get that would need to be delivered?" Andy asked, still stunned.

"It's just a drum set."

"Hope, please, is the Sears Tower just a building? Andy, she got a Remo Mastertouch!"

He stared at her, stupefied. "No, you're lying, you have to be!"

"No, this is a sweet drum set," Hope smiled.

"Andy, you should hear her play! This woman can pound the skin!"

"Before you ask, too, I didn't say anything because it never came up. Plus, it's not like I was able to play with the cast on my arm."

"Dude, she has some real musical juice in her."

CHAPTER 9

The next day, Andy told Hope and Davy it would be okay to go home. After a week in the motel, he figured that Nick would think they had all fled the area, going underground. Plus, Andy's captain had spread it around the bureau that they had all been relocated to Seattle, placing Andy on a month's paid vacation, not that he needed the money.

It felt so good to be home.

"Hope, I will have the drum set delivered here instead of the restaurant. It's only a few blocks away, and I will give them a hundred dollar tip to do it," Davy said.

"All right, sweetheart. Have a good day. I love you!" She leaned up and gave him a kiss, and he went to his car. She couldn't help but stare at him, her heart swelling with love and awe. He might be filthy rich, but he still went to work every day like every other man.

"I love you too, Hope."

She spent some time cleaning her bedroom and took a hot shower. An hour after Davy left, as she headed to the kitchen to start making spaghetti sauce for tomorrow night's dinner, the doorbell rang announcing the delivery of her drum set.

"Miss McLeod, do you need us to put it together for you?"

"No, thank you. I can do that myself."

She went ahead and put it together in the living room. As she was putting the snare on its stand, there was a sudden, deafening explosion that shattered the windows and shook the walls! She pressed herself against the wall beside the window, hoping it would give her some protection from the glass.

Andy raced out of his bedroom, screaming her name.

"I'm ok!" she hollered through the echoes of the deafening reverberation. A sick feeling went through the pit of her stomach, making her want to vomit as Davy's face flashed in front of her. Terror as she had never known it, coursed through her veins, and she just knew she had to get to the restaurant now! She had to know for sure that he was okay!

"Andy, I have to get to the restaurant! I have a really bad feeling!" She grabbed the keys and started out to the Beamer.

"I'm going with you!" he said in a tone that left no room for argument, coming up from behind her.

Sirens wailed from all around them, echoing the screaming in her heart. The closer they got, the higher the flames seemed to be reaching for the atmosphere, and they made an honest attempt to suck the oxygen from the heavens.

"Andy, I really don't like this! It has to be the restaurant!"

"It is the restaurant! Hope, stop the car!"

"No! I have to get to Davy! I have to make sure he's okay!" Hope knew somehow he wouldn't be. The explosion had been too powerful, but she had to see for herself. She couldn't help but hold out some kind of hope that he survived, that he got out somehow.

"Hope, you will blow up the car if you get any closer! Pull. Over!"

She pulled over to the side of the street and got out. She slammed the door and ran toward the fire. Another loud explosion rent the air, knocking her to the pavement!

She screamed Davy's name, but couldn't hear it through the deafening booms. Smoldering debris fell all around her like lava bombs. Hope felt Andy throw his body over hers, shielding her. Once the wreckage stopped falling, she made him move off of her. She leapt up and frantically ran toward Davy and the restaurant. She felt Andy grab her around the stomach before she could get into the vicinity of the intense heat radiating from the fire. He pulled her to him, trapping her in his arms. "No! Let me go! Davy's in there!" She struggled against him, feeling herself lose control. She had to get to him, so the man she loved didn't have to die alone!

"Hope, he's gone," Andy said into her ear as he pressed her face into his chest.

His words sank into her determination, turning her blood to ice. "No!" she screamed, long, drawn out. She felt her knees buckle, and she went down slowly, Andy helping her down.

They sat there for hours as the firefighters got the fire under control, their tears mingling. Davy couldn't be dead, he just couldn't be!

Several hours later, once it was merely smoke coming up from the absolute destruction of the building, the Captain walked up to them, removing his mask and helmet. "Hope, Andy, I'm sorry. We found Davy. He was lying against the far wall in the dining room, blown away from the kitchen. I'm so sorry, he's gone." His tears mingled with the soot on his face, making tracks.

Hope felt every bit of her sanity wither and die with every word from the captain. Andy just held her, his tears falling into her hair.

"Andy, he can't be gone, he just can't! We're getting married in October!" Her consciousness just couldn't grasp it, couldn't conceive that her fiancé was dead.

"I know, honey," he choked out a sob, and they sat there and cried, holding on to each other for dear life.

Once her tears dried up, the Captain returned to Andy and Hope. "I'm so sorry you two. God, I can't believe it! I never thought he'd go out this way." Hope looked up, and the rest of the firefighters were huddled together, hugging each other, each one sobbing.

"The department will give him a burial with full honors," the Captain choked out, and broke down crying. She stood up, and just held him, as she broke down yet again. She felt Andy's arms go around both of them. She couldn't begin to estimate how long they stood there, their arms around each other, sobs wracking their bodies.

As their tears subsided, she let go of the Captain, and let him return to his job and his men.

"There's nothing we can do here, Hope. Let's go." Andy quickly steered her away from the shell of the building. She saw some people bring a body bag out of what used to be the front door. "Davy!" she screamed, and broke out of Andy's arms, running toward the men.

"Hope, no! You don't need to see it!" Andy grabbed her around the waist and held her tight against him. He turned her head away from the sight of Davy's body being put into the waiting ambulance, resting her cheek against his chest. After a few moments of pure shock coursing through her body, they turned around and walked away. It was at that moment that she truly knew without a doubt that the only people left in her life were Andy, Tristan and Chris. Without them, she was utterly alone.

Nick got exactly what he wanted.

Andy and Hope slowly walked back to the car, their arms around each other as if they were to let go, they would both fall to the ground. Carefully, Andy turned the car around, and headed toward Tristan and Chris's house. They had to be told.

Andy opened the door, and Tris was watching television while Chris made something for them to eat.

"Andy, dude, what's wrong? You two look like you've been through a fire," Tris asked.

"Chris, you need to come in here," Andy called out, not answering Tristan.

"Hey Andy, Hope," he greeted us. "Where's Davy?"

"Chris, sit down," Andy nodded toward the couch.

Once Chris planted himself, Andy started. "Boys, there was an explosion in the restaurant. Davy was caught in it. He's…he's dead," he choked out

They sat there for a moment, their eyes shut tightly with pain. "No, I can't…..I can't believe it," Tristan said softly.

"It's true, I saw….." She couldn't finish, her throat closed up, and she fell into a fresh bout of tears. Her legs collapsed out from under her, and Andy picked her up, putting her on the opposite couch. They merely held each other and cried.

Once they could cry no more, she looked at the brothers. "I wanted to tell you something. It may come down to me disappearing. If it does, I want you both to know that I love you like you are my little brothers. Please, never forget that, or forget me."

"We could never forget you, Hope. We love you, too." Chris wiped the tears from his face with his shaking fingers.

"You aren't going anywhere, we won't allow it," Tristan said.

"You may not have a choice."

She went over to Davy's keyboard, and couldn't help but touch the keys. She pulled up a memory of her childhood and sat down on the stool. She hadn't played a piano since she was ten, and she flubbed the notes somewhat, but she played a small, classical tune that was taught to her by her old teacher. Fresh tears fell down her face as she pictured Davy behind this same keyboard.

Tortured sobs came from the couches as the guys watched her. It was her goodbye to Davy, and deep inside, she knew this was the last time she would ever see these two sweethearts again. She had to get out of here somehow, someway, or everyone in this room would be dead, including her. Nick would make sure of it.

He killed Davy, she knew he did.

A few hours later, Hope and Andy left for their house and she realized that most of the night had gone by in a blur. She couldn't remember anything that happened after she played.

"It's too late to start making the plans now; I will start making them in the morning," Andy said as they walked into the house.

She looked around the house at the damage. Every window facing the street was shattered, including the one in her bedroom. She felt dissociated, utterly numb, as if she was watching a movie and this was happening to someone else.

They put up as much plastic over the windows as they could, even cutting up a tarp that Andy found in the garage, both of them in silence.

"I will call tomorrow to have the windows replaced," she said; her voice as hollow as the rest of her.

Davy wasn't going to come home any second and kiss her. They weren't going to have a wedding to rival Princess Diana's. He was never going to see his baby grow up, get married, and have babies of his or her own.

Her hand went instantly to her stomach at the thought of the baby as if she could protect it. "Mommy isn't going to let anything happen to you and neither will your Uncle Andy. We both love you so much already, and you're not here yet," she said softly to her baby.

She went down the hall to the main bathroom, needing to relieve herself, and then washed the soot off her hands and face. When she came back, she started to pass Davy's bedroom, but before she knew what she was doing, she slowly went inside. The Yamaha keyboard she bought him was sitting on a stand next to his bed and the room was still as neat as a pin. It was like nothing had changed; his room was merely waiting for him to come back. He only left eight hours ago, yet it felt like a full lifetime had gone by.

Hope couldn't help but lie on the bed, his scent thick on the pillow like he'd just gotten out of the bed. She pulled the second pillow into her and breathed, smelling him as if he were right next to her, a mixture of man, and *Cool Water*, his favorite cologne.

She felt the tears start up again and let them go. She felt rather than heard Andy come in and lie down next to her, wrapping his arms around her.

"Why, Andy? Why did it have to be him? Why couldn't it have been me? He was such a good man, so kind and generous," she asked without turning around.

"I don't know Hope. I wonder the same thing, only the 'why not me'," he said in a voice that didn't seem his own. It was deeper, huskier.

"I know this is hugely inappropriate, but will you sleep next to me tonight? I don't want to be in my bedroom alone. It's where we conceived the baby, where we slept." She gave a laugh. "I think he liked my bed better than his own."

She felt him give a jerk, then he said, "Sure, Hope. I will always be here for you."

They lay there for several minutes, too numb to cry, too shocked to speak. All she could think about was Davy. She couldn't help but to send out a prayer that he never knew what hit him. She couldn't handle the thought that he might have been in excruciating pain when he died alone.

The air in the room felt charged, different somehow. Any little noise seemed exaggeratingly loud, warped like the music at a carnival fun house. Her world felt like it was careening off its axis and there was nothing she could do to stop it. Maybe she was losing her mind, or having a nervous breakdown. She realized then how much she loved Davy; she likely always would. She cannot even begin to fathom a life without him. She knows that she needs to get out of this room, right now--something felt wrong, something felt off.

Hope truly was not hungry, but she had to keep this little bit of him alive, it would help to keep him immortal to the rest of the world. "We need to take care of business. First order, we need to eat. We haven't eaten all day, and I have a baby to feed. Plus, Davy would be pissed if he knew that neither one of us have taken care of ourselves."

He gave a chuckle. "Yes, that's true."

"Well, I don't feel much like cooking. What do you want to eat?"

"Let's go to the Diner down the street. It's.....It's the opposite direction."

"Fast food it is then." She stood up and felt the room spin. "Whoa, I think I stood up too fast," she said and sat back down.

"Put your head down as far as it will go," Andy said, rubbing her back.

She followed instructions, and as soon as she felt better, she tried it again, only this time a bit slower. They took quick, separate showers, and changed their clothes. She grabbed her purse this time before running out the door.

Hope let Andy drive. She then remembered something. "Andy, you need to let my family know about....about Davy, and the baby."

"I will. I will call them tomorrow. I just.....I can't...right now."

She grabbed Andy's hand, the one that wasn't holding the steering wheel, and he squeezed hers in return.

"We will get through this together. Davy wouldn't have had it any other way."

He suddenly broke out into laughter.

"What's so funny?" I asked, not affronted, just wondering.

"He asked me just a few weeks ago to take care of you if anything happened to him. It was the night before he changed his will. I would have done it anyway, but he made me promise. He always was an intuitive son of a bitch!"

Andy pulled into the restaurant just as the sun set below the horizon. They got a seat in the back, where they could talk alone.

This night seemed surreal, like she was walking through a nightmare. How was she supposed to make it through this? Yes, she now had more money than the law should allow, but money couldn't bring the love of her life back.

She sat down and looked at the menu. Maybe she would just get a half-order of Sweet and Sour Shrimp since was honestly not all that hungry.

Hope thought that maybe she should go back to school and get a degree of some kind. She needed to contribute instead of only spending the money that Davy had left her. That was not fair to him.

The server came to take their order and left.

"Andy, I think once this is over, I am going to go back to college, get a degree."

"What kind of degree are you thinking about?" he asked, curious.

"I don't know. Maybe I could get it in music somehow."

"That sounds good." He smiled and took her hand. "I want you to know that whatever happens, I will stand behind you in every decision you make about your future. I want to be there for you and the baby. Hell, I will even babysit the ankle-biter while you go to classes."

"Thank you, Andy. That means a lot to me." She gave a pallid smile.

"Hope, do you want to sell the house? I will completely understand if you do. That place holds a lot of memories for me, and I just don't know if I can handle it."

"I....I don't know yet. I haven't even thought about it. It's just too early to know much of anything. Let's give it some time, ok?"

He nodded, and looked down at the table. "I can't believe he's gone. I was such an asshole the last month or so. I wish I could go back and change it."

"Andy, you had no way of knowing this would happen. Besides...." She felt the tears welling back up again. She tried hard to bite them back. "Besides, it's my fault he's dead. You were right from the very beginning. I destroyed him; I destroyed his life."

"Hope, no! I *never* want to hear you say that again! It's *not* your fault. You didn't force Davenport to kill him! We don't have the proof right now, but I *know* he did it. You are as innocent in his death as I am. Davy and I were *blessed* the day you came into our lives! I am so sorry for saying that when we first met, but you have to understand. His last girlfriend was a money-grubbing bitch that tried to take him for everything."

"No, Andy, it is I who was blessed. But hell, I never wanted anything from him. I hate the thought that I now own half of his estate."

"I think I know why he left you half."

"Why?" She couldn't help but ask.

"He felt that you have gone through so much that you could use it for something good, turn your experiences into something to help others."

She never thought of it that way. Maybe she could open a domestic violence shelter.

The server came with their food, and Andy let go of her hand to eat. As he brought the first bite to his mouth with the chop sticks, he looked at Hope. "He really did love you, you know this don't you?"

She nodded. "I loved him too; I think I always will," she said, her eyes filling with tears again. She blinked them back and concentrated on her food.

They made small talk through dinner, neither one of them wanting to think about the day, and how their hearts were shattering. She also knew that she would tell her daughter or son about his or her father every day. She would never let this baby forget what a truly special man Davy was.

When the check came, Andy grabbed it without giving her the chance, and paid for it. Without a word, they went out to the car, hand in hand, both of them needing the physical touch.

She went to her room to change clothes, and saw a piece of paper lying on the bed. Thinking that Davy might have left it before he went to work, Hope picked it up, and screamed Andy's name when she saw the letters cut out of a magazine!

ONE DOWN, TWO AND A HALF TO GO

Andy came tearing into the room. "What is it? What's wrong?"

She handed him the note and watched the color drain from his face. "Hope, we have to get the hell out of here, now! We have to get out of Chicago, out of Illinois itself."

"Where are we going to go?"

"I don't know, but we have to pack up some stuff that is the most important to us, and get the hell out!"

"Get into Davy's safe, and get the papers out of it. I'm not leaving his will behind!"

He nodded. "I have to call my boss first."

He went tearing back out, and into his room. Hope grabbed Davy's suitcase out of the attic, and started throwing clothes and her favorite books into it. She grabbed her makeup case and other toiletry items out of the bathroom, and threw them into an overnight bag. She grabbed the picture from Davy's nightstand of him and Hope laughing together at the last band practice, and shoved it into her purse.

Andy grabbed the Voodoo Stratocaster, along with some clothes, and they put them into the Beamer. She cried, looking back at the house. She just knew that it was the last time she would ever see it.

"My boss is getting us plane tickets to Corpus Christie. We will be met by an FBI official there, and given the royal treatment. Hope, we are going to have to pretend to be married."

"I don't give a damn what I have to do to keep you and my baby safe, Andy. I couldn't stand it if I lost either one of you."

Andy tore out of the driveway, and started heading to the highway toward O'Hare.

They just barely made it to the plane before the attendants closed the terminal doors. Andy put the Stratocaster in the overhead compartment, along with Hope's overnight bag, and sat down. They were both breathing heavily from their race across the airport. Andy took Hope's hand and held it tight with both hands.

"I think we can relax now, Hope," he said, his eyes scanning the plane.

A flight attendant approached them, checking to see that their seat belts were fastened, and to ask if they needed anything.

"We only need two pillows and blankets, and something to drink, but only after we get into the air," Andy said, continuing to hold her hand.

Hope looked around, and realized they weren't flying coach, they're in First Class. She had never flown this side of the curtain before.

She watched out the window as the plane began backing away from the terminal. That was when she truly started to relax. She felt her shoulders sag, feeling the loss all over again. She bit back the tears, not wanting to cry in front of people even though the section was almost empty. She leaned into Andy, and he wrapped his arm around her, holding her close.

She thought about Tristan and Chris, and her heart broke all over again. She sometimes hated being right.

This was yet another senseless death in Hope's life. In the short two years of his life, her little brother had become her best friend. His asthma kept them from doing a lot of playing, since any kind of exertion would throw him into an attack that would take weeks for him to recover from. His last attack was the worst of all. His little lungs just couldn't take it when he came down with the croup. She found him in their shared bedroom, gasping for air. She ran to get her mom; even at the tender age of five, she knew something was horribly wrong. Mom came tearing out of the bedroom, with him wrapped up in a blanket. She called Hope's aunt that lived right down the street, and she came to babysit her and Grace. Two hours later, Hope's Mom called the house to let her aunt know that Corey was gone.

Dad lost it. Hope's aunt called him at the nearby base, and he came straight home. He started beating his head against the wall, unable to take it. Hope didn't know how to take any of it, since she really didn't know what death was. She just knew she wanted Corey to come home and play with her again.

Dad's grief overtook him; and not knowing what he was saying or doing, he looked down at Hope, and said: "This is your fault, you little bitch, you should have found him sooner!" That stayed with her for years.

Finally, after years of counseling, Hope finally realized that Corey's death wasn't her fault, that his body was just too weak to handle it. While his death was a horrible loss not just to her, but her family also, Davy's death hit her even harder. It was something that she didn't know if she would ever recover from. Davy meant everything to her.

She also thought about Elaine, and realized that she never truly mourned for her best friend. She would have to assure Andy that she did love Davy, with all the stupid deaths in her life, she just needed him to know.

"Andy, I have to tell you something, and I don't know why. I hope you know that I really did love Davy; hell, I think I always will. He meant everything to me. I don't know if I can ever come out of this one."

"I know, Hope. I'm glad he got to find out what love truly feels like. You are a wonderful woman, and he was lucky to have had you for the time that he did. You will come out the other side of this, just like I will. You just have to give it time."

"I don't know, Andy. I think I am the lucky one," she said in a small voice, trying not to cry as Davy's face flashed in front of her eyes. She thought about all the stuff they did over the last month, and it brought the tears back into her eyes, but she blinked hard, trying to hold them back.

The flight attendant broke her out of her reverie. "Here are some earphones, sir, and ma'am." She handed plastic pieces of crap to them, looking Andy up and down like a prize bull at a county fair.

Hope gave her a wry smile, full of anger. The sudden surge confused and startled her. Here Hope was scared, depressed about her fiancé's death, and she's getting pissed off that someone was flirting with Andy. What the *hell* was wrong with her?

Andy never even looked at her, and once she left, he turned to Hope. "I want you to know that I will give my life to protect you and the baby."

"I know you would Andy. If it comes down to it, I will also give my life to protect you."

He shook his head. "No Hope, if it comes down to it, you get the hell out. I want you to leave me there. You and the baby have to live at all costs, if you don't, then Davenport goes free to do this to someone else. That cannot happen."

"Andy, let me get this straight with you right now. I will not leave you to die; I don't give a damn! Got it? I already lost Davy; I am not going to lose you too! I won't survive it!"

"You would survive it, Hope. You are stronger than you give yourself credit for."

"You don't get it, do you? I have lost my family, my fiancé, my friends, and my home; everything I know and love is gone. All I have left is you and my baby. So do not give me that shit about leaving you there to die! Fuck. That."

Hope's body trembled uncontrollably. Maybe the adrenaline was wearing off, or she was going into a full-blown panic attack, but she couldn't stop the violent shaking.

Andy's eyes grew wide at the sound of her cursing, since she hadn't done it in front of him before, and just held her even closer. How messed up was it that it was as comforting as it had been when Davy held her?

"It's all right, Hope. Nothing is going to happen to either one of us, I promise."

She felt the plane start to rev in preparation for take-off.

"Did I ever tell you that I hate to fly?" Andy said suddenly with an edge of panic.

"Its okay, Andy. It's the safest form of travel, even safer than a car."

"If humans were meant to fly we'd have wings!" he said, freaking out as we were plastered against the seats when the plane started down the takeoff strip.

She held his hand close to her heart. You would think they were together by the way they had been constantly touching since...since the explosion. Maybe subconsciously it was their way of confirming that they were alive, maybe it was truly comforting each other. Either way, it felt so good, so *right*.

Once the plane hit cruising altitude, Andy relaxed. He didn't have many fears, but flying was one of them; and how messed up was it that he was able to take so much comfort from Hope?

The flight attendant came back to give them the pillows and blanket that he requested.

"What would you like to drink?" she smiled at both of them.

"I would like a jack and coke."

"I want a glass of ginger ale."

He looked at Hope, unable to take his eyes from her. She was right; she had lost everything to Davenport. The depth of pain in her eyes seared his soul, and he just wanted to take it all from her. He felt like a piece of shit for macking on Davy's woman, but damn it all, he couldn't help it. She grabbed a piece of his heart and soul, and she wouldn't let go! When she walked away, and they all do, it was going to take a lifetime of intense psychotherapy to get over her.

The flight attendant left with the cart, going back to coach. His eyes widened as he heard two words come from her mouth that he never thought he'd hear.

"Damned slut!"

"Huh, what was that, Hope?"

"Don't tell me you didn't notice how she was flirting with you, trying to get you to meet her eyes."

He couldn't help but to smile. "No, I didn't. I had other things on my mind."

She rolled her eyes and looked away.

He didn't know why but he found her exasperation endearing. The thought that she was jealous made his cock jerk in response to the images going through his head.

She put her pillow up on the back of the seat, and moved her body so she was facing him. "What are we going to do, Andy? How are we going to live?"

"It's going to have to be day to day, Hope. That's all we can do. Once we land in Corpus Christie, I will no longer be an FBI agent; I will be a witness to a crime that is on the run."

She nodded and closed her eyes. "I'm scared, Andy. I'm afraid for my baby. We will never be able to go back, and we will be on the run. What kind of life is that for Davy's baby?"

"He or she will be alive, Hope, just as we are. That's what is important."

Her voice turned small, thick, and sleepy. "Andy?"

"Yes, Hope."

"Please don't ever let me go," she said in a soft, exhaustion-filled voice. An instant later, she was asleep.

He gently caressed her beautiful face with the backs of his fingers. "I won't, Hope. Not ever."

He watched her sleep. For the first time today, she was truly relaxed, almost at peace. "Sleep well, Hope. You've earned the rest."

His thoughts returned to the events of the day. He had never been so afraid in his life when he heard that explosion, then Hope scream. He didn't know what to expect when he ran into the living room, but that woman had some amazing instincts. She'd flattened herself against the wall so that the glass wouldn't spray her completely. She knew immediately that Davy had been…..had been killed. Maybe they'd had some kind of psychic bond together that she could feel him. Who the hell knew? All he knew was that he wanted Hope more than he had ever wanted anyone. He had since he met her and had fought it for just as long. Even now, she was Davy's, and he would never do that to him.

Andy felt his eyelids grow heavy, so he put his pillow under his head, and faced Hope. He knew that he echoed her sentiments, that he would never make it if something happened to her.

His last thought before sleep claimed him, was that maybe he truly loved her.

He found himself back in the house. He knew he was dreaming, but it felt so real, so tangible. Hope's drum set was over by the window that he and Davy put their Christmas tree at, half-assembled. Shards of glass littered the living room floor; he could feel them crunch under his shoes.

"Andy." He heard a familiar voice behind him. He turned to see Davy, bathed in an almost blinding white light.

"Davy? What is going on?" he asked, stunned.

"I don't have much time. I came to tell you something about Hope."

"What about her?"

"I know how you feel about her; I've known it all along. I've seen the way you look at her."

"Davy, she is your woman, even now. I won't hurt you like that!"

"I know that, Andy. It's okay. I'm not angry about it. I want you to love her; I *want* you to be with her. She is a wonderful, truly special woman. Just please, love her, and take care of her. You two are meant to be together, not her and me. Yes, I fell in love with her, who wouldn't? But she's your destiny, not mine. She needs you just as much as you need her. Love her, Andy. Just let yourself love her. She's worth it." His voice faded as he did.

Andy jumped in his seat, startled. How creepy could that dream possibly be?

"Are you ok?" Hope asked, worried.

He took a deep breath, and ran his hand along his face, calming himself. "Yah, I'm fine."

"I....I dreamed about Davy," Hope said in a small, pain-filled voice.

"Yah, I did too." He rubbed his face with the palms of his hands.

"What did he say to you?" she asked, more to her tone than just curiosity.

He shook his head. "It's not something I want to talk about right now. It's not the right time or place."

"Andy, he wants me to love you."

His head snapped up to look at her. "Hope, I don't think it was a dream."

"What are you talking about? Ghosts don't exist!"

"Hope, he told me the same thing. That can't be just a coincidence."

"But how, *why*?" She didn't seem to be capable of completing a full sentence.

"I don't know, Hope. He told me a bunch of things that I cannot fathom right now."

"Attention passengers, this is your Captain speaking. We are beginning our descent into Corpus Christie, Texas. The sky is cloudy, since there is a hurricane approaching, but don't worry, it is still a few days away. The temperature is a sultry eighty-nine degrees, and the local time is six twenty-seven in the morning. We should arrive at the terminal in about twenty minutes. I am turning on the fasten seat belt sign so please put your tables in their upright and locked position. Please enjoy your stay and thank you for flying with us today."

Hope fastened her seat belt just as the bell went off for the sign.

"A hurricane is approaching where we are going to live? Andy, what the hell was your boss thinking?"

"He likely made other arrangements. Corpus Christie is a diversion for those that may follow us, or check into where we are. That is where we will receive our new identities."

She nodded and threaded her fingers through his. Her hands lightly trembled as they descended into their new, unknown future.

An obvious government agent waited inside the terminal for them when they deplaned. Andy knew it wasn't an FBI agent. The agent saw Andy and approached.

"I am with the U.S. Marshals, Agent Newcomb. Would you and the lady follow me, please? Do you have any luggage besides what you have on you?" The guy had quite the affront to his voice as if they had interrupted something more important that he needed to do.

Andy bristled, wanting to tell the asshole where he could shove the *how dare you bother me* bullshit.

"Yes sir, it should be down in the luggage area soon. Are we going to be allowed to pick it up?" Hope asked.

"No ma'am, we will do that. It would risk too much exposure," he all but snapped at her.

She took Andy's hand, seeming to take some comfort. The Marshal noticed. "Good, keep it up. You two are now happily married," he said, opening the door to the security office.

They followed him to a desk, where he picked up two files, then herded them into what seemed to be a holding room. The Marshal tossed the files onto the desk, and told them to have a seat as he took the one facing them.

"Agent Newcomb, you are now Jackson Connor. You served for 15 years in the United States Marines, and made it to Captain. You are retired now, and want to own your own business. You are thirty-four years old, born in Staten Island, New York to Catriona and Joseph Connor. Here is your birth certificate, service records, DD214, credit cards, driver's license, bank account information, marriage license, and your new social security number."

The Marshal turned to Hope. "You are now Brooke Connor, Jackson's wife. You two have been married for five years. You can make up a story about how you two met. Brooke, you are a restaurant manager, you are thirty years old, born to Edna and Ian Campbell in San Diego, California. This is your first marriage. Here are your credit cards, joint bank account information, birth certificate, driver's license, and new social security number."

The man leaned back in his chair and crossed his arms. "Now, we have done something unprecedented. We took all of your money from your old bank and transferred it into your new account. Essentially, we hacked it, stole it, and gave it back to you. The way we did it is completely untraceable, and no one will ever find out. Your old boss is moving you out of your old house as we speak, and putting your things into a storage unit under a fictitious name so that is also untraceable. Once this is all said and done, you will keep your new identities, but all of your stuff will be yours again. You will never see that house that you just left again. You both have excellent credit, so you will have no problems finding a house once this is done. For right now, we are transferring you both to a small town in Louisiana named Slidell. Don't worry; the hurricane is not headed there."

"Andy…." Hope all but sobbed with fear.

"No, his name is Jack, not Andy. As far as the rest of the world is concerned, Andy Newcomb and Hope McLeod are dead. From this point on, you are Jackson and Brooke Connor. You may as well get used to it now," the Marshal almost barked.

"I….I'm sorry."

Jackson's eyes narrowed. "Marshal, she has been through enough. There is no need to treat her with such blatant disrespect and hostility. She is already in danger; the least you can do is show a bit of compassion. She is not the criminal here. She is the *victim.*"

"So she had nothing to do with the death of one…." He checked his records. "David Alexander Marshall?" he asked drolly.

Hope sucked in a noisy breath next to him, her hand fluttering to her mouth.

"No, she did not! I was with her when he died, and she definitely did *not* kill him! He was killed in an explosion in a restaurant he was trying to open."

"It says here that yes, he died in an explosion, but an incendiary device was found in the wreckage of the restaurant. It was planted near the stove in the kitchen."

"Oh god, no!" she cried and broke down, sobs wracking her entire body.

"What the hell are you thinking, Marshal?" Andy got up and wrapped his arms around her.

"I think you both killed him so you could get his money and be together. That's what I think."

"Careful there, Marshal. When it comes out that we didn't do it, and it will, I can have your ass in court for slander, libel, and have your badge. I can and will do it. In fact, call my old boss with the FBI, and ask for some tapes. After Nickolas Davenport, the real criminal, broke in the first time, I installed video cameras all over the house so that if something did happen, we had proof. Well, something happened; we have proof. Then, after you watch the tapes, you can shove them straight up your ass!"

The Marshal sat there blustering for a moment. "I…I am sorry."

"Too little too late, I want your supervisor's name, direct number, and your badge number. I may no longer be employed by the Bureau, but I still have connections. This is the last victim you will treat as a criminal."

The Marshal took his notebook out of his pocket, wrote down the information, and handed it to Jackson/Andy.

"By the way, if you reported us as criminals to Slidell Police, and we're harassed, I will personally sue you for everything you own. Then the Bureau will get in touch with you." He grabbed his and Brooke/Hope's paperwork, and started toward the door.

"Here are your plane tickets to New Orleans." He handed the papers to Jackson/Andy. "Also, here is the address to your new home, along with the keys." The Marshal handed Jackson/Andy an envelope. "Again, I am sorry."

"Not yet, you're not. But I promise you, you will be."

"Wait, before you go…instead of flying, why don't you drive? It's only about eight hours, so there's no use in flying. Plus, it will get you used to your new names and identities."

"No, thank you. I wouldn't want the Federal Marshals to get worried when we don't show up at the airport. I know how they have itchy trigger fingers. I have worked with enough of them during my career," Jackson/Andy said. He picked up his guitar, and gave Brooke/Hope her bag. He took her hand, and walked out.

Inside he was positively seething. How dare that sorry piece of shit treat Hope like that, and then try to set them up! If they hadn't have shown up at the airport at the designated time, then there would have been a nationwide all-points bulletin out for them! They would have been tossed out of the program, and possibly jailed. The bastard was trying to hide what he did, and cover his own ass.

"A….Jackson, slow down please, I can't keep up with you."

"I'm sorry, Brooke. I didn't mean to do that." He stopped, leaned down and kissed her cheek. "Good job in remembering the new name," he whispered in her ear. "Don't worry about using the whole name, just call me Jack."

Within a few hours, Brooke and Jack were exiting the plane in New Orleans, and were met by another Federal Marshal.

She had never felt so nervous. After the last Marshal, she didn't know how to deal with this new one, so she let Jack handle it. The Marshal took them to another Security office, and brought them into another holding room. "Jackson and Brooke, it is so nice to meet you. Jack, we talked to the FBI agent in charge of your case in Chicago. We are sorry for your loss, both of you."

"Thank you," he said, taking her hand again. Her racing heart immediately slowed, and her hands stopped shaking.

"Now, this is how this is going to be handled. There are Federal Marshals outside in a couple of moving vans with some furniture and other things that you are going to need. There are several of them, so don't be nervous. We will have you moved in to your new home in no time flat. I am going to act as a cab driver, bringing you from the airport. The *movers* will give you the rest of the information you need."

"I have a question for you, sir," Brooke asked.

"Sure, Brooke, ask away."

"An….I mean Jack and I were in a band up in Chicago. Is it possible for us to start doing that again?"

"Of course, you can do whatever you want for work. You can just never contact your old band again. You were in the news last night, with the story that you were in a car accident and both killed."

"Oh, poor Tristan and Chris, they must be beside themselves," she said, her heart breaking for them.

"Is there anything else?"

"Yes, I have a question," Jack said. "What if one day, Hope and I truly fall in love, and want to get married?"

"Jack, she isn't Hope anymore. She is Brooke. She is your wife, legally. If you wish to have a ceremony, then plan a renewal of vows. But she is your wife. If you guys don't wish to be married, then you will have to get a divorce, but not until after Nickolas Davenport is caught."

"Then we need to get wedding rings as soon as possible," he said. "That way, it will at least be legit to us."

"That is up to you."

"Oh, how would I go about filing a formal complaint about the last Marshal we dealt with? He treated Brooke with contempt, and then tried to set us up by offering to let us drive down here instead of taking the plane."

The Marshal's eyes darkened and narrowed. "I will take care of that myself. You aren't the first witnesses he has treated like that. I can promise that you will be the last. I will show up at your home at nine o'clock tomorrow morning in the cab. I imagine you want to find a vehicle of some kind for you and your wife. We could go car hunting, and I can take your statement about the other Marshal.

"Oh, if I may make a suggestion, Brooke, do something to change your appearance. Get your hair cut and colored. You are a very beautiful woman, and you tend to stand out because of that. Changing your hair style and color can make you look completely different."

She honestly didn't want to cut her hair; Davy loved it. However, if she had to, she had to, and she refused to even acknowledge the fact that the marshal said that she was beautiful. She just couldn't see it. "There is one thing you need to know, Marshal. I am pregnant."

"Yes, we know. Congratulations, you two."

"I am not the father," Jack said.

"I know that, and you two know that, but for legal reasons, you are the father."

"I can't give the baby his father's name?" she couldn't help but ask, panicking.

"You can, just not the surname. You can always give the baby two last names, maybe hyphenate them."

"Marshall-Connor....It does have a nice ring to it," she tried it out.

"Now, shall we get going? We have a lot to do, and very little time to do it in." The Marshal said.

"Yes sir; and thank you for everything," Brooke said sincerely.

"You're welcome, Brooke." They stood up, and walked out after the Marshal grabbed their things for them. Brooke and Jack reached for each other's hands at the same time, not even thinking about it.

She could not believe how comfortable they had become with each other in such a short time. Could it truly be that Davy was right in her dream last night, that he knows how she feels about Andy...er.... Jack? Could she be in love with him? She knew that there had been an attraction, at least from her side since she first met him, but love? No, she loved Davy, didn't she?

She could hear Davy in her mind, repeating what he said last night. "I know that you love me, but we were not meant to be. You truly do love Andy, and its okay. Go to him, Hope. You deserve nothing less than happiness. Let yourself love him."

She couldn't go from one man to another! That just wasn't in her genetic make-up! Yet here she was, married to another man without agreeing to it. How could that possibly be legal? Andy pointed out time after time that he was protecting her because she was Davy's fiancée, although yes, they were friends. She supposed there were some marriages that began with much less and stood the test of time.

Before she realized it, they were at the cab, and getting in. Less than twenty minutes later, they were pulling up in front of a beautiful antebellum plantation house just outside of Slidell.

"Welcome home, Jackson and Brooke."

"Is this our house, or does the Government own it?" she breathed. She fell in love with it immediately.

"Oh, it's in your names. You own it, lock, stock, and barrel, so to speak."

She got out of the cab and slowly approached the house. She never thought in her wildest dreams that she would own a piece of real estate like this. She looked around at the trees lining the drive. The row of Bald Cypress trees had Spanish moss dangling from their leaves, giving it an old world feel. The house itself had wisteria vines attached to one side, trimmed neatly around the windows. The rest of the house had been painted in white, including the wood on the wrap-around porch. She felt like she was looking at a modern day *Twelve Oaks* from *Gone with the Wind*, and it was hers and Jack's!

"Go ahead and go in, Brooke. It's waiting for you."

Brooke slowly climbed the wooden steps, and went into the house. Never had she seen anything more gorgeous in her life! Davy's house was large, and beautiful, but this....she almost expected to see southern belles in bright colored dresses with hoops and whalebone corsets come gracefully down the stairs.

The front entryway had a large crystal chandelier hanging from the ceiling, the brass shining as if it had been recently polished. Off to her left stood large, sliding doors into another room. She opened them and entered into what had to be the parlor at one time. A large stone fireplace stood proudly against the far wall, almost begging to be lit once again.

"Brooke, this house dates back to the Civil War. It has been restored numerous times to its original state. It had been looked at to become part of the Historical Registry, but because of how many times it had to be rebuilt, they denied it," the Marshal said.

"Why did it have to be rebuilt so many times? Jack asked as he wrapped his arms around her waist from behind.

"Once, because of a hurricane, and the rest because people would just abandon the house for unknown reasons throughout the years and it would stand empty for a long time. But I must be leaving. The Marshal that will be handling your case here in Slidell will be here shortly. It was a pleasure meeting you both, and I wish we could have met under better circumstances."

"Thank you." She smiled, and shook his hand.

"You're welcome, Brooke. You two have a nice life, and a nice marriage." He pumped Jack's hand, and walked out the front door. As he pulled out of the driveway, four huge moving trucks came down the long driveway.

"What are we going to do?" she asked, scared. This house seemed to be so large, so beautiful; she couldn't help but feel that they wouldn't be here long. She could never be this lucky.

"I don't know. I'm sure we will figure it out though."

"Jack, do you hate it that we are married? I mean, you never even indicated that you wanted me in that fashion, let alone had feelings for me," she blurted it out without even thinking.

"Actually, I couldn't think of anyone else I would rather be married to," he said, and looked into her eyes. She thought for a moment that he would bend his head down and kiss her, but the moment was broken from the *movers* coming up the front steps.

"Hello, Mr. and Mrs. Connor, welcome to Slidell, Louisiana."

This Marshal was huge! He stood at least six-foot-four, and had to weigh in at two-forty! His hair was cropped short, military style. All of the Marshals were dressed in overalls with a moving company logo stitched on the arms and chest.

"Shall we go inside so that my men can move you in?"

Brooke gave a small smile, and went inside the house. She wanted to see the upstairs to pick out her bedroom, so she climbed the steps, and went down a long hallway. She passed six other rooms, deciding to start at the far end of the hallway and work her way back. She turned around, and noticed that the hall went down both sides of the stairwell. Jeez, how many rooms were there in this house?

She opened the door at the far left corner. It was obviously the master bedroom, with another massive stone fireplace against the wall facing the driveway, nestled between two picture windows. The mantle of the fireplace was made of cherry oak! Hope almost cried remembering the shopping trip when Davy bought the bedroom suite that she had left behind.

"Brooke?" She heard Jack's voice echo down the long hallway.

"I'm in here, last door to the left," she called out, her voice echoing in the emptiness.

"Good, I'm glad I found you, and could spend a moment with you alone. Look, I think we should act like a married couple and at least sleep in the same room so that we could at least appear married. If we sleep in separate rooms, we will still have an invisible wall between us, and people will pick up on that."

She nodded, only hearing half of what he said. She couldn't get over the size of this room. Three of her old apartment, the one she had lived in with Nick, could fit in this huge space.

"So you don't mind the idea of us sleeping together?" Jack broke through her thoughts.

"What? No, I don't mind us sleeping together. It makes sense." She turned around and froze. He stood directly in front of her, with a light in his eyes that she had never seen from him before. He stared back, only it wasn't at her eyes. His eyes were transfixed on her lips. "Andy...." Her breath started coming in fast pants, her hormones going into overdrive.

"Hope, we shouldn't do this," he whispered, just as breathless.

"No, we shouldn't," she said as his lips started descending. She took in a sharp breath as her stomach jumped, and an intense, heavy ache formed instantly between her legs.

His lips touched hers, and her body exploded. She wrapped her arms around his neck, latching on for dear life. His tongue traced the outside of her lips, begging her to open for him. She did, and when his tongue touched hers, her legs gave out, weak with a longing she'd never felt before. They both moaned, and Hope knew she wanted so much more than just this kiss. She wanted to feel him pound into her; hear him screaming her name as he shot his seed deep into her. Most of all, she wanted to hear him tell her that he loved her, which was one thing she knew she would never hear from him. The thought was like a splash of cold water on her, and she pulled away. "Andy....Jack, we can't do this. Davy just died yesterday. Yes, you are one hell of a kisser, but I can't do this. It's too soon."

"Oh god, you're right. I'm so sorry Hope....Brooke. I am going to have to get used to calling you that." He ran his fingers through his hair and paced the bedroom. "I have wanted to do that for so long. It's why I used to get pissed so often, I was trying to hide it from you, and most of all, myself. I have wanted you from the first time I saw you in the hospital, lying on the bed in a coma."

She stared at him, her surprise complete. He didn't hate her? He truly as attracted to her? Her stomach did a somersault, still feeling the positively devastating effects of the kiss. She couldn't help but compare the kiss to Davy's, and she felt horrible when she realized that Davy's fell way short.

"I have to go back downstairs; I need to help the movers." He leaned back down and gave her a chaste kiss, then left.

As he walked out the door, the room began spinning, then went faster and faster. She tried to get over to one of the walls but was too weak. She started to sit, but felt herself start to lose consciousness. She called out for Jack as the floor rushed up to meet her.

She woke up to his face above hers, worry clouding his eyes. "Oh, thank god, Brooke."

"An...Jack...what happened?"

"I don't know, Baby. I was hoping you could tell me."

"Mrs. Connor, how long has it been since you've eaten?" one of the Marshals asked.

She had to stop and think about it for a minute. "It's been since we were in Chicago."

"All right, we have emptied one of the trucks, so I am going to take that one into town and get some food. You just relax."

Jack helped her up, and walked her down into the parlor since she was still weak. The furniture the Marshals had gotten them had been neatly arranged in the room in a U-shape facing the fireplace. The furniture was absolutely stunning, all antique. The couch and chaise lounge had been made of coffee-colored velvet; the cushions overstuffed and comfortable-looking. He helped her to the chaise, and lay her on it. One of the Marshals brought her a glass of water, which she gratefully sipped.

A few minutes later, the Marshal came back with McDonald's. She didn't realize how hungry she was until the scent hit her nostrils. She inhaled the fish sandwich and fries, and started to feel a bit better.

"Well, we can't let that happen again, Mrs. Connor. We don't wish to starve your baby."

"Well, it isn't like I was given a choice."

Jack almost choked on his last bite trying not to laugh.

"Well, Gentlemen, let's get the rest of this stuff inside so these two can get some rest tonight," the head Marshal said as he stood up.

"Are you feeling better, Brooke?" Jack asked, worry still in his eyes.

"Yes, I am. Thank you, Marshal, for the food."

"You are most welcome, Brooke."

"Come on, *honey*, let me show you the rest of the house," Jack said, holding his hand out to her.

She took it and let him lead her to the other side of the staircase and into the kitchen. She stood in the center of the room, slowly turning in a circle as she took it in. This room was gigantic! Three of the kitchens in Davy's house could fit in here! Men came in with boxes, placing them near the cabinets while one looked at her. "We are bringing your dishes in, and if you would tell me which cabinet you want them in, I will put them away for you."

Brooke showed him the cabinet that she thought would be best, and he began to put everything away for her.

"Mrs. Connor, which bedroom do you want so that we may set up your furniture?" the head Marshal asked.

"The one you found me in," she told him. She stopped for a moment, realizing that it wasn't just her in there anymore. "Is that okay, Jack?"

"Yes, of course it is, darling. Whichever room you wish is fine with me." He smiled. "Besides, it is a beautiful room."

The Marshal nodded, and left. Before long, grunts and heavy footsteps climbed up the stairs.

She went up to Jack, and whispered in his ear, "This place is way too big for us. It's a beautiful house, but there is just too much room!"

"We will make the best of it. I found another room we could set up for band practice if we find another band. It is on the other side of the hall from the parlor. We could use the parlor as our living room, and the true living room for the band. Hope, it is enormous."

"Show me," she smiled. He took her hand, and led her to another pair of sliding doors just where the staircase ended. He opened them, and she sucked in a deep breath as she entered. The room that Jack thought was a living area was large enough for the entire town of Slidell to dance in, with today's population! Mirrors lined one wall from floor to ceiling. On the other three walls, moulding made of cherry oak lined the crevice between the wall and ceiling, with intricate patterns etched into them. Small statues of the heads of cherubs were bolted into all four corners, and the rest of the walls were lined with beautiful wall paper, the curly-cues made of soft velvet that also had to date back to at least the nineteen thirties. The wood floors gleamed and sparkled as if newly cleaned and waxed.

"Andy...er....Jack, this wasn't the living room. This was the ballroom. This is where they would have their parties back during the civil war, this is where they danced! You are right, it is perfect! We could build a stage over there by the mirrors and put our instruments there. The acoustics in here had to be phenomenal, since everyone in the house had to hear the orchestra that would play during the balls."

She twirled in a pirouette, almost feeling like a ballerina. "Jack, when we get our vehicle, I want to go shopping for instruments again. I won't get anything as nice as the other drum set, but I want to start on this room as soon as possible."

"What kind of vehicle do you want, Brooke?"

"I don't know, I haven't thought much about it. When I was in high school, I had a 1971 Cutlass SS, but I haven't thought about what I want now. I think I want something sporty for driving around, but maybe a van for any gigs we might have when we find a band."

"That is a very good idea." He looked at Brooke, and pulled her into his arms. "I'm not sorry about the kiss. I am sorry you fainted, but I will not apologize for the kiss. It was beyond anything I ever imagined. You will never know how you affected me."

His comment took her off guard. She didn't know how to respond, except with honesty. "I don't regret it, either. It is only that, it isn't the right time. If what you suspect is true, and Davy came to us while we were on the plane, then let's give each other time to mourn. We just lost him, and it feels like a betrayal to jump into something this quickly."

"You're right. We just have to learn to act like we are in love around everyone else. That is why I think we need to sleep together, and why I think we should just touch each other whenever others are around. I don't know about you, but it helps me, it comforts me, makes me feel alive."

"It does the same for me." She leaned up and kissed his cheek.

She decided to explore the rest of the house. She returned into the kitchen and opened the first door to the right which led to the basement, so she went down. At the bottom of the stairs, hung a bald fixture with a light bulb that she found when she cracked her head on it. Brooke found the pull and the basement lit up. A wine rack filled the entirety of the far wall, which spanned the entire length of the house! Inside lay more bottles than would fit into a liquor store, all of them covered with a thick layer of dust. She took one out, and the weight told her that it was full. She wiped the dust off the label and it was a bottle of Scotch, from Nineteen twenty-four! Maybe she and Jack could drink it, since she had heard nothing but good things about aged Scotch through the years. It would be good for celebrating their escape from Nick and toasting Davy.

The rest of the basement was empty, nothing but old planked walls, and cemented floors. She assumed the cement had been put in by the former owners, since it was a more recent invention than the Civil War.

She went back up to the kitchen, and looked through another door to find an empty pantry. The other door led to the back yard, so she just closed it too, and went back upstairs to the bedrooms. She opened the door directly in front of the stairs. Another set of narrow stairs led to an attic. Each step creaked and groaned as she stepped on it. When she got to the top, she looked around to find boxes, trunks, and an old-fashioned armoire. Her curiosity got the better of her, and she started to rummage through them. After all, this was hers and Jack's house now, and everything in it they now owned.

The inside of the armoire smelled of moth balls. Inside, there were three of the most beautiful gowns she'd ever seen hanging on a bar. They were period dated, during the civil war! The fabric, although faded, was in perfect condition, as if they had been recently placed in there.

Brooke sucked in a deep breath, and took one off of a hook. The taffeta rustled in her hands as if glad someone was actually paying attention to it again.

"Brooke, where are you?" she heard Jack's voice float up from the hall downstairs.

"I'm up here, Jack. You need to come up here and look at this!"

He came up, and took in a deep breath. "Oh, wow, this stuff is amazing."

She held the gown to herself, and turned around. "What do you think?"

He stared at her for a moment. "Brooke, you look beautiful!" he breathed shallowly. "Did you find this here?"

"Yes, there are two others in the cabinet!" She replaced the dress back on the hanger, and opened one of the trunks. Inside were books, old magazines, chipped dishes, and many other things.

She heard Jack lift something and he said her name. She looked over to find him holding up a picture of a woman wearing the same dress that she had just held up! She had her hand on the shoulder of a man who was wearing a Confederate uniform!

"Brooke, I think I want to go into town and find out the history of this house! This is remarkable!"

"Jack, this stuff would be worth millions on the antique market! I don't understand why no one has tried to sell these!" She again looked at the boudoir. "I think I want to have the movers bring this downstairs into our bedroom. I want to refinish it and use it! I will put whatever else is in it into a trunk and leave it up here."

"I don't think anyone has been up here in a very long time," he said, and shrugged his shoulders.

Brooke noticed for the first time that there were several inches of dust on the floor, with no footprints but theirs.

"Jack, I never want to leave this house. I want to live here for the rest of our lives. I am falling in love with this place."

"I love it, too. Maybe one day, we can fill it with our own children."

They went back downstairs, and were met by the Marshal's supervisor at the door to the hall. "We are finished, Mr. and Mrs. Connor. Here is your paperwork and if you need anything, don't hesitate to call me. We also left you something in one of the nightstands to help you for protection in case we can't get here in time. Also, you are going to have a security system installed the day after tomorrow."

"I am so sorry to be such a pain, but I found an armoire up in the attic. Would you and your men mind bringing it down to my bedroom? It's too heavy for Jack to handle himself," she asked, praying that they would.

"We would be happy to, ma'am." A few men went upstairs and moved it into the room, putting it near the window.

"Is there anything else?" the supervisor asked.

"No, I think that's it. Thank you for everything, Sir. You can't know how much we appreciate it."

"You're most welcome, Mrs. Connor. We will check in on you every day, in one way or another. If we do not hear from you once a day, then we will assume you are in danger and come running. We also noticed that you still call each other by your old names. It is sagacious that even when you are alone, you call each other by your new identities so that you do not slip up and say it around other people. You must get used to it; your lives depend on it."

She looked at the floor, feeling awkward. He was right. "We will; thank you."

"Have a good first night in your new lives."

They saw him out onto the front porch. Jack wrapped his arm around her waist, and waved at the Marshals as they were pulling out of the driveway. Slowly, they went back in, and found a bunch of food sitting in plastic bags just inside the parlor. They took the food to the kitchen and put it away. Brooke decided to start dinner, and looked around the cupboards for the stuff she would need. She noticed that they had plugged a microwave in at one corner of the counter, so she looked around for light switches.

She found one just inside the doorway and flipped it on.

Jack came back in, and wrapped his arms around her waist. "You are safe now, Brooke. I know Davy would be happy. That is all that mattered to him."

At the mention of Davy's name, she turned in his arms, and held him. "I still can't believe he's gone. But at least he will live on in the baby."

They stood there for quite a long time, just holding each other, their memories overtaking them. When they looked up, it was dark outside.

"Well, it is about eight o'clock, so we need to get some dinner in us. Let me cook it, Brooke. You just relax and you can cook tomorrow."

"All right, I won't argue with that." She kissed his cheek, and went back upstairs. She wanted to see what furniture the Marshals had gotten them for their bedroom.

Brooke walked in and sucked in a breath. To accommodate Jack's height of six-foot-four, they got them a four-poster California King Bed, with neutral-colored sheets and blankets. The furniture in the room, including the headboard and footboard were all cherry oak, keeping with the theme of the trim in the room. A large, expensive-looking Aubusson rug ran most of the expanse of the room. She must admit that the government had taste.

"Brooke, let's just catch a cab into town....Oh wow!"

"That's exactly what I said when I walked in here!" She went over and sat on the bed. It was even softer than the one she had in Maywood! "Oh, Jack! Wait until you sit on this!"

He groaned. "Not yet, I won't want to get up. Let's go into town and get something to eat. I really don't feel much like cooking, and I know you really don't either."

"Isn't that dangerous, considering?"

"Baby, we are thousands of miles away from Davenport. We will be okay. Besides, we need to stick together. If Davenport's smart, then he will try to divide and conquer. We aren't going to let him do that."

Jack awoke the next morning to Brooke lightly touching his shoulder. "Honey.....I'm bleeding."

"Wha...what does that mean?" he asked, groggily.

"It may mean nothing, but coupled with the cramps I am having, I could be miscarrying." She said, her eyes wide with fear.

He jumped up and headed downstairs to call an ambulance. She followed him down, and a knock came at the door. It was the first Marshal that had met them at the airport in New Orleans.

"Are you two ready for your car shopping?"

"No, Brooke is spotting and cramping. I was about to call an ambulance."

"I will take you. Both of you get in. We will have to go to New Orleans."

Two hours later, it was official. She had miscarried Davy's baby. His heart broke, for both of them. She cried in the hospital bed, devastated sobs wracking her tiny body. He had never felt so helpless in his life.

"I failed him, Jack," she wailed.

"No honey, you didn't. Don't blame yourself for this. You've just gone through too much stress. The poor guy didn't have a chance," he choked out, tears forming in his own eyes. He already loved the little guy and had looked forward to raising him.

He held Brooke all the way home, scared for her beyond reason. She just lost her fiancé, and now her baby. He prayed that it was something she could recover from, but he really didn't think she ever would. He was at such a loss of what to do. He knew he was falling in love with her, but he just wasn't ready to admit it to anyone yet, sometimes even to himself.

They got into the cab to head back home, when the agent looked at them. "I will have a car delivered to you tonight. It is a rental, but you can use that until you are able to buy one. I feel terrible that you didn't have one when you needed it."

"It's ok, Sir. You had no way of knowing, none of us did," Jack said.

"Jack, please call me Louie. I am not old enough to be a *sir*."

"I was beginning to think we weren't allowed to know the names of our case managers."

"You technically aren't, and should anyone ask, you know nothing."

"Know what?" Jack smiled.

They pulled into the long drive leading up to the house. Jack and Louie helped Brooke into the house, since she was feeling weak. They took her upstairs and lay her in the bed, where the sleeping pills the doctor gave her at the hospital took effect almost immediately.

Quietly, the men went back downstairs into the parlor. "I am going to hide the cab in the stables out back. I will return shortly," Louie said.

He returned just a few minutes later. "So, how do you like your new home?"

"We love it! I never in my wildest dreams would think that I could own a mansion!"

"Well, it is yours. We don't want it back," Louie joked.

"Do you know anything of the history of this place? Brooke went up into the attic and found a bunch of stuff left by the previous tenants."

"The previous tenants are long since deceased. It was handed down from family member to family member, and the last one died in nineteen seventy-five. Sure, it has been rented from time to time over the years, but no one wanted to stay. It has been standing empty now for around five years. I wish I could live in a place like this." Louie looked around the parlor. "We had originally bought it for another couple on the run, but they didn't follow directions, and the ones they were running from found and killed them before they could move in. Since we had already bought all the furniture, and had it cleaned from top to bottom, we gave it to you and Brooke. We just had it transferred into your name. There are no mortgage payments, and the government got it on a steal--less than a hundred thousand dollars."

"You bought this mansion for less than a hundred thousand?" Jack asked, shocked.

"Oh, it's said the place is haunted, but do you really believe that? I certainly don't."

"Honestly, with everything I have seen recently, I'd believe anything," Jack said, thinking about the possible visit by Davy the night he died.

"Look, I have seen the clinical version of what has happened. I want to hear the humanized version. What has this poor woman upstairs gone through?"

Jack gave him all the details he had. He had never listened in on the wiretaps, so all he had to go by was what she told him, and she wasn't much for talking about anything. "She lost her family now since they are also in the program, her fiancé, and now the baby. I am all she has left."

"This is one of the worst, most heartbreaking stories I have ever heard, and I have been working for the U.S. Marshals for twenty years."

"She is truly something special, Louie. I didn't want to like her when I first met her, but here I am, falling in love with her. I have seen some shit in my time too, working for the FBI. I didn't want to trust her. But Davy made a good choice in bringing her into our lives, he did the right thing. Now I can't remember what my life was like without her in it. There isn't another woman on earth that I see, only her."

"Sounds like you are already in love with her, my man."

"No, not yet, but I'm getting there. I just want her to be happy, and safe. Right now, neither one of us is ready for a relationship. Yes, we are married, but only because you made us that way."

"Well, we are giving you two more liberties than we would anyone else, only because you were an FBI agent. You are more than capable of protecting her. We have informed the local police department of you two, and the clinical version of what happened is in their hands, so they can watch things here. They know the importance of keeping this a secret from the people of the town."

A horrified scream from upstairs set Jack's legs pumping. He beat Louie up the stairs to find Brooke writhing in bed, in the throes of a ruthless nightmare. Her eyes still shut, she screamed "No, Andy, don't you leave me too!"

"Brooke, I'm not going anywhere!" he said gathering her into his arms. "Honey, I'm not leaving you for the world!"

She opened her eyes, and shrieked shrilly and full of agony. Her eyes were opened so wide, with terror deep in their depths that he thought they would pop out of her head.

"Brooke, honey, you're okay. I'm here, baby. I'm never going to leave you," he crooned soft noises as she cried, near hysterics. He rocked her in his arms, and looked over at Louie.

The Marshal signaled that he was going to leave for the night and would return tomorrow. He quietly went back downstairs.

"You looked at me with such loathing, just like you used to, and told me to die," she sobbed.

"I promise you, I will never leave you, and I would never tell you to die. I....I care about you too much; you have become a large part of my life, and I need you."

She leaned up and wrapped her arms around the back of his neck. She pulled him to her, and kissed him with a fire that he never knew she had. He instantly felt himself harden to the point of pain. Losing all mental faculties, he pulled her closer into him, and before he knew it, she was laying crossways on the bed, with him on top of her.

Oh god, she is pure heaven! The feel of her soft skin under his almost drove him to the point of lunacy. Her kiss was of the sweetest ambrosia sent from Olympus. He knew he had to have her, or he would die, right then and there.

A moment of clarity seeped through and he pulled away. "Brooke, we cannot do this. You just had a miscarriage, and it isn't safe for you right now."

"Jack, please, I need you. I need to feel you," she begged, desperation dripping from her voice.

He shook, trying to calm his raging body, and just held her closely. "I want you too, Honey, but I will not do anything that is going to hurt you, and it will physically hurt."

She nodded against his chest. They both lay the correct way on the bed, and he just held her until they both fell asleep.

CHAPTER 10

Brooke awoke the next morning alone in the bed, ashamed of herself for how she had acted with Jack. She had no right to demand something like that of him. They had both decided that right now wasn't a good time to jump into sex or a relationship; that they were going to give it time, and she had all but attacked him. She wouldn't blame him if he never wanted to be around her again.

Mother Nature was calling, and she was a bitch when she wasn't answered, so Brooke put her slippers on, and did her morning routine. She went downstairs and found Jack in the kitchen, making breakfast.

"Morning, Brooke," he smiled.

"Morning, Jack. I'm sorry about last night."

"I'm not. You did nothing to be sorry about."

"Yes, I did. I had no right to come on so strong. It won't happen again."

He let out a long sigh. "Brooke, if you were in better shape physically, you're damned right I would have. I truly do not want to hurt you."

"That's not the point, Jack. I acted like a slut up there!"

"No, you didn't, Brooke! I think you're entitled to it! Damnit, woman, you have been to hell and back in the last few months! You have every right under the sun to want to feel desirable and needed! By the way, I do want you, and I do need you, but right now, your body needs time to heal! So you can stop the 'I acted like a slut' crap, because you didn't!" He pulled a waffle out of the waffle iron, and slapped it on a plate. "Here's your breakfast," he said sullenly, and slid it over the bar.

Miserable, she put a little syrup on it, and ate small portions at a time.

He poured some more batter into the iron and closed it.

He placed his hands on the top of the island. His voice turned deep, matter of fact. "Look, I'm sorry for yelling at you, but you need to give yourself a bit of a break. I am not Davenport, and I will never touch you out of anger. You are the most stunning, magnificent woman I have ever known. One day, when we are *both* ready, it will happen, but not until. So please, Sweetheart, stop with the crap of putting yourself down."

He was right; it served no purpose for her to think only the worst about herself. "All right, I will work on it. I'm sorry."

They heard a car coming down the driveway, so he flipped up the top of the iron and unplugged it in one fast motion. "Get upstairs, *now*."

She ran up, and stayed at the top, just in case it was actually safe. If not, she could run into one of the rooms and hide.

A moment later, he called her back down. "It's the rental car."

"Oh, thank god!" She came back down the stairs to stand beside her husband. Her husband….that sounded so anomalous to her ears. Just the other day, she was supposed to marry someone else; now she was married to his best friend. How strange and twisted life could be some times. She had to wonder if she would ever have her wedding ceremony, the one every girl dreamed about.

Jack was still tense; she felt it in his arms as he wrapped them around her waist from behind, putting on a show for the driver of the rental car.

Another car followed behind to bring the driver back.

It was only a matter of moments, and the driver was gone. "Do you feel like a drive?" he asked her, hopefully.

"Sure, just let me change my clothes, and grab my purse."

Brooke slipped on a pair of faded denim shorts with a tank top and a pair of sandals, and grabbed her purse. She inhaled sharply as the engagement ring that Davy had given her smacked the door jamb. Maybe it was time. He was gone, and was not coming back. She went back into the room and put her purse on the bed. She looked at it one more time, her heart breaking all over again, and slowly slid it off her finger. "Goodbye, Davy. I am so sorry," she said softly, kissed the stone, and put it into a holder in the bottom drawer of her jewelry box.

She came back downstairs, and her face must have told Jack what she was feeling.

"Are you ok?"

"Yes," she said, and lifted her left hand to show her bare finger.

He just held her for several moments. "It's going to be okay, Brooke. I know that must have hurt." He took that hand and kissed the finger. "Where would you like to go?" he asked, changing the subject.

She stopped when she saw the car: an '89 Mustang convertible, cherry red body, with tan leather seats. "Oh, Jack, she's beautiful!"

She popped the hood and looked at the engine. "Oh, she's pretty much factory specs, a 2.3-liter Inline, and a four-cylinder engine. She gets about 90-horsepower, and 135 pounds per feet of torque. She can do zero to sixty in about thirty seconds. It's so not impressive." She looked at Jack, and he was staring back at her with wide, shocked eyes.

"What?" she asked, wondering why he would look at her with surprise.

"You…..how do you know about engines?"

She sighed, "Just because I am a woman doesn't mean I don't know anything about cars, Jack. My father was a backyard mechanic after he got out of the army, and he taught me plenty. He wanted me to learn so that I would never be ripped off by a mechanic. The only thing I cannot work on is something with a computer chip in it, and that is only because I don't have the right equipment." He tossed her the keys. "You are full of surprises, aren't you?"

"If people wouldn't think that just because I'm a woman, that I don't know anything else besides raising babies then no, I wouldn't be."

He chuckled, "I guess that is true."

"Piece of advice Jack, don't take me for granted. I am intelligent, and know a lot more than just cars, drums, and raising children."

"What else do you know about then?" he asked as she started the car. She turned it around in the horseshoe shaped driveway, and pulled out. "I also know about computers. I took some classes on them in high school. I can program DOS, and I can build computers from the ground up. I can put up drywall, build just about anything wooden from scratch, and I can paint this house. I can also fix some plumbing problems. The only thing electrical I can do is replace the wiring in a lamp. I play piano, drums, and can use a tambourine. I am also good with weapons. I know how to use several different kinds, how to clean and maintain them. I was the stereotypical tomboy as a little girl."

"I have to admit, I am impressed."

"You will be even more so when you see me actually do it instead of talk about it."

She pulled into town and just drove around.

"Where is it you are headed to, Brooke?"

"I'm not really going anywhere to speak of. This is how I learn a town, just by driving around." The town really was beautiful; it had a lot of nineteenth-century charm, mixed with modern. "All right, now, what do you say we go to New Orleans? I want to get us some wedding rings, and it wouldn't be a good idea to do that here in this small town."

"That's a very good idea."

She headed back toward the house and the highway leading down to New Orleans. She absolutely fell in love with the beauty of Lake Pontchartrain as she drove beside it.

"Do you remember the Interstate we took coming out of New Orleans?" she asked.

"No I don't, but there is a map in the glove box."

He read the directions off for her, and they got to the French quarter with no problems. She found a parking spot, and they decided to try some walking.

They found a beautiful jewelry store right on Bourbon Street not far from where they parked. They went inside and looked around.

"May I help you?" A stunning saleswoman made a beeline for them with dollar signs in her eyes. Her long jet hair fanned out around her as she turned around, and her olive complexion shone with a radiance that could only come out of a spa. With the way she was eyeing Jack, her long, lithe body seemed ready to pounce, desperate for a sale, or for the perfect specimen of manhood, and she thought the man right beside Brooke was it.

"Yes, thank you. We are looking for wedding sets," Jack said in his best charming voice.

"Wonderful! Congratulations you two!" she said in what sounded like a faked line, like something she had to learn to do her job. "Is there any cut of diamond you are interested in?"

"I was thinking of the brilliant cut. Nothing is too good for my lady." Jack's smile was as brilliant as the diamond he was thinking of as he wrapped his arms around Brooke's waist, taking her hands in his and lacing their fingers.

"That is an excellent choice, sir! If you will please follow me, they are right over here." She took them about ten feet to the rings as she swung her hips like they were double jointed. "Now, when is the big day?" she more purred than asked.

"It just happened, but my husband's best man lost the rings just before the wedding, so we wanted to replace what we had." Brooke smiled coldly at her, and then looked up at Jack. She really didn't like this woman; she was looking at him like she wanted to eat him for dinner, and it made Brooke's neck bristle. She realized he was drop dead gorgeous and all, but if he was in a jewelry store looking at rings, it meant he was off the market! Brooke wanted to scratch the bitch's eyes out!

When the sales woman blatantly looked him up and down, Brooke dropped Jack's hand. "I'm out of here!"

She looked at the slut. "Here is a piece of advice, woman to skank. If a man brings in his woman to look at wedding rings, he's off the market!" Hope turned around and walked out.

"Brooke, wait! He ran up from behind her as she walked out the door and kept going. "What the hell was that about?" he demanded from behind her.

Brooke stopped, and looked at him, fire in her eyes. "Don't bother trying to pretend you didn't notice the blatant invitation she gave you. She looked at you like you were a filet mignon and she hadn't eaten in a month."

He had the audacity to laugh like it was the most hilarious joke he had ever heard. "You're jealous!"

She blustered, so irate she couldn't get a word out. When she was finally able to think coherently, she turned, and started heading back down the street. "For your information, I am not jealous. I didn't care for the blatant disrespect she showed me."

"That may have been part of it, but you are jealous! Come on Brooke, admit it!" he cajoled and grabbed her arm in a loose grip.

Brooke stopped and turned to him. "So what if I am! What the hell difference does it make?" she demanded.

"I would have been jealous too, Brooke. Yes, I noticed how she was looking at me. Yes, I was getting angry, and I was about to walk out too when you beat me to it. I just wanted to hear from you the reason why."

"Well, now you know!"

"Babe, wait, please. Listen to me for a moment." She stopped trying to pull away, and looked at him. "When we get home, we will have a nice long talk. But until then, I think this will suffice in letting you know how I feel for you." He yanked her into his arms, and kissed her with so much heat, Brooke thought she would burst into a roaring inferno of raw emotion! She wrapped her arms around his neck, while his were around her waist, holding her up. Certain parts of her body flooded, and swelled to the point of crossing the threshold into agony. Her breath came out in pants, and one of them moaned.

The world around them ceased to exist, at least to her, until she heard someone say from beside them: "Get a room!"

Jack broke off the kiss, and said, "Yah, I guess you've never kissed *your* wife."

"Come on, let's go get our rings." he smiled and took Brooke's hand. Now, she knew for certain, she was falling in love with Jack, and there wasn't a damned thing she could do about it. She composed herself as they walked down the street, and forced her breathing back to normal.

They found another jewelry store and headed inside. She smiled when she saw the silver-haired gentleman, knowing this was going to be nothing like the last place they went into.

The place was clean, with display cabinets made of dark oak bases, and sparkly clean glass. The carpet wasn't worn, but standing up as if it had been recently placed. The store itself was all but empty, save for a woman looking at watches. She quickly walked out.

"Good afternoon, you two. How may I help you?"

"My wife and I are looking for wedding rings. We just got married, and my groomsman lost the set that we were going to use." Jack must have liked the story Brooke gave to the last place.

"Well, that's too bad. Our rings are right over here." He brought them over to the display, and took out several ring holders. "If you don't see anything that you like, then we can always have one of your design made in no time."

Brooke did see something that she liked, immediately. It was a sapphire, surrounded by smaller diamonds set in a twenty-four carat gold ring. The band was in a wrap, surrounding the sapphire and diamonds. She took it out of the case and tried it on. It fit perfectly, and she was already falling in love with it. It wasn't gaudy, but actually quite classy. It wasn't heavy, and it seemed to scream at her to buy it. It reminded her of the ring she just took off her finger this morning, but it really was different in a lot of ways.

"Ma'am, you have excellent taste. That just arrived this morning, the first of its kind made by a local jeweler."

"Honey, I don't think I need to look any more for myself. Let's find yours."

The salesman smiled, and grabbed the men's rings. Jack picked one that seemed to not only match Brooke's; but also complement it. She took hers off, and let him ring up the sale. Jack handed him his credit card, then the salesman went in back to clean the rings.

Once he returned, it was with two ring boxes inside of a white paper bag with small ropes for handles.

"Mr. and Mrs. Connor, I thank you for your business. I recently opened within the last few months, so please tell your friends and family about me."

"We certainly will, sir. Thank you so much for the beautiful rings," she said as they were walking to the door. Brooke reached in the bag just before they reached the entrance, and took Jack's out. She wanted to show the man how much they loved them. She took it out of the box, and put it on Jack's finger. He in turn, did the same for her. Brooke looked back, and smiled at the gentleman. The poor guy had tears in his eyes.

"Thank you again, sir," she said to the kind salesman.

"No, thank you for that, I never get to see it. It's nice seeing two young people truly in love come into my store."

Brooke and Jack looked at each other and almost laughed, but didn't. She turned back to the salesman, and said, "Have a wonderful day."

"I certainly will, after the two of you."

They turned and walked out.

"Let's go and get something to eat while we're down here, and take a look around," Jack suggested.

"We can go ahead and eat, but I'm getting really tired here. My stomach is starting to really hurt." She couldn't help but wince as a sharp pain shot through her. She also knew she had to change something before she started leaking.

Two weeks later, Brooke decided that she'd had enough of eating out, since she was starting to gain weight. She went downstairs and started making sauce for tomorrow night's spaghetti, and took the wax paper off the fish for tonight's dinner. She seasoned it, and stuck it in the oven. She started on the potatoes when Jack came downstairs from cleaning the attic.

"I got the boxes organized and some of the broken stuff thrown away."

"Thank you, sweetheart." Brooke smiled as he leaned down and kissed her cheek. "Could you do one more thing for me, please? Down in the basement is an old bottle of Scotch I thought we would be able to drink tonight with dinner. Would you go get it?"

His mouth formed an *o,* and he flew down the basement stairs. A few minutes later, he came back up with the bottle. He cleaned it off, and popped the cork. "Most of the stuff down there will probably be vinegar, but we can open one here and there to find out. Some of it is likely a collector's item."

"That's okay, we can always restock it."

"But for tonight, we celebrate! We are safe, and together. That is all that matters to me."

He grabbed a couple of crystal snifters, and put some ice in them, then poured the Scotch. He handed a glass to Brooke, and raised his. "This is to us. We started out as enemies, and turned into best friends. The future and the world are ours."

She looked at him over the top of her glass and took a drink. "Is that what I am, a friend?"

"Oh no, you are much more than that, Brooke," he said in a low voice as he looked her over. He quickly turned away, and sat down at the table.

She downed her glass, and put it on the table without flinching. The stuff was fantastic and went down smoothly.

"Wow, you really are full of nice surprises." He stared at the glass. "Most women can't handle a strong liqueur such as Scotch."

"I can handle anything that has alcohol in it, except tequila. That stuff makes me beyond mean."

He laughed, "I'll keep that in mind."

There was a kind of tension in the air, as if a bomb was about to go off. She told herself to tread softly, that she may not like it if it went *boom.*

Jack got up and poured Brooke another glass as she drained the potatoes, and got the hand mixer out to mash them. He came up behind her and moved her hair. He placed a gentle, but devastating kiss on her neck, and she just leaned into him, as if it came naturally. Butterflies took to flight in her lower stomach, and nervous, she leaned back up and grabbed the glass, taking another healthy swallow. Her pulse pounded, and her knees wanted to collapse, so she locked them, keeping her in place.

Every single day, that man grew more and more sexy, more devastatingly gorgeous. Plenty of times since they got back from New Orleans had she wanted him to kiss her like he did on Bourbon Street, but she held back, not wanting to get turned down again. She still got weak in the knees when she thought about that day. Right now, she truly didn't want to cook food. She wanted to cook something else, yet another thing that involves fire, but of a different kind. She couldn't keep her eyes or her hands off of him, yet again, she had to tread carefully. If she didn't, she was going to lose her heart once and for all.

She heard the water boiling, so she turned it off and put the vegetables into a serving bowl. He finished setting the table for her. She brought everything over and told him to dig in.

"Brooke, it smells delicious!"

"Oh, hang on a second!" She forgot to cut up a lemon for him to spread across the fish. She did so quite quickly, and put them on the table next to the fish. She knew she was stalling, but sitting next to him made it even more difficult to keep from throwing him on the floor and giving him a meal he would never forget.

"Now, you can dig in." She sat down at the opposite end of the table from him, and watched as he took his first bite of her cooking. He closed his eyes, and chewed slowly, moaning with ecstasy. "Oh god, Brooke, this is fantastic! This cod melts in my mouth!"

Her body reacted to his moaning strongly, she could feel herself getting wet, desperate to hear him moan for a different reason.

She grabbed her glass and took another swig. This stuff was getting better and better the more she drank it.

He got up to throw his bones in the trash, rinsed his plate in the sink, and put the plate in the dishwasher. As he came back, Brooke couldn't stop staring at him.

"Brooke, you haven't touched your dinner," he said, his brow creased with worry.

She stared at his belt buckle, trying not to go further south. "I guess I'm not hungry."

"Brooke, do you see something you like?" His voice sounded far off, funny.

"I always do when I look at you," she answered without thinking.

She shook herself, and looked up into his face. "Talk to me, Jack. Why is there so much pain in your eyes all the time?"

"Brooke, Davy was like a brother to me, the brother I never had. Yes, it hurts, bad. He's dead, and I couldn't do a damn thing to save him."

"It has nothing whatsoever to do with Davy. The pain in your eyes was there way before he died."

"No, oh hell no, we are not going there! That is a topic that is off limits!" he said fervidly.

Okaaaay, she would never tread those waters again. She started the dishwasher, and straightened up the kitchen.

Jack came up from behind and wrapped his arms around her waist. "I'm sorry for snapping at you. It is such a touchy subject for me, and hard for me to even think about, let alone talk about."

She nodded, and turned around. She had to hug him, silently letting him know that he could always talk to her. Her body melted into his, painfully aware of his solidness, his hard contours and muscles. Her hands roamed his back of their own accord, wanting to feel every inch, every hill and valley of his back. Her mind conjured images of his hips advancing and retreating while over her. Her body tightened painfully, so to get her mind off of it, she took another drink of scotch.

Grabbing the bottle, she left the room, turning off the light on the way out.

They headed up to the bedroom, and as she saw the bed, she wanted to collapse with exhaustion. She changed into her night clothes and looked at the bottle, still half full. She went over and picked it up. She upended it, taking a healthy swallow. She couldn't get over how good this stuff was.

"Honey, you need to slow down on the sauce."

"No." She changed her mind on the sleepiness. "I intend to get good and faced tonight. I think I've earned it."

"Yes, you have, but you don't want to drink sixty year old scotch like its beer."

"I will drink it how I want. This is some good stuff!" She placed the bottle back down on the nightstand, and went to turn back around and stumbled. She righted herself, and slowly went to Jack. She needed to feel him in her; in fact, she needed to feel him all around her! Her body started boiling from all the pent-up frustration emanating from her core. She had to have him now, tonight, or she knew she would explode all over this room, and gore would not be a good look for these beautiful walls. She wrapped her arms around his neck, and pulled his head to her. Liquid courage was a wonderful thing!

She knew she had won when she felt his arms surround her waist and roughly pull her to him. She could feel his erection against her stomach and it did things to her body that she never thought could happen. "Andy, make love to me, please," she begged.

He picked her up, cradling her against his chest, and lay her down, climbing above her. "I thought you'd never ask, Hope. I know that we're not supposed to use those names anymore, but I don't give a damn. Tonight, we are Andy and Hope, not Jack and Brooke. I also don't intend on stopping at one. I am going to make love to you for the rest of your natural life!"

"Andy, just shut up and do it!" Hope demanded, not wanting to hear him talk. She wanted action! She wanted *Andy*!

He complied by removing her nightgown. When his hands touched her bare skin, she hissed at the sensations going from where his fingertips touched straight to the center of her being. She pulled his mouth to hers, to show him how much she wanted him. She wrapped her legs around his, almost involuntarily.

"You are stunning, Hope." he said, his voice low, husky with need. He splayed kisses down her throat to her breast, leaving a trail of fire in the wake of his lips. She almost screamed when his mouth latched on to her ultra-sensitive nipple.

He got up, and unbuttoned his jeans, then kissed a path down, down, down to her swollen cleft. This time, Hope did scream as he created a delicious suction around her. Her legs shook and vibrated as he brought her to the point of exploding, then stopped.

They both panted, looking into each other's eyes. "I can't wait any longer! I want you now!" he growled.

"Then take me, Andy. I want you so bad I ache!"

Andy gave a shout of pure bliss as he entered her, pushing through her moist tightness. She again surrounded him with her legs, pushing him in even deeper. He began to thrust, slowly but deeply. Within just a matter of moments, her whole world shattered around her, and to keep from screaming as love collided with lust, she bit his neck, not hard enough to draw blood, but hard enough to keep her from losing complete control of all faculties. She felt herself writhe, and tears dripped down the sides of her face as wave after wave of intense pleasure washed over her.

He started to pound into her, thrusting as hard as his hips would allow. "Hope!" He chanted her name with every movement, every breath. Another orgasm built and exploded a second time from her very soul, or was it a continuation from the first? He roared, and arched backwards, screaming her name at the top of his lungs. At the same moment, she screamed his name in answer, losing control, her own body arching up to meet his as he gave one more brutal push, and stayed there as he emptied himself deep into her.

Andy collapsed on top of Hope, praying he wasn't crushing her. He knew it would be good with her, but he had no clue, he truly didn't. He just drove himself straight into the: *I'm in deep shit* zip code. The only way that he could make it out of this intact was if she agreed to stay married to him, for the rest of eternity, whether they are Hope and Andy or Jack and Brooke; he didn't give a hot, wet monkey's ass. He also knew he had to tell her the truth about his former partner. It was eating him alive, and he was so afraid that he was going to lose her too.

He gathered the strength to roll off of her, and took her into his arms. "Honey, I need to talk to you. This is so hard for me, so please do not interrupt me until I am done, or I am afraid I will lose my nerve." He took a deep breath, and started.

"When I first started with the bureau, I had a partner. He was awesome, the best partner a person could have. He would help a homeless person by taking them out for a meal, then go out and bust a dad that had just taken his kid from the custodial mother. But, he had his own demons. He had two major addictions, gambling, and sex. The first one, he was getting help for with gambler's anonymous, the bureau made him go as a last ditch effort to be able to keep him on. The second cost him his marriage and children. One day, he was caught by our supervisor having sex with the wife of a suspect. So, Caleb got suspended without pay, pending an investigation into whether or not to keep him. Three days into the suspension, Caleb called me up talking a bunch of crazy shit, things like how there was a traitor in the bureau, and this traitor had been trying to get Caleb fired for several months now, and how the mob is infiltrating the FBI. I figured he was talking in a drunken stupor, so, I hopped into the car, and drove over to his house. Just before I got to his front walkway, I heard a shot come from inside. I broke down the door to see a whole lot of blood, and brain matter. Caleb had shot himself in the head, using his sidearm from work. It was lying next to him, near his hand.

"Brooke, he had begged for my help, and I laughed at him, telling him that he was going to be just fine, that he just needed a couple of beers and a good night's sleep. But, I still went over there, hoping that I could calm him down enough to maybe seek some counseling. I didn't get there in time. His death is my fault."

"No, Jack, it's not your fault. Caleb was hurting badly enough that he didn't want anyone to know. He didn't even confide in you until he was well past helping. If someone is determined to kill themselves, they are going to do it regardless of what anyone else says or does. It sounds to me like he was living alone, and wanted someone to find his body. So he waited until you got there to shoot himself. Honey, there was nothing you could have done."

He thought about what she said. Davy had said the same thing to him, almost verbatim, but it made more sense when she said it. Maybe they were both right.

"Honey, you did not stick the gun to his head and pull the trigger. He did it, it was his choice. You couldn't have stopped him, even if you were in the room when he did it. Yes, his death is tragic, senseless, but he was determined to end his suffering one way or another."

"I...I never thought of it that way." He held her even closer, his breathing a bit more even. He then had a realization that floored him. He thought that they would have to pretend to be married, but the Marshals made it to where they actually were, and he couldn't be happier! A year ago, he would have panicked and ran the other way at the thought of the *M* word, but today, he wouldn't have it any other way!

Dear god, he fell in love with her! When the hell did that happen? He thought about saying something to her, but decided against it. For one, he was certain that she did not feel the same way. Two, love was a weakness that he could not afford to have known. After all, it destroyed Caleb, or at least it helped to, although he never thought for a moment that Brooke would ever destroy him. He wasn't scared anymore that she was going to hurt him; he was now petrified that Davenport was going to find her, and kill her. If he still had a contact within the Bureau, then he could find her at any moment, and kill her. That was the only thing that could destroy him now.

He heard her breathing deeply beside him, and knew either she passed out, or simply fell asleep. He chuckled, thinking about how drunk she was. She really could hold her liquor. She had four large juice glasses full of the stuff, and didn't give the ice time to water it down, then was drinking out of the bottle. She'd had four to his two! That was damned impressive! She was just a tiny little slip of a thing, only around five-foot-five, and one hundred five pounds soaking wet! He just got bested by a woman half his height and weight in a drinking bout! She truly *was* incredible!

The final thought he had before he joined her in sleep was that he needed to take her tomorrow to go car hunting and instrument shopping.

The next morning, Jack awoke in the bed alone. It didn't surprise him since it seemed no matter what time Brooke went to bed, she was up at the ass-crack of dawn.

He smiled and stretched his muscles thinking about last night. Sex had never been as good as it was with Brooke, and he was never exactly celibate. Davy used to call him the "man-whore" of the two of them. He was usually content to sit at home and read while Jack went out partying, even after he got on with the FBI. It was his biggest pickup line for a while. After a bit though, even that became tedious. Women wanted him only because he was an agent, thinking he had money and some kind of glamorous lifestyle. Then along came Brooke. She didn't give a damn if he was the Pope, or the president of Russia, she put him in his place but good and kept him there. Granted, she was terrified at first of standing up for herself, but she got used to it, and had been doing it ever since, and honestly, how *hot* was that?

He got up and slipped on a pair of sweats. He worked his morning routine, and went downstairs to find Brooke sweeping the parlor floor. She had been busy this morning; the entire room gleamed with recent polishing. A lemon scent made his nose tingle, the smell reminding him of his grandparents' house as a child, bringing back memories of fresh-baked cookies and lots of love.

"Good morning, Brooke." She gave a loud moan as his lips brushed the side of her neck.

"Morning, Jack."

"Listen, I was thinking, it's Saturday. Let's go get us a car, and some musical instruments. We can get a van or a truck so we could haul the stuff."

"That sounds like a fantastic idea. Let me change out of these grubby clothes, and we can go." She smiled, then leaned up and kissed him full on the lips. He inhaled sharply as his body started swelling. He couldn't resist grabbing her as she walked away and pulling her to him. He gave her a kiss right back and she wound up melting into him. When he pulled away, they were both panting.

"Jack, last night was....I...." she stammered.

"Last night was incredible, Brooke. I have never felt like that in my life."

She blushed deeply. "I thought I was amazingly inadequate."

"Inadequate? No. That is not a word I would use to describe you; beautiful, phenomenal, yes, those would be more accurate."

She blushed even deeper, making her more beautiful than ever before. "Come on, go change before I take you back to the bed and keep you there all day."

He followed her upstairs just so he could look at that tight ass as it swung side to side, and also to put something on more suitable--a nice pair of black cotton Brooks Brothers dress slacks and a white button down shirt. A few minutes later, she came out of the bathroom in a long multi-colored skirt, with a black blouse and black high-heeled leather boots.

He couldn't take his eyes off of her. Whether she was in a pair of jeans and a shirt-shirt, or dressed to the nines, she was the most divine woman he had ever laid eyes on.

He couldn't move, couldn't speak, then she kissed his cheek and broke the spell. "Are you ready, Jack?"

"I'm always ready for you," he murmured and they went back downstairs, where he opened the front door for her.

He took them to a dealership in town, where they found a nice, brand new Ford Aerostar LS. He let Brooke do her thing, and she looked the van over. As she popped the hood, a salesperson came over to them.

"Hi there, I'm Steve. I've never seen you around these parts before. How may I help you?"

"I'm Jackson Connor, and this is my wife Brooke. We just moved into town a few weeks ago."

"Oh, where do y'all hail from?"

"I was born in New York, but raised on the west coast, and met my wife while I was in Boot Camp in San Diego."

"Oh, Navy boy, are you?"

"Oh no, Sir, I am a Marine all the way!"

"Semper Fi, my brother!"

"Do or die!" He offered his hand to Jack with his fist up, and he clasped it, showing solidarity.

"Gentlemen, I am glad you can bond on the Corp, but can we do that later? In fact, I will even invite you to the house, Steve, so you can get to know my husband and me. Right now, all I am interested in doing is buying this van."

"Oh, the lady is a hard hitter! I like that!" Steve smiled. "My wife will, too!"

"Thank you." Brooke smiled.

"She's a beaut, ain't she? She's fully loaded, automatic locks and windows, AM/FM cassette, rear defrost and wiper, and y'all will be the first owners!"

"That's great, but is there a power-train warranty on it, or is it as is? Are all the bugs worked out of the transmission, or is it the original that Ford put into these a few years ago that happened to be recalled?" she asked, and Steve's jaw hit the ground.

"Ma'am, you're good! Yes, the bugs are all worked out; they decided when it was recalled that they would put a better system into it, so it didn't blow up any more. And there is a full power-train warranty on all our new vehicles, for one hundred thousand miles, or five years whichever comes first. You can buy an extended warranty, which I don't recommend, because these babies are top of the line, built to last. Chevy couldn't compare to our power-trains."

"Well, I would like to take it for a test drive, if that's ok," she declared.

"Of course, let me go get the keys." He smiled and walked back toward the show room.

"I'm impressed, babe! You actually do know what you're doing!" he said as soon as Steve was out of ear shot.

"Did you have any doubts?" she asked, her eyes narrowing.

"If I did, I certainly don't anymore."

Steve came back with the keys, and handed them to Brooke.

Jack could tell that she already had her mind made up, but she didn't want to seem too eager. She played with all the knobs and switches, adjusted her mirrors, put it into reverse, and took off. Steve sat in the passenger's seat, with Jack in the bucket seat behind Hope. She took it down winding roads, testing the drive train itself, then onto the highway to test the acceleration.

She turned the van around and came back to the dealership. "Let me talk to my husband for a few minutes, and we will come inside the show room to let you know."

"Certainly, ma'am." He walked back toward the show room.

"So, what do you think, Brooke, not that I really need to ask."

"The left front tire is a bit low, but that's easily fixed with a stop to the gas station. I think we should get it. Do you think we should get the other two while we're at it?"

"I don't see why not. I am sure he wouldn't mind delivering two cars while one of us drives the van, and the other gets the 'Stang."

"Or, I'll finalize the deal, and you can call the rental shop, they can come to get the Mustang, and the three of us can drive the vehicles back to the house. Then, we can just go get the instruments," she shrugged.

"Sounds good to me, I like the way you think." He grabbed her and gave a short peck to her mouth. He stared into her eyes for a moment, lost in their depths. He cleared his throat, trying to keep his thoughts from replaying last night, and broke off the contact before he embarrassed them both.

They walked hand in hand back to the showroom, and chose two other Mustangs-- one red, one black, both convertibles--then found Steve at his desk. "We are going to take the van, and those two Mustangs." Steve's jaw hit the ground, again, when Hope told him the news. "Will you take a check, or cash?"

"Will your credit allow that?" he asked.

"No, you don't understand. We are going to buy them outright." Jack smiled. "I was also wondering two other things: may I use your phone to call the rental agency to come and pick up the rental car, and, will you be able to drive the van back to the house for us? There are only two of us after all."

"I would be happy to! Let me get started on the paperwork for the state, and I will have one of the other salesmen call about the rental car. There is only one rental car place in town, so it's obvious where you got it."

"I appreciate it, Steve."

Steve laughed. "Brooke and Jack, you have no idea what you have just done for me; and the dealership also, but me in particular. I would walk to the ends of the earth for you two right now."

A woman's voice came over the loudspeaker: "Steve DuPont, line three please, Steve DuPont, line three."

"Excuse me for a moment." He picked up the phone. "Steve DuPont…..yah….I can't talk right now, I'm in the middle of a sale…..let's just say Sally that we have just saved the house…..yah…..I have to go, I will tell you when I get home…..I love you too…..bye babe."

Jack shot Brooke a questioning look, one she picked up on right away. She smiled and nodded her head. She started writing a check, as Steve took a deep breath and started writing out the sales paperwork. When she was done, she handed it to him. He looked at the five thousand dollar tag, and nodded at Brooke, giving her a thumb up.

"Oh, by the way, yes, we will take a check. We will just have to verify the amount with the bank before we can release the cars."

"That's fine, and the bank is local," Jack told him.

Steve punched some numbers into the adding machine, and ripped off the piece of paper, handing it to Brooke. She looked at it, smiled, and handed it to Jack. She wrote out a check for the amount, and passed it over to Steve. He smiled, and took it into the back for the accountant.

A few minutes later, his phone rang. "Steve DuPont…..yah…..you've got to be kidding me…..Ok, thanks!" He turned to Jack and Brooke. "It's verified, you have yourself three vehicles!"

He went over to a large box, and pulled out two other sets of keys. "Now, who gets the red Mustang?" he asked.

"My husband gets it. Mine is black, not that it really matters. They're both going to the same place," Brooke smiled. "I want to stop somewhere and fill them up with gas. I don't like to let them below half, especially in the winter."

"With as much money as you've just spent, I think I can have them completely filled here." He held his hand out for the keys, and went in back to have the cars taken care of. Jack noticed that Steve had one hell of a spring in his step now. Well, he would too if he just made several thousand dollars' worth of commission.

About twenty minutes later, the cars were ready to be driven home.

Steve looked at the invoices, and noticed the address. "Wait, you guys live at the old Beauchamp place?" he asked, stunned.

"Yes, is that a problem?" Brooke asked.

"Oh no, no problem whatsoever, I just didn't know anyone moved into it is all."

"Yes, we just moved in a few weeks ago. It was....given to us as a gift," Jack said quickly.

Steve chuckled. "That's a nice gift! I've always wanted to see the inside. The Beauchamps have a name around here, and it was well known that you don't go over there for anything, except if invited."

"Well, Brooke and I live there now, and you are more than welcome to come up there any time you wish. Oh, is there a place here in town we could go to and pick up musical instruments?"

"Sure, right downtown. Do you guys play?"

Jack chuckled. "You might say that. I play lead guitar, and Brooke plays drums, keyboards, and sings. Why, do you play anything?"

"Yup, I am a keyboardist, and I also sing."

Brooke and Jack looked at each other. "Do you know any other musicians in town that may be looking to form a band?" Brooke asked as she turned back to Steve.

"I may know a few. What are you looking to play?" Steve asked, obviously excited, but trying to hide it.

"We were thinking some of today's music, maybe with some sixties and seventies thrown in," Brooke said.

Steve smiled widely. "Let me make some phone calls, and I will get back with you say...tomorrow night. Now, let me take you over to the music store. Then we can head on up to your place. The rest of the day is mine; my boss gave it to me with the big sale I just made."

Jack dropped a whole bunch of money from his half of Davy's fortune since Hope paid for the cars. He let her pick out what she wanted for the house, which was everything needed for a band. A keyboard, another drum set exactly like the one that was in storage in

Chicago, a bass guitar, another guitar for him, amps, leads, and another mixer. She got three more microphones, complete with stands and clips, along with another headset and batteries for each. They would have to make two trips for everything, but it wasn't like the store was very far from the house. The smaller stuff they were able to put into the mustangs, but the bigger equipment had to be put into the back of the van, and the seats had to be taken out for the largest equipment. Everything was top of the line, nothing but the best for Brooke and any band she belonged to, he made sure of it.

They brought Steve into the house, and he helped Jack unload everything and bring it into the ballroom as Brooke called it. Steve and Jack took the rear seats out of the van, and the three of them went back to town to grab the rest of the equipment. As the equipment was being loaded, Brooke bought a bunch of song books with today's music, along with some more classic stuff like Queen, Led Zepplin, and Lynyrd Skynyrd.

Brooke let Steve call his wife, and invite her down to the house, which she immediately accepted.

As Brooke set up the instruments, Jack approached Steve with the check. "Oh, no, I can't take this, dude!"

"We heard you tell your wife that you now have the money to save your house because of our sale. We want you to be okay for a little while. Get some food; pay off your utilities for a bit. If you need anything, Brooke and I want you to come to us, ok? The only thing is you can't tell anyone where you got this. We don't wish to become the Connor bank of Slidell."

"That's great and all, but I really can't take it. I don't take charity!" Steve blustered.

"It's not charity, Steve. Brooke and I were....blessed by someone we both loved dearly, and we only want to help someone less fortunate than we are. We can't think of anyone better than you. You were the first in this town to talk to us, to welcome us, and it is the least we can do."

"I'll tell you what. I will take it on one condition. You let me come up here once a week and I work it off by doing odd jobs....grounds keeping, repairs, whatever you need."

"You help Brooke and I get into a band and you can consider it paid."

"I need to hear you play first."

Jack thought that Brooke was going to get whiplash by listening to them negotiate.

"Honey, grab a mic. Let me tune my new guitar real quick, and we will let the good man hear us."

It only took a matter of minutes to tune the guitar, and Jack started a riff from Ac/DC's *You shook me all Night Long.* Brooke already had her drum set put together, so she joined in on them, and started singing. When they were done, Steve asked to borrow the phone again. They let him, and as he hit the door to the parlor, he asked them to play again, so that they could be heard on the phone.

When he was done, he came back in, and they stopped mid-song. "It's done; the guys are on the way." He looked at both of them. "You guys are really good! Are you sure you two aren't professionals?"

A knock came at the door. "That would be my wife." He grinned ear to ear. They let him answer it, and bring her into the ballroom.

Sally was a pretty woman around twenty-five, with long blonde hair cascading down her shoulders, and bright green eyes. "You guys have an incredible stereo system…." She stopped when she saw Jack with his guitar slung over his shoulder. "It wasn't a stereo, was it?"

"No, Honey. This is Jack and Brooke Connor. They are the ones that saved our asses."

She immediately burst into tears, and ran up to Brooke, hugging her. "You don't know how much we appreciate it."

"It's okay," she crooned. "We just bought a couple of cars."

"Try three," Steve said.

CHAPTER 11

A few minutes later, two guys came to the door.

Steve brought them into the ballroom. "Brooke, Jack, this is Jeremy and Craig." Jeremy had a 4-string bass guitar. He made Brooke think of Neil Schon from Journey with his tight curly hair. Craig had a pair of drum sticks in his hand, so Brooke got up while Jeremy plugged his guitar in. Sally grabbed the wireless microphone, and stood in back over by the drummer.

Jeremy tuned his bass, and within moments, they were ready to jam.

"Baby, *Shadows of the Night*?" Jack suggested. Brooke smiled and nodded. This song had quickly become her favorite song to sing. It described her relationship with Jack perfectly, and even she had to admit, with all the practice she had been putting in, she was really improving her vocal skills, rocking this style of music.

She broke out into the opening chorus of the song, and she could feel all eyes on her for a moment. Then Jack joined in, along with Craig and Steve, and they absolutely knocked the song out of the park! Even Sally had a beautiful voice for background!

When the last note faded, there was absolute silence in the room for several heartbeats. Then Sally, Jeremy, Craig, and Steve all started high-fiving, and loudly cheering. Jack looked at Brooke and winked. She couldn't help but smile and wink back.

"So I guess we're in then?" Jack asked, feigning ignorance.

"You bet your ass you're in!" They all said together. "We haven't heard anything like you two in a long time, in fact, since our last Pat Benatar concert!" Sally boasted.

"Do you guys want to try something nice and easy?" Brooke asked.

"Yah! Let's get back to our instruments," Steve said and rushed back to the keyboards.

"How about we do *Faithfully* by Journey?" Brooke suggested.

"Wait, isn't Journey a bit...high in pitch?" Steve asked.

"Trust me Steve, Brooke can do it." Jack looked at her, and blew her a kiss. She wanted to collapse right then and there; her knees going weak.

"This I would like to hear!" Craig said dryly.

"Then Steve, start us out," Brooke answered, ignoring Craig's tone. He'll eat his words!

She stunned them all, including herself when she held the long note without her voice cracking, or running out of air.

"Brooke, can you sing any Def Leppard, or even Prince?"

"Can you play *When Doves Cry*?" Brooke asked, sarcasm thick in her voice.

Jack again winked at her, and started the opening guitar solo. She could only stare at him, stunned for a moment. She knew he was good, but holy shit! That man can play! He made that guitar wail!

She recovered, and started singing.

Once it was over, Brooke wanted to try something. So, she asked permission.

"Brooke, since you can sing like that, you can try anything you want!" Craig said.

"Ok, Jack, I know you can sing; I've heard you over the years. For the next song, I want you to sing it. Steve, you sing the second man's voice, and I will sing Wendy's part. I want to do *1999*."

Brooke, Sally, and Craig all did the clapping parts of the song, and Brooke started it out. When they came together, it was wicked fantastic. Then, Craig surprised them all, and did the bass voice at the end. When it was over, they were all celebrating.

"Holy shit, I'm so glad you two came to Slidell! You guys rock!" Steve yelled, happily.

Suddenly, Jack broke into the opening guitar riff of "Wanted Dead or Alive" by Bon Jovi, and the rest of the instruments joined in. Brooke started singing right away. Steve, Jack, and Sally joined in as back up. Brooke decided she was really going to let go, and cranked it out. When the last note faded into obscurity, she was out of breath. "I think we have the name of the band: *Dead or Alive*," she suggested.

"Hell yah!" Everyone agreed, including Jack.

"I want to try one more thing. Sally, come up front, please, hon." When she stood beside Brooke, she asked Steve to start the opening notes for *Desperado* by *The Eagles*. Jack, Steve and Brooke did the backup voices for her, and Brooke added a few soft *ohhhs* where there were none in the original song, making Sally's voice stand out even more. Sally sang so beautifully that it brought tears to Brooke's eyes. "Sal, that's your song. I want you to sing it at any gig we go to. You really are very good!"

Sally blushed, but didn't reply.

To take Sally's mind off of her obvious embarrassment, Brooke said, "Jack, I'm going to go to the basement and grab a bottle of wine. This calls for a celebration!"

"Brooke, do you mind if I go with you?" Sally offered.

"Not at all, Sal, come on," she smiled.

"Wow, Brooke, you really have a set of pipes on you!" she said as they went down the stairs.

"Thank you, I really appreciate the compliment. That is very kind of you. I have actually just recently started singing with bands. Jack was gone so much with the Marines that I just didn't care much about it." Brooke hated lying to her new friend, but she didn't have a choice. She didn't want to put her in danger too.

"You recently started singing? You've got to be kidding me! That is some serious talent!"

It was Brooke's turn to blush, thinking that she just lit up the basement with her red face alone. "Sally, you have got some serious talent going on too. You have an astonishing voice! I meant what I said; I would really like you to sing *Desperado* at gigs.

"You really would do that for me? I thought you were just being nice." Her voice dripped with shock, and some fear.

"Sure, why not? I think you have a talent that needs to be used also. Do you think Stevie Nicks sings all of Fleetwood Mac's songs? Christie McVie sings too."

"Well, let me think about it, okay?"

"Sure sweetie, take all the time you need. It's not like we are going to be doing any gigs tomorrow." Brooke grabbed one of the Burgundies, and brought it upstairs.

She poured six glasses, which took almost the entire bottle, and called everyone into the kitchen.

Brooke raised her glass in a toast, and everyone followed suit. "To new friends and business partners, may darkness never descend on neither!"

"Hear, hear!" they responded, and drank. Each of their eyes widened, and then slowly closed when they tasted the wine. When it touched Brooke's tongue, she did the same. This was the best wine she had ever tasted!

"Let me order a pizza or something; any good recommendations?" Jack offered.

"That sounds like a plan," Steve said.

Brooke didn't hear what place he recommended, she was too busy looking at her husband. There had been a lot of times lately where she just could not take her eyes off of him. He was not the same man she met three months ago. He had been angry, volatile. Now, he was the sweetest, caring, most loving individual she had ever known, and she was truly falling in love with him. God help her, but she was.

While she knew he was attracted to her, he had made that abundantly clear, she just didn't know if he loved her. How could she? He still tended to keep his emotions close to his chest, although he was getting better at showing them.

The real difference between what she felt for Davy and what she felt for Jack was that it wasn't born out of gratefulness as it had been for Davy, but from weeks of being on the run for their lives. However, she just didn't wish to make a fool out of herself telling a man that she loved him if he doesn't love her in return.

Brooke never thought how easy it would be to show someone affection, let alone to Jack, but since Davy's death, it had been quite easy. They were constantly touching in one way or another; it was almost second nature to them now. While she loved every moment of it, it was just strange in a way, since she'd never seen, or done anything like it.

Brooke tore her eyes away from her eye candy, and made a large salad, offering it to everyone.

"You girls and your rabbit food," Steve joked.

"Well, we have to keep our girlish figures, or we wouldn't be married for much longer," Sally joked right back.

"I would love Brooke no matter what she looks like. I didn't marry her for her looks, I married her for her *heart*."

Brooke blushed deeply, even though she knew he said it to make their marriage more believable.

"See, Steve, that's a real man!" Sally joked.

"Yah, well, you love me and you know it, Sal."

"Yes, I do," she leaned over and kissed him.

Brooke could only look at Jack. He smiled and winked at her. She leaned in and gave him a chaste kiss on the lips, keeping the illusion of a loving couple.

It's not that she wasn't happy being married to him, she just didn't feel it since they hadn't had a ceremony.

After they finished eating, everyone went back into the practice room, but just sat around talking.

"Where do you guys want to go with this? Do you want to just do this for fun, or do you want to get gigs once we get used to each other, maybe go pro later down the road?" Brooke couldn't help but ask.

"Music has always been everything to me," Steve said, carefully watching his wife for some reason. "I would like to take this as far as we can go with it."

"I honestly don't know," Sally piped up. "I just don't think I am good enough. I've never had any kind of lessons, and I think I would only be good for backup."

"Sal was abused horribly growing up; she was told that she would never be good enough for anything, except for a wife."

Brooke shot Jack a questioning look, and he gave an almost imperceptible nod. She told Sally mostly the truth: "Sal, I was with someone before I met Jack who also abused me like that. It took Jack and…a mutual friend to show me that I am good enough. I also have never had any lessons, at all. But Jack and I can help you with that. I think with practice, you will be phenomenal, to be perfectly honest. You have beautiful pitch and control of your voice. If you want, you can come over every day, in fact, all of you can, and we will practice for no less than three hours a day."

"You would do that for me?" she asked, stunned.

"Yes, we would, in a heartbeat!" Jack said.

"Honey, I will drop you off every day before work, and pick you up, if this is what you truly want to do."

She gave an emphatic nod. "Yes, this is what I want," she laughed, and hugged Jack and Brooke. "I don't know why you are being so kind to us, but I love you both already!"

"Sally, you four are the first to welcome us into this town. Jack and I have been here for three weeks, and no one has ever come to the door, or waved to us on the street. We have the love of music in common; therefore, we would walk through the fires of hell for all of you," Brooke said sincerely, pointedly looking at the entire band.

Brooke stood up. "Let's do another song, guys."

Everyone jumped up, making her feel like the unspoken leader. "Do you guys know *What About Love* by *Heart*?

"Oh yah, it's one of our favorites!" Jeremy said.

"One, Two, Three Four." Brooke counted out the beat, and everyone started playing at the same time. She belted it out, mixing the styles of Ann Wilson and Pat Benatar. Sally sang an octave higher than she did, and they rocked out the song!

"Sally, you were perfect!" Brooke ran to her, and hugged her. "You are much better than you thought, and I have to say, sweetie, the person that told you that you are horrible lied to you! And I'm going to prove it!"

She went up to Steve, and whispered into his ear, "*Hold Me* by *Fleetwood Mac.*"

"Oh Brooke, that's perfect!" He smiled, and she ran back to her microphone and stand.

"Sal, you get the lead, it's going to be your song, and the rest of us are going to harmonize with *you*." Brooke nodded to Steve, and he started playing. Everyone gasped for a moment, including Sally, but she sang like a trooper. She went flat in a few notes, but Brooke didn't stop the band, she just let her go. Once the song was over, she looked at Sally. "Sal, this may help. Do not sing in your normal voice. Sing an octave either higher, or lower. That is why you go flat; it is that you subconsciously revert to your speaking voice."

She nodded, beaming. "I love this; you don't know how much I appreciate it. Do you mind if I try a different song though?"

"Not at all, which one do you want to try?"

"I want to do *Crazy for you* by *Madonna.*"

"Oh, that is a good choice!" Brooke praised Sally, and meant it.

She sang backup for Sally, while the guys played. When the song was done, Brooke couldn't speak for a moment, she was so stunned. "Sal, that was beautifully done, you were perfect in pitch, rhythm, and beat. You did a great job! Tomorrow, we're going to step it up, and you're going to do *Vogue*."

Sally beamed. "Do you really think I could be as good as you are, Brooke?"

"You already are. You just need a few lessons. Don't feel bad; I need some also. I don't know how to read music. Everything I have done is from memory. But, with what Jack and I are going to teach you, you will be even better than I am."

"I seriously doubt that, but thank you."

Jack and Brooke sat down in the parlor after everyone left for the night to watch some television, but she couldn't concentrate. Brooke kept thinking about the band, and last night with Jack. That was the heaviest on her mind. To say it had been incredible was an understatement.

"Brooke, what's on your mind? You're just staring off into space, not even watching the television." he asked.

She blushed deeply. "Trust me, you don't want to know."

"Yes, I do….Oh, you're thinking about…."

"Yes, last night." She blushed even harder.

"It's been on my mind all day too. God, Brooke, I have never had anything so phenomenal in my life." He grabbed the remote control and turned the television off. "We need to talk."

"Y….yes, we do," Brooke stammered, suddenly nervous. When a conversation began like that, it never boded well for the one expected to listen.

"Listen, when this is all over, I don't know what it is you want, but I want to stay married. I….I consider you a good….a good friend, and marriages have started off with a lot less."

I can't believe he just said that to me! "So, let me see if I have this right. You said you want to stay married to me because we're good *friends*?"

"Well, yes. Isn't that important in a marriage?"

"So, what was last night then?" She ignored his question. "Am I just a friend with benefits, or was it a charity fuck?"

"No, damn it! You're misunderstanding me…."

"No, I think I understand clearly, *Jack*. If you don't love me, and don't think you ever will, just tell me! I think I deserve that much!" She stood up, and went upstairs, wanting to cry her eyes out, but refused to give him the satisfaction. She grabbed something to change into for tonight and tomorrow, and went into the bedroom across the hall that had been set up just in case they decided to sleep apart. She slammed the door shut, and went over to the bed. She didn't want to look at him, let alone sleep next to him.

She lay on the bed, and curled into a ball, the tears flowing. She would *never* let him know how much he hurt her!

The bedroom door opened slowly. "Brooke, I'm sorry. Please, may I come in?" he asked tenderly.

"What?" she snapped, facing the opposite direction.

"That came out all wrong," he said, coming closer. He sat on the bed next to her, nervous energy coming off of him in waves. "Honey, I honestly don't know what it is I feel for you. I know that whatever it is, it's so damned powerful. But for what it's worth, I do want to stay married to you. If you want a divorce when this is over, I will give it to you, no questions asked. But I have become attached to you. You are a part of me that I didn't know I was missing. I don't want us to part ways, not now, not ever."

She turned around, the tears still streaming down her face. "I don't know what I feel for you either and I never asked for you to tell me. But the way you put it downstairs is that you didn't think you ever would. I don't want to live the rest of my life with someone that isn't in love with me. I did it for seven years; and it was a worse level of hell than you could ever imagine."

"I understand Hope, I truly do." He also had tears streaming down his face. "I hate it that I hurt you. It's killing me."

"Sorry to put it this way, but *good*. You deserve it."

"Yes, I do. Now please come downstairs and watch the movie with me."

Brooke nodded. "Let me wash my face first, and I will be right back down. Actually, let me take a shower."

He went to the door, and put his hand on the handle. "Hope, I have to be honest. I think I am falling in love with you." He walked out of the room.

She scrambled off the bed, and ran after him. "Andy, you can't say something like that and just walk away!" she called.

He startled her when he whipped around and grabbed her. He pulled her to him roughly, and gave her a thorough kiss that set her on fire! He picked her up and took her back to their bedroom. He put her down inside the threshold, and again kissed her, pushing her against the wall. His next words sent her spinning; reeling in a place that she never knew existed. "I am going to brand you. I am going to make you mine!"

"Oh god yes, Andy!" He yanked her jeans off, then all but ripped his own off. His manhood stood tall and thick from between his legs, almost scaring her with its size. She would have been utterly terrified had he not already made love to her once. He lifted her by her ass and impaled her with his length. She wrapped her legs around his powerful hips as she screamed his name. Her fingernails dug deep into his shoulders as he thrust hard, causing such an exquisite pain that she couldn't breathe, couldn't think. Hope knew nothing else except the pleasure that Andy was giving her.

She heard their grunts mixing, and found them laying long way on the bed as he continued to pound himself into her. "Hope, oh god!" He yelled, as he gave one last, brutal thrust. She felt herself career over the edge, and her world exploded as he buried himself into her, spilling his seed deep into her womb. Her back arched as wave after wave of pure, intense pleasure ripped through her. She screamed his name long, loud, the sound reverberating from the walls. Her tears came for a different reason this time, for the emotions that were so foreign to her as they coursed through her veins.

After a few minutes of trying to get his breathing under control, he slipped out, and she moved lengthwise on the bed, making room for him. He lay beside her, and she laid her head on his chest, as their breathing slowly returned to normal.

"Now do you understand how I feel?" he chuckled.

"I heard that loud and clear," she smiled widely.

"Oh, before I forget again, I want you to take your purse with you wherever we go from now on. One of the Marshals came by early this morning while you were still sleeping. He dropped off two tracking chips. One is to be kept in your pocket or pinned to your bra at all times, and the other is in your purse. If Davenport gets ahold of you, we will be able to find you."

"Okay, is there something going on that I don't know about?"

"He hasn't been seen in the Chicagoland area for the last three days. He was seen talking to the guy that I suspected was the mole. It turns out that I was right. The mole is Davenport's cousin. Davenport's cousin has been arrested, and bail has been denied."

"Oh god, he could be coming here!" Brooke sat up in full panic mode. "We have to get out!"

"No, Brooke. We are well-protected. There are Marshals on the property watching the house as we speak. We are fine. If Davenport even sneezes toward the house, he will either wind up in jail, or dead, preferably the latter."

She shuddered at the thought of having to bury Jack too. That thought almost sent her into a full blown panic attack! However, it occurred to her that since he had worked for the Bureau, he had the training in all manners of defense. Nick truly didn't stand a chance. She found herself hoping that Jack put a bullet through Nick's forehead. "Wait, didn't the Marshals say that they left us something for defense in the nightstand?"

"Yes, come to think about it, they did!"

They went for their nightstands at the same time. Brooke found a black, shiny, SIG Sauer .38.

"Jack…." She showed him the pistol.

"I have the rounds." He pulled out a box of ammunition. "Do you know how to load and use it?"

She took the box, grabbed a bullet, and shoved it into the chamber. She then pulled the hammer back, and handed it back to him, handle first. "You tell me."

He looked at her with another impressed grin on his face, and released the hammer. "I think we should keep it in there, just in case. There is also a clip in the stand. I am going to load it."

She sighed, "Just give me the damned thing, and I'll load it."

She grabbed the clip, took the pistol, and looked at him. She took the bullet out of the chamber, shoved the clip into place, cocked back the hammer to reload the chamber, and slowly released it, with the safety on, all without looking away from Jack. She handed it back to him, again with the handle out.

"What a woman!" Andy breathed.

"Honey, my father was a Sergeant in the Army. He taught me well. I can take one of these apart and put it back together in sixty seconds flat. Dad made sure of it. I just haven't done it in a while," she shrugged.

"Is there anything you *can't* do?"

"Yes, I can't survive if Nick kills you," she said, looking at the pistol.

Brooke put it back in the drawer, and lay back in the bed. He pulled her flush against him, and held her there tightly.

"I won't survive if he kills you either. I wouldn't want to," he said softly in her ear.

"Andy?" she asked, looking down at the blanket, picking lint off of it.

"Yah?" he returned sleepily.

"I think I'm falling in love with you too," she said, and reached over, shutting off the lamp. She scooted down into the covers and he wrapped his arms around her again, and whispered into her ear, "That is the best news I heard in my entire life."

Jack woke the next morning, smiling ear to ear. Brooke still lay next to him, sleeping like the dead. He lay there for a bit longer and just watched her.

"Davy, wherever you are, I thank you for this angel, my man!" he whispered, caressing her beautiful face with the back of his hand. She gave a low moan and a slight smile, leaning into his touch.

Mother Nature started torturing him with a full bladder, so he got up and emptied it, then brushed his teeth. He went downstairs to start making breakfast and noticed they were out of some things that they were going to need for the next few days. He didn't want to leave Brooke alone in the house for even a moment, so he decided when she woke up they would go to the grocery store.

He stood with his hands on the counter, thinking about last night. He wanted to jump for joy knowing that she was falling for him. Hell, he wanted to go to the nearest mountain top, and shout out to the world: "Hope McLeod is falling in love with me, and I love her too!"

Only, she wasn't Hope McLeod any more, and not just in name. She had come a long way in the last few months. She went from a shy, introverted victim to an outgoing tough-as-nails survivor, one that didn't take any bullshit from anyone! He never would have thought it was possible in such a short time! However, it felt like an entire lifetime ago that he first saw her lying in the hospital room in a coma. Hell, it was a lifetime ago! They both had changed!

He no longer had Caleb's death on his shoulders. The day she made him see that it wasn't his fault, it felt like the weight of the world had been lifted off.

He went into the ballroom where all the instruments were set up, completely alone. He went over and touched her microphone that she used last night. Damn, that woman could sing! He thought about the first time he heard her; he could barely speak for the shock!

That woman had perfect pitch, rhythm, and control, which was something that most have to train years to achieve! And her range.... dear god, she had at least a five-octave range! She could go from singing Genesis to Whitney Houston without skipping a beat! She was as much of a powerhouse as Joan Jett or Pat Benatar! Brooke could really go places with her voice, if she wasn't in so much physical danger right now. Maybe once this was over, she could send *Dead or Alive* straight up to the top, and hopefully take him with her! He never thought about going pro in the music industry until he lost his job with the FBI. Now, if he wasn't thinking about Brooke or the situation they were in, he was thinking that he wanted to make music full time, and it was all because of her. He was also quite impressed with the way she gave Sally lessons. Damn, that woman can sing too, she just needed a little self-confidence, and Hope was helping her, even though she was going through her own brand of hell. *What a woman!*

He picked up his Stratocaster, and started playing at chords, something he hasn't done since he was in high school. He used to be good at writing music, just not the lyrics. He stopped playing when he realized that he was still plugged into the amp. He unplugged it so he didn't inadvertently wake Brooke.

"It's okay, Jack, go ahead and play." She padded in, covered in her robe with her eyes still droopy from sleep. "I think I will watch you instead of singing."

"It's just some stuff I played around with in High School." He put the guitar back in its stand. "How did you sleep?"

"Like a rock," she smiled, and yawned.

He went over to her and took her into his arms, giving her a slow, gentle kiss. "Good morning, Sweetheart."

She gave a long, pleasure-filled moan. "Good morning, Jack."

"I've been doing some thinking. I want us to try and go pro with the music. I hate sitting here doing nothing. Yes, we are set for life, as are our children, but I've never been lazy, I have to work. I can't go back into law enforcement, it's too risky, but I want to make music. It has always been my first love, and it helps me to de-stress."

She sighed in a way that he didn't know how to take it. "I know you're damn good on that guitar, Jack. I heard you play some stuff yesterday that told me you should have been on the circuit long ago. As for me, I am not good enough for the professional circuit. I told Sally the truth last night when I said I didn't know how to read music, or write it. I honestly don't think you want to cover someone else's music for the rest of your life."

"Okay, then once you wake up, you and I will start your lessons. I want you to feel completely comfortable should you decide to do this."

"I would love to. We will just have to wait and see."

"Are you sure?" he asked, wary, but hope shining in his eyes. "I don't want to do anything that is going to make you uncomfortable."

She gave him a wan smile, and sighed, "I can't remember when I have been happier than I am when I am singing. The only exceptions to that are when I am with you, and when Davy was alive. You and the band are the only things I have to look forward to now. I don't have my family anymore, and I won't get to see my niece grow up. I won't be able to see her take her first steps, go to school, take her to get her prom dress, get married and have her own children. And I really miss my mother. I have to make my own family now. I will never see mine again." A lone tear fell from her eyes, and slid down her cheek. He pulled her face to his chest, keeping his hand on the back of her head as his heart ached for her.

She was right; she really had nothing to look forward to. It was a wonder, and a miracle she hadn't had a nervous breakdown yet. She didn't even seem close, but, strength comes from when impossible situations are met and overcome, and she had overcome a lot.

He kissed the top of her forehead. "Come on, put on something nice. You and I are going to go out for the day, just the two of us."

"Where are we going?" she asked, wiping the tear from her cheek.

"New Orleans. We are going to go to the Garden District and the French Quarter again. I want to try some of those beignets, and take my wife on a date."

"I have to call Sally and let her know that we have to go out for the day." She smiled, and ran upstairs. He followed her so that he could change too. She looked through the closet, rummaged through her sparse dresser, then sat on the bed with her head in her hands. "I have to go clothes shopping. I am tired of wearing the same things time after time. I left everything in Maywood."

He laughed, "We will take the van then. I think we both are going to need to get new clothes, I don't have much either. We'll go over to North Shore Square."

"Okay, sounds good to me. I think I also want to get a haircut and coloring. I haven't had one since way before the accident."

"If I may make a suggestion…go red. It will fit your temperament," he smiled.

"Are you saying I have a lot of fire?" she asked, a wide smile on her face.

"Oh yes, Baby, that's exactly what I'm saying." His voice turned low, husky as his eyes dragged themselves up and down her body.

"Can I just put on a pair of jeans for the shopping, and we can come home, change clothes, and go?"

"Oh, I suppose," he said, acting like it was a big deal. Fact was he liked her in jeans. She had a nice ass, and he liked to stare at it.

"I…er….would also like to get clothes to wear for gigs."

"What are you thinking?" he asked, cocking an eyebrow.

"I'm thinking leather, lots of leather."

Inwardly he moaned at the thought of her wearing leather. She was sexy enough in jeans, but she was going to be positively devastating in leather. He was going to punch holes in his poor guitar, and he wouldn't be using his fists. "Brooke, I think you are purposefully trying to drive me insane," he laughed.

"Maybe I am." She also laughed and grabbed a pair of jeans out of the closet. He snuck up behind her, and as she bent over to put them on, he grabbed her waist, and pulled her into his erection. She gasped, and he moaned at how good she felt. She had a way of turning him on like no other woman had ever been able to do. He could never get enough of her no matter how many years they would be together. Then he had an idea; it would be painful, but the result would be worth it.

"Let's wait until tonight. I know we both want it, but the wait would be worth it."

"Oh, now that's just sheer cruelty, Jack," she complained.

"Yes, but if we do anything now, we're never going to get out of the house, because I am going to make love to you slowly, taking hours."

Her right knee gave out, and she caught herself before she could go down. "Then we had better get a move on, hadn't we? And you can forget about New Orleans. We will go to the mall, shop, eat, and then we're coming home!"

She threw on her jeans, then oh god, she dropped her robe. He watched her hips gently sway, and looked at her spine as it showed through the satiny skin of her back. He wanted to pick her up, throw her on the bed and ram himself home until they both were weak and shaking.

She went over to her dresser, grabbed a bra, and put it on, covering her perfectly formed breasts. She put the tracking device inside the bra and threw on a shirt. "What are you doing standing there watching me? You aren't exactly getting dressed either."

She grabbed her hair brush, and ran it through her long hair, tying it up in a ponytail. "I guess I will have to leave the room for you to get dressed." She threw him a sassy smile, and grabbed her makeup case. As she passed Jack, he grabbed her and gave her a kiss that promised what he would do to her later. She dropped her makeup case, and wrapped her arms around him, pressing herself against his erection.

They both moaned, and she broke off the kiss. "I'd better go and put my makeup on."

"Yes, good idea. I'm about to throw you down on the bed and say to hell with the shopping."

He couldn't help but to stare at her backside as she walked away. God that woman was dazzling! She could make the pope forget about mass!

He took a deep breath and calmed his furious hormones. "This was your idea, stupid!" he chided himself, and dressed.

A little bit later, she came back in and put her makeup case back in the closet. "I think I may need glasses. It was a bit hard to see to put some of my makeup on."

"We will find you an Optometrist, and get it taken care of. I should probably have an exam too."

"I am actually thinking about contact lenses. They've recently come out with soft ones; my sister has them."

"Well, let's get going. If we don't, trust me, we're not leaving any time soon."

She grabbed her purse and threw it over her shoulder, purposefully swinging her rear end to the point where she looked double jointed. He gave another moan and followed her. She was going to torture him for the rest of the day.

Within just a few minutes, they were pulling into the mall parking lot. For being such a small town, the place was packed. Brooke bought herself some more jewelry since she had to leave what Davy bought her in Chicago, along with some more clothing, makeup, and shoes. She and Jack went into Dillard's for men, and she insisted on spending an obscene amount of money on him. Then again, he paid for her stuff, so she thought it was only right. She bought him two suits, one in blue and one in black, along with ties, jeans, dress shirts, and T-shirts. They took what they had bought so far to the van, and went back inside.

She then grinned evilly, and went inside Victoria's Secret. Oh hell no, he's not going in there! She will do nothing but torture him! "Babe, before you go fully into that store, I am going to take a look inside Sears. We need tools for the house."

"Ok, hon." She gave him another sly smile, and kissed him. "Just wait until we get home." She gave him an impertinent wink, and went inside.

He found her soon after inside the Regis hair salon, looking through the books. "What are you going to go with?" he asked, curious.

"I don't know yet, I'm thinking of a long bob, to my shoulders, and coloring it strawberry blond. Since I never colored my hair before, I am likely going to have it donated to cancer victims."

They called her back into the chairs, and she came back out three hours later looking like a completely different woman. The strawberry blonde complemented her, as did the cut. He could do nothing but stare, she was positively stunning!

"What do you think?" she asked shyly.

"I think you are the most beautiful woman that has ever existed," he breathed.

"Jack, what's the date today?" she asked as they left the salon. She knew his birthday was coming up soon, but for some reason, today's date completely escaped her.

"September twenty-second," he answered.

Oh, it's tomorrow! "Honey, could you do a favor for me and go put these in the van? There's one more thing I have to get."

"Brooke, I know what you're doing, and I don't want you to buy me anything for my birthday."

"Tough. Shit. I'm going to do it anyway." She gave him a light kiss and walked away.

A few minutes later, she came out carrying a long box with a handle. "I know it's a day early, but I am going to get a few more things for you later. I want to give this to you now. Happy Birthday, my sweet husband." She shyly handed him the box.

He took it, but before he looked at it, he had to let her know something. "Honey, you didn't have to get anything for me. You have already given me so much that is worth more than any physical gifts. That means everything to me."

Her eyebrows knitted together in confusion. "What are you talking about, Jack? I haven't given you anything but three months of fear."

"You gave me you, Brooke. These last few months were not filled with only fear, but also with utter elation. There is no one else I would rather spend the rest of my life with. There isn't anyone else on earth that I would want to grow old with, have children with, and hold until I am dead and gone." He leaned down and kissed her. "But thank you. I do appreciate this, and I want you to know that I appreciate *you*!" He put the box on the hood of the van, and opened it.

He sucked a deep breath in through his teeth as he pulled out a Civil War collector's sword. His head shot over to Brooke. "This is gorgeous!"

"It is galvanized steel. It isn't battle ready and will break if it is used, but I thought it would look good over the fireplace in the sitting room."

He put the sword into the back of the van with the rest of their stuff, and took Brooke into his arms, then whispered into her ear, "Thank you, Baby. I love it." He felt her shudder a bit, and held her even closer. It was on his lips to tell her how much he loved her, how much she meant to him, but he just couldn't bring himself to do it. He would lay down his life for her if it came down to it. His heart swelled with pride that she had put so much thought into his present, that all he wanted to do was hold her, for the rest of his life.

He remembered thinking that he wanted someone just like her. Now, he had her, and he wasn't going to ever take advantage of her, or purposefully hurt her in any way. He just wanted to worship her as she deserved, and never give her a reason to doubt how he felt. He pulled away awkwardly, and wiped away the tears that had formed in his eyes.

"Come on Babe, let's go get some lunch." His voice came out husky, shaky.

He found a steak house where the lighting was low, and they got a booth in the back corner so they could be alone. She sat beside him, and without thinking about it he put his arm around her, pulling her close. She rested her head on his shoulder while they shared a menu. For the first time in his life, he was content, complete, a cold case solved.

The server came and took their order, and Brooke ordered a strawberry daiquiri with her lunch. Once the server left, she kissed his cheek, and excused herself to go to the bathroom. He couldn't help but watch her as she walked away. God, she has a fine ass! His zipper tightened around him as he felt himself harden. So help him, when he got her home, he was going to make her orgasm eight ways from Sunday!

A few minutes later, she came back, her hands still slightly damp from being washed. She put one on his thigh, and leaned into him again. He slightly shifted, trying to relieve the pressure behind his zipper.

"Am I crowding you?" she asked sitting up.

"Oh no, you could never crowd me." He smiled, and discreetly rearranged himself as he returned his other arm to where it belonged, around her.

Belonged? Yes, it did belong around her, just as his heart officially belonged to her.

"Here is your strawberry daiquiri and your coke. Your dinner will be out shortly," the server said, startling Jack out of his head.

"Thank you," Brooke said, smiling innocently up at the male server. He looked at Brooke a bit too long, raising the fine hairs on the back of Jack's neck.

"I think that will be all. Thank you," Jack said pointedly, his jealousy meter spiking a serious woody, one that was as big as the one behind his zipper.

The smart waiter beat feet away from the booth.

About ten minutes later, their lunch showed up, and Jack felt a cool rush of air as Brooke sat up to be able to eat. Damn, he didn't realize how she warmed him.

He sat in a seat three booths back from Hope and that bastard she's banging now. It didn't take her long to get with two other men. One has been taken care of, now it's this bloke, her, and that mutant she is carrying. He is going to follow her around for the rest of her life, and take out anyone she ever gets with, and her spawn, until she comes back to him! She is his, damn it! No one lays a finger on her but him! He owns her lock, stock, and barrel. She will pay for what she has done to him!

He watched as their waiter brought out a cake for the pig that she was with, and the staff sang "Happy birthday". He watched as the fucker turned beet red, and Hope laughed.

He heard the retard say; "I'll get you back for this! You have a birthday too!"

Laugh it up, asswipe; this will be your last birthday!

He spent the last week getting to know this podunk town, biding his time until he could get his revenge on her. If it hadn't been for Allan, he would never have found the whore, and by tonight she will *be his again, or she will be dead.*

"I can't believe you did that, Babe! When did you get the time to let them know? Jack asked Brooke as they were leaving the restaurant.

"When I went to the bathroom to wash my hands, I took our server aside and told him. It's my revenge for you being such an asshole to me for those two months," she laughed.

"I think we're even now." He couldn't help but laugh with her.

"Oh, not nearly, Jack. That one was for the blowup at the party when I got my casts off. I still have fifty-nine more days to go!"

Jack pulled out of the parking lot, and looked down at the gas gauge. "Oh, we're almost at half a tank; I'm going to have to fill her up. I know how you are about that," he smiled at her.

Once they were done, he headed back toward the house. He was looking so forward to the rest of the day, spending it with her, worshipping her. That was all he wanted for his birthday to begin with. The best present he could ever have hoped for was her.

He turned on the street that led to the driveway, and a large SUV pulled over into their lane, and headed straight for them! He heard Brooke scream his name just before he jerked the wheel over. The van veered off, and went nose first into a deep ditch, and Jack saw stars as he banged his head into the steering wheel. He heard her scream once more just as total blackness took over.

CHAPTER 12

Brooke awoke in a dingy, disgusting motel room, tied spread-eagle to the bed. "It's about fucking time you woke up. You always were lazy," a familiar voice cut through the fog.

Oh dear gods, Nick! "I have never been half as lazy as you are, asshole!" She was rewarded with a stunning blow to the jaw. She saw stars and tasted blood, but it still didn't deter her from standing up for herself.

"Yah, sure Nick, hit me while I'm tied up. Are you afraid I can fight back now? God, you are such a poor excuse for a man, let alone a human being."

Nick's face turned red with fury. "I am more of a man than that sorry piece of shit you're banging now, you whore!"

"If I am a whore, it's because you turned me into one. After all, you forced me to sleep with people for money, Nick."

All she could think about was Jack. Oh god, let him still be alive! She sent up a silent prayer for the man she really did love.

"Bitch, I am going to torture you before I kill you! You are *mine*! How dare you leave me? How dare you have me *arrested*?"

"I didn't, Nick. You threw me into a coma when you hit me. You fucked up and got yourself arrested."

"You ruined my life, bitch, and you will pay!" His eyes dull with insanity, he turned around, grabbed a gun from the beat-to-shit dresser, and moved toward Brooke.

"So, you're going to shoot me when I'm tied up? How cowardly of you. But then I can't expect much more from a man that beats up on women. Every last one of those kinds of men are weaklings." She has to keep him busy, keep him talking. If she could do that, then she might have a chance. If not, she was dead.

"Are you calling me a coward?"

She rolled her eyes. "Gee, do you think so? I said all men that beat women are cowards! Even doctors think so, or mine wouldn't have called the police on you for sending me into a coma, you stupid shit!"

"So now I'm *stupid?*" His voice rose to a fever pitch, almost screeching.

"Hey, he finally gets it right! Give the boy a kewpie doll!"

His eyes narrowed to fine slits. "I'm not that stupid; I killed fire boy and found you and that sick pig you're banging even though you changed names. Seriously Hope, what the hell kind of name is *Brooke?*"

"Oh, so you admit killing Davy then? God, you really don't have a brain! Not only that, we are not together anymore. What I do with my life is none of your business! Besides, he isn't my lover, he's my *husband!*" She couldn't help but bait him, and she completely ignored the asinine comment about her new name.

"Bitch, you are mine! You are my property, and you will come home with me, or I will kill you right here, right now! I also told you to never cut or color your hair! How dare you!"

"Fuck you, Nick. It's my hair; I have to take care of it! As for you taking me back to Chicago, that will be hard to do while I am tied to this bed."

"So you will come home with me then?" he asked, surprised.

"Y…yes, of course. I just wanted you to see that I felt like I was being taken advantage of and abused."

"I have never abused you, Hope. If you would just remember your place and stay in it, I will never have to beat you."

"Where is that place, Nick? This time I want everything laid out on the table before I jump back into it. I don't want to take the chance on being hit again." She would just have to keep him talking long enough, and get him to untie her so she could get the gun on the top of the dresser. She knew that Jack and the U.S. Marshals were coming, and when they burst through the door, Nick would be stupid enough to go for the gun just two feet from him. Jack wouldn't shoot as long as he was anywhere around her; which gave Nick a distinct advantage over him.

"Your place is to do what I tell you to do, when I tell you to do it. This is a man's world; even the *Bible* says that women are to be complacent, to listen to their men. First you listen to your father, then to your husband. Your brain is smaller than a man's is; therefore, you know a lot less. You are also weaker than a man is, and are highly emotional. You know this, Hope. We have discussed it at length."

"The only thing I know for certain Nick, is that you are so full of shit. You want to keep women under your heel. What you don't realize is that even back in biblical times, women ruled the household. They paid the bills, kept the house clean, killed for food, kept the children in line, and still had time to work in the fields. We were forced to become slaves for not only the hierarchies, but also for our men. That was bullshit. Just because our brains are smaller, doesn't mean we're not as smart; it means that our skulls are smaller. Now untie me, or you are going to have to sleep in a wet bed, because my bladder is full."

Nick untied her hands and feet. She slowly stood up, rubbing the circulation back into her wrists, and slowly lowered her arms which felt like they were permanently stuck above her head from lying like that for god only knows how long.

Oh God, let her be able to get back to Jack! Brooke swore that she would never take advantage of him, and she would love him with everything she is for the rest of their lives! Please let him still be alive! Don't let her lose another that she loves, she would never live through it! Jack was her whole world, her life, her *love*!

Different points of the last few months with him ran through Brooke's head like a movie, from his anger in the beginning, until today, when he cried from her birthday present to him. He touched a place deep within her that she never knew existed, and thawed her frozen heart. Davy was right, she did love Jack! If they were still alive at the end of the day, she would tell him! He would never have a reason to doubt it!

"As soon as you go to the restroom, we can leave for home. It's time, Hope," Nick broke through her reverie.

She wasn't going to go anywhere with this poor excuse of a man, but she had to stall as long as she could for Jack to get here. "Well, you paid for the motel room for the night; it would be a shame to waste the money. Let's just stay here tonight and head back to Chicago tomorrow."

"That's a good idea, Hope. For once, you're using your head."

She heard the police cars pull up out front, so to distract Nick, she said: "Nick, I *have* to go to the restroom. Will you please move out from in front of the bed so I could get past you?"

He moved between the beds. She went past him, and quickly grabbed the gun. Whipping around, she pointed it at him. "Do not move, you sorry sack of shit! You put me through hell for seven years, and you really think I'm going back with you? You are a fucking idiot!"

"Give me the gun, Hope, before you blow your leg off. You don't know how to use one," he said quietly, with more than a touch of fear.

"Fuck. You," she said, meaning every word. "Even if I didn't know anything about guns, which I have forgotten more than you will ever know, any idiot knows that I couldn't possibly miss from this distance." She pointed the gun at his junk. "Do you really want to take that chance?"

"Hope, you're acting crazy. Give me the gun." He started toward her, and she raised the gun, squeezing the trigger. The shot echoed in the room, almost blowing her eardrums out. He staggered back a couple of feet and landed against the nightstand when the bullet entered his chest. He looked at her, stunned for a heartbeat, and fell to the floor, dead.

She dropped the gun as the door flew open, and Marshals rolled in, with Jack in tow. She raised her hands in surrender, as her knees wobbled, and the tears started streaming down her face.

"Andy....he....he...." She couldn't get the words out.

"I know, love, I know." He wrapped his arms around her. "You couldn't wait for me to get here? You just had to steal all the fun?" he joked, and her knees collapsed.

"Whoa, I've got you, love."

"I....I just killed someone," she said out loud. "Oh god, Andy, I just took Nick's life!" She looked down at him, his eyes staring blankly up at her, accusing her of murder.

"Mrs. Connor, we need to ask you a few questions," said one of the Marshals as he came up to her. Hope answered his questions as honestly as she could under the circumstances.

"Ma'am, it is clearly an open and shut case of self-defense. It is over for you now. You have your life back, only with a new identity. Live it to the fullest, Mrs. Connor," said the supervisor of the Marshals.

"I intend to, thank you," she said, wiping her cheeks with her fingers. She didn't know if she would ever get over the fact that she took a human life, but she didn't have any other choice. Nick was going to kill her, and since it was either him or her, she had to make damn sure it was him.

Jack had woken from the accident to find Brooke gone from the van, and he went to a house near the scene. He begged to use their phone, and called the Marshal's office to tell them what had happened. His head burned where he had hit it on the steering wheel, but he didn't give a damn if he was bleeding or not, he had to get to Brooke!

He wasn't nearly as afraid as he had been when he heard that gunshot come from the room! His mind immediately went to finding her on the floor, dead. He knew now that he loved her, and he always had. If she was dead, he would tear Davenport apart with his bare hands, and then pull a suicide by cop.

When he saw her alive, her hands in the air in surrender, he felt like crying with relief. Instead, he went to her and just held her, grateful that she was still alive. He could feel them both shaking, and she fell apart. He could feel the hysteria rising up in her, and he knew he had to get her out of there as fast as possible. She didn't need to be there to see his body anymore. He turned them toward the door, and….

"Newcomb!" a familiar voice called from the vicinity of the bathroom. There, in front of the mirror stood Allan Collins, Davenport's cousin, and FBI mole, a .45 aimed right at Jack's chest.

"Collins, what the hell are you doing here?"

"Getting revenge for all the years I put into the bureau, getting passed over for promotion after promotion, while little pukes like you get everything handed to you on a silver platter! Hell, you even get the girl, don't you?"

Jack put Brooke behind him. "Damn straight I do!" Damn it, he had become too complacent without his sidearm, and didn't bother to grab it before he left the house.

"Collins, I worked for every promotion I got. You just wanted to sit behind a desk, not wanting to do paperwork, or any part of your job. Why would you expect to be promoted?"

"You fucking liar! I did more than any of you fucking field ops!"

"You're right Collins; you did a lot more than we did, in getting people killed! My best friend is dead because of you!"

"So is your old partner, you sorry sack of shit!" he lowered his sidearm to brag.

Jack's blood froze in his veins. "What did you say?"

"You heard me, *I killed Caleb Sessions*! I broke into his house, made him call you to tell you what was going on at the bureau headquarters, then as you pulled up to comfort your little butt buddy, I shot him in the head, planted the gun, and ran out the back door! I know the Mob infiltrated the FBI, because *I AM THE MOLE!* You, that fucktwit Davy, and that skank behind you took everything from me! My cousin, my job, my *freedom*! Now, I'm taking her, and I am also taking your life!"

In slow motion, he brought the gun up, and a loud retort came from behind Jack. Collins fell, blood seeping through the belly of his shirt, dead before he hit the floor. Jack whipped around, and the love of his life was lying on the floor behind him, holding a smoking pistol in her hands.

He could only chuckle. "That makes twice you've taken my fun, Babe!"

"Next time, get the hell out of my way!" she demanded in a weak, shaky voice, and promptly passed out from shock, throwing Jack into a terrified frenzy.

When she regained consciousness, he got her the hell out of there. He decided on the way home that he was going to tell her exactly how he felt, and then ask her to truly be his wife by having a ceremony. Not another moment will go by that she didn't feel exactly how much he loved her.

Once they walked through the front door, she turned to him. "Andy, I need to talk to you."

"I need to talk to you, but you first," he said, his heart sinking. Here it comes, she wants a divorce.

"Andy, I love you, with my entire being. When I woke up tied to the bed, I knew then exactly how much I love you, and I didn't want to die before I had the chance to tell you."

His heart leapt with joy! She loved him! "Oh god, I love you too, Hope, Brooke, whichever name you want to go by now. I have loved you since the first moment I saw you in the hospital bed in a coma. I just couldn't do anything, since my best friend wanted you. I just don't operate like that. Now, I know I can't live without you. You are the part of me that I never knew had been missing." He ran his hands through his hair, and nervously got down on one knee. "Hope, please marry me, for real. I want us to have the works. I want us to *feel* married."

"I already do, Andy. Yes, I know I loved Davy, but that was in such a different way than I love you. It is like night and day, just like the two of you were. Yes, I will marry you, but I already feel it, right here." She put her palm on his heart. "You are the air I breathe; every beat of my heart belongs to you."

He took her into his arms, and kissed her, full of all the love and devotion in his heart. "I love you, Hope."

"I love you too, Andy."

The front door flew open, and he shoved her behind him, ready to take a bullet for her. Instead of it being someone that wanted the two of them dead, Steve and the rest of the band came barreling into the parlor.

"We heard what happened, are you two ok?" Steve demanded.

Andy looked at him, stunned.

"Yah, good news travels fast in small towns," Sally said, hugging Jack.

Brooke came out from behind Jack. "Yes, we're fine." She looked up at him, and said, "I have to tell them. I can't keep this up. They are our closest friends."

He nodded, understanding.

"Maybe you guys should sit down; this may take a while."

Together, Brooke and Jack told the story of what led them to this area. Shock registered in each of their eyes, right into the part where Brooke had to kill Davenport and Collins to stay alive.

Sally jumped up and took Brooke into her arms, throwing her off guard. "So you're not angry with us for lying to you?" she asked, shocked.

"How could we be? You had to lie to protect everyone, especially yourselves!" Sally said. "Brooke, I am really glad you killed those bastards, they deserved it."

"Thank you Sally. Oh, there is one more thing. Jack and I are going to have a wedding ceremony, and I would love it if you would stand up with me. We didn't have one; we were only told we were married legally."

Sally gasped, and covered her mouth with her hand, tears welling up in her eyes. "I would be honored!"

"So Jack, what was your original name then, you never told us," Steve asked.

"It was originally Andrew Jacob Newcomb the Third." He smiled, wrapping his arms around Brooke's shoulders, pulling her close to him. He kissed her forehead, just reveling in the fact that not only was the nightmare over, but she was strong enough to end it and live to tell the tale. A more perfect woman had never been born for this tired old cop.

"Newcomb? Was your mother's name Caroline Newcomb?" Steve asked.

"Yes, why?" Jack asked, confused.

"Was her maiden name Beauchamp?"

"Come to think of it, it was, yes."

Steve laughed, "Jack, you are the only living descendent of the Beauchamp's. This house is yours anyway, by inheritance!"

EPILOGUE

June 25, 1990

Brooke, Jack, Sally, Steve, and the guys approached the stage at one of the more prominent bars in New Orleans. They had come in earlier in the day to set up their instruments, then left to get food. While Brooke looked out onto the packed floor, the guys tuned their instruments, and Sally came up from behind her. "Are you scared?"

"I'm absolutely petrified. I don't know if I can do this! What if I screw things up but good? This isn't just my life here, this involves you guys too!"

"Brooke, if the producer didn't think we were any good from that demo we sent, he would never have offered to hear us in person. Trust me, you're not going to flub. You are too good!"

Once the guys were done, Jack approached the girls. "Are you ready?"

Brooke could only nod, still scared shitless. He grabbed her hand and gave it a reassuring squeeze. "I love you."

"I love you too, Jack. Let's get this over with." Brooke grabbed the mic with trembling hands, and took a deep, cleansing breath. The people in the bar started clapping and cheering when everyone noticed they were ready. She took another deep breath, and started the opening refrain of *Shadows of the Night*. With every gig, they started with this song, to pay tribute to Davy for helping to change their lives for the better, and for bringing Jack and Brooke together. It was because of him that they were even standing here with their hearts still beating. The further they got into the song, the more relaxed she became, until she was finally able to just explode all over the stage.

They finished the first set and took a break. Brooke looked out into the audience, and saw five familiar faces that brought her to her knees, tears streaming down her face. Her mother, sister, Kenny, Tristan, and Chris were all sitting at a table together, clapping as if they had just heard the best band ever playing, tears coursing down their own faces. She jumped off the stage, and bolted to them at full speed. The crowd moved aside, and she hugged her family tightly. Brooke never thought she would see them again, and it made the last year of hell worth it, knowing they were all perfectly happy and healthy.

"Wow, Hope, you look great!" Kenny offered, hugging her.

"Yah Ken, I'm surprised too, since she begged the driver of the truck that hit her for the maximum amount of pain before he hit her. Guess he didn't deliver," Grace said sardonically while looking at her sister.

Brooke couldn't help but laugh. "That's it, Grace! Looks like you finally got the hang of sarcasm!"

"Brooke Connor?" she heard a vaguely familiar voice behind her.

She turned around and saw a younger looking man with long, flowing brown hair and impossibly bright blue eyes. She wiped her tears, and said, "Yes, I am Brooke."

"Let's go up to the microphone, all of us." He looked at her family, and at the rest of the band. They followed him, and he took the mic. "I am Trevor Jacquard, a music producer. I want to sign *Dead or Alive* to a five album deal with my company! I have the contract right here if you guys wanted to take some time to look it over."

Brooke's mother and sister broke out into ecstatic screams, leading the rest of the crowd in loud cheers. Brooke shook the man's hand, and took the contract. The rest of the band approached her, Jack wrapping his arms around her waist. They hugged, unable to believe this was actually happening. Jack and Brooke looked over the contract and decided not to wait. It was all in order, exactly as was discussed on the phone with the gentleman. The whole band signed it, and Brooke took the mic. "Mr. Jacquard, on behalf of the band, we accept the contract. Ladies and gentlemen, we are on our way, thanks to you!" The room again erupted in loud applause and cheers. "I also have a surprise for two members of the audience. Tristan and Chris, you are coming with us! You are not getting left behind again!" The boys closed their eyes, and leaned their heads back, stunned. When they opened them again, they were filled with tears.

Jack started the opening riff for *Celebration* by *Kool and the Gang*. Chris and Tris rushed to the instruments while Sally and Steve took their places, and they rocked the house while the audience and Trevor Jacquard did the parts of the song that involved the cheering. Brooke always believed in getting the audience involved in a gig, since they sang with them anyway. She loved to show them how much the band appreciated their loyalty, and love for them.

By the end of the night, they were all exhausted, and Brooke and Jack brought her family, along with Tris and Chris back to the mansion. They filed into the ballroom, where they had set one corner up as a relaxing zone with the leather furniture that had been in Davy's living room.

"Hope, I am so proud of you. Nick put you through so much, yet you overcame it all with such strength and dignity. Now look at you. Your dreams since you were a little girl have finally come true. I remember when you were little, you would run through the house with a hairbrush in your hands, pretending it was a microphone, and singing your little heart out. I wanted to get you voice lessons then, but I just couldn't afford it," Mom said, her eyes filling up with tears.

"Mommy, it's okay. I know you couldn't afford it. You did the very best you could for Gracie and me, and you did a great job raising us. I love you so much! I'm just glad grandma was able to give me the piano lessons." Brooke stood up and hugged her mom, and opened her arms for her sister. The three of them stood there for such a long time, hugging and crying. Her life was complete, a brain teaser solved, and she didn't think she could be happier. Hope had her family back, the love of her life at her side, and a career where she was going to make her mark on the world. She had her ultimate revenge on Nick; she made something of herself. She then had an idea, something well-deserved. "What do you say that we all take a vacation? We don't start recording our album for a few months, and I just want to spend some time with my family. After this last year, we deserve it. By the way, Tris, Chris, and the rest of *Dead or Alive* are our family too. Maybe we could take a cruise to Hawaii, or we could go to Vegas."

"I agree. We could use this time for me to get to know them, and for you to catch up."

A collective gasp resounded. "Are you serious?" Tristan asked. "You would take all of us on a vacation?"

Brooke stood up, and kneeled in front of him. "Tris, I want to explain something to you. Andy and I didn't leave because we wanted to. We didn't want to leave you behind, but we didn't have a choice. Our lives were on the line, and because you knew us, yours would have been too. To make up for what we did, and to show you that you are a part of the family, hell yes, we will take you!"

"Hope, we knew what was going on, remember? Yes, we believed the news reports that you and Andy were dead, but we found proof that you weren't when our bank accounts started showing up with money out of the clear blue. That was how Andy helped us to survive while you were away. There was no other contact, nothing, until he called to tell us that the danger was over, and sent the tickets."

"You two are like the little brothers that I wasn't able to have after mine died so long ago. I love you guys!" she said, and hugged them.

Once they broke apart, she wanted to do something for her mother, and told the rest of the band to fall back, she wanted to do this *a Capella*. "Mom, I am going to put this on the album, but I want you to know that it is dedicated to you, for all I put you through when I dated Nick, and to show you that I love you." She grabbed her sister, and whispered the song in her ear. They harmonized beautifully, singing a cheesy but lovely song by *The Carpenters, On Top Of the World,* a song Mom used to sing to them when they were little. By the time they finished, tears were falling down everyone's faces like rain. "I love you, Mommy."

Brooke's mom stood up, and grabbed on to Brooke like she was afraid she would disappear again. "I love you too, Hope."

She leaned her head into Jack's shoulder. "Thank you for giving them back to me, Jack." Brooke looked at her baby sister. "Did you bring my niece with you?"

"Yes, she is upstairs with one of the local ladies that Jack had set up to watch her. I'm surprised he didn't tell you we were coming!"

"I wanted to surprise you for your birthday." He smiled down into Brooke's eyes.

"Oh my lord, I forgot that it's my birthday!"

"Honey, I wanted to give you something that money couldn't buy. I knew you missed your family, and I was witness to the love that you all have for each other. I wanted you to have that back."

Brooke's mother looked at her. "I'm so glad you have everything you ever wanted, honey. I am so proud of you. I am also so sorry about Davy and the baby. He was a really sweet guy."

Brooke couldn't hold in her excitement any more, she had to tell everyone, especially Jack. "Speaking of babies, I have something I need to tell everyone. I'm pregnant." She looked at her family. "I'm due in November." She stared into her husband's eyes. A joy so profound lit them up, and he wrapped his arms around her. "I love you, Jack, with everything in me. I never thought I could be this happy."

"I love you too, Sweetheart. You have made me the happiest man that could ever walk the face of the earth. There is no one like you. You have the kindest heart, the most beautiful soul I have ever known."

She went up the stairs to finally meet her beautiful niece. She lay on her stomach, fast asleep. She ran the back of her finger along the baby's chubby little cheek. "I love you, Davianna. I can't wait until you wake up so I can hold you. You are one special little girl." Brooke gasped as Davianna moved her cheek into her finger, scared that she woke her up. Instead, the twelve-month-old toddler took two deep breaths, and let out one exhale as she slipped deeper into her dream.

The next day, Brooke stood just outside the mansion in the back yard in her wedding dress. The entire town had shown up to watch as Jack and Brooke "renewed" their vows, while Tris and Chris both gave Brooke away. This should have been her father's job, but he had died of a heart attack three months ago, not that they were ever truly close to begin with.

Brooke rounded the corner to where the boys were standing, and a five-piece orchestra played the wedding march. When she spotted Jack standing under the gazebo in the back yard, she almost stopped in her tracks. He wore a black tuxedo, with a plum tie and cummerbund, with a black shirt, that made his azure eyes pop. His raven hair was tied back at the nape of his neck, and the tux fit him like a glove. Dear god, he was beyond gorgeous!

Brooke almost broke into tears when she saw the posters standing up on easels on both sides of the altar, one of Davy on Jack's side of the aisle, and one of her father on hers. Even though they weren't with them anymore; they were still there, watching her and Jack get married. Jack stood in the center of the altar, his hands folded in front of him. He turned to look at Brooke, and his eyes swam with tears. He grabbed onto Steve's shoulder, who was serving as his best man. It was almost as if he was using Steve as a crutch to continue standing.

Before she knew she had taken another step, she was standing beside him, and handing her sister the bouquet. Brooke took both of Jack's hands as they had rehearsed yesterday, and the justice of the peace had her start the vows.

"Jackson Andrew Newcomb-Connor, we have been through so much together. There has never been another man born such as you. We have triumphed over every adversity, and have grown closer because of it. I have told you that I loved you since we lived in Chicago, and that isn't true. I loved you since I was a little girl, dreaming of the man I would one day marry. You are the man of my dreams in every way conceivable, and then some. I will love you for all eternity. I promise to love, honor, and cherish you, until I am laid to rest. I will spend the rest of my days doing everything in my power to make you happy."

"Now, Jackson, you may say your vows," the Justice of the Peace said.

"Brooke Hope McLeod-Connor, you are the most amazing woman ever born. Your original name fit you so well; you have given hope to so many people, including me. I have needed you for so long, and when you finally walked into my life, I knew I was in trouble. You complete me. I promise to love, honor, and cherish you until the end of all life, above, and below the earth."

As they went back down the aisle, Brooke grabbed Davianna from Grace's arms, and held her all the way back inside so that they could let the party rental crew move the chairs and put up the tables for the reception, and the band that they hired could set up. Brooke looked into the sweet little face, and watched her little eyes light up. Brooke's eyes welled with tears, thinking about the day she was born. The proof that it was only a year ago was in her arms, but it seemed like such a long lifetime ago.

"Bookie...." A singsong voice came from Davianna as she looked into her aunt's eyes. Brooke's eyes filled with tears as she heard her name come from her niece's lips for the first time.

"Another generation starts, Grace. Let's hope her life is better than ours was."

"If I have anything to say about it, it will be." Jack wrapped his arms around his wife. "I meant what I said in my vows, Baby. I will love you until the end of all life." He said, and tickled Davianna's tummy.

She gave a squeal, and put her head into Brooke's shoulder while looking at her uncle. "Andy!" Davianna scolded.

"I love you too, Andy. Not until I die, but for the rest of eternity."

THE END

AUTHOR'S NOTE

Okay, let's get this out of the way. I am a domestic violence survivor. I started *Shadows of the Night* back in 2003 when my son was still a toddler; (incidentally he's in his 20's now). But I was told that it was horrible, and I threw it away. I was told I would never be a writer; that I really sucked at it, and I just gave it up. I started writing other novels years later, but somehow I couldn't give Hope's story up. It haunted me, nagged at me for years.

Now that her story is told, I wanted to give a few pieces of advice from someone who lived it. A spinal fusion later from having my neck broken in nine places, this story was too important for me to give up on.

There are many forms of abuse. Spiritual, Sexual, Physical, Monetary, Emotional, and Mental. You see all of them in this novel. Spiritual abuse is when someone won't allow you to practice your religion. They try and force you to become their religion, or have no religion dropping yours.

Sexual abuse is...well....rape. You absolutely CAN be raped by your spouse. When you say no, that means NO, and if they force it, it's rape, and also sexual abuse. It can be violent, but it can also be coercion. Several minutes of "But BABE.....come on....please???" and when you continue to say no, and they persist, that is coercion.

Now for the monetary. This one is a bit tricky. This is when they refuse to give you money for doctor's visits, medications, food, clothing, etc. Now, I have to say this. If you have a closet full of clothes, or food in your refrigerator, but you see a sweater or a pair of shoes you like and want, or you want to go to Longhorn for a steak, but you really don't have the money, then NO that is NOT abuse. You have food in your pantry, and plenty to wear.

Now this next one is how everything starts. EVERY TIME. They isolate you, take you from your family, your friends, and your support system. They perceive your family as wanting to take you away from him when they don't like him. It's usually sentences such as "It's them or me!" They may even try it with your children! They will alienate your kids, making them seem horrible, and driving them out of your life. It will seem cute at first, as in they want you all to themselves, and later, once everyone is out of your life, then the beatings begin. This is called Emotional abuse

Mental abuse is tied in with Emotional abuse. Sometimes it can be hard to tell them apart. Its name calling, such as "You're worthless!" or "You're stupid, you'll never amount to anything!" The abusers will tear you down, little by little until you have no self-esteem left. It's stomped into the ground with a boot heel, and kept there. Then they have you, hook, line, and sinker.

We all know what physical abuse is. But let me tell you something. ONE SLAP is how it starts. They are never sorry, not truly. They may cry, they may convince you that they are, but if they are going to slap you, it means that they are FORCING you to see things THEIR WAY. They are changing your mind using violence, and that is NEVER ok. No one has the right to lay their hands on anyone. It's bullying, and its abuse even if it is just a slap.

Those are the many forms of abuse, and once they start, 89 chances out of a hundred, they never stop. There are always signs in the beginning, ALWAYS. If you see these signs from anyone, don't walk, RUN away.

To get help and support, and to find out the signs, go onto the internet to the National Coalition Against Domestic Violence site at www.ncadv.org. It is confidential, and easy to get out of if your abuser comes into your room. You can also go somewhere safe and call the National Domestic Violence Hotline at 1-800-799-7233.

I beg you....if there any of these signs, please get out. Your abuser isn't worth your life, or your children's lives. One out of 3 women, and one out of 4 men are beaten in the United States and every 30 seconds, someone is assaulted or killed by their intimate partners. This isn't a joke, or a laughing matter. Please, I beg you. Get help.

Phoebe Rae

CPSIA information can be obtained
at www.ICGtesting.com
Printed in the USA
LVHW04s1602140818
586955LV00002B/428/P